THIS WILL NoT LOOK GooD on my RESUME

Also by Jass Richards

The Road Trip Dialogues

The Blasphemy Tour

License to Do That (forthcoming)

THIS WILL NOT LOOK GOOD ON MY RESUME

Jass Richards

Magenta

Published by Magenta

This Will Not Look Good On My Resume
Second Edition

ISBN 978-1-926891-48-4

Cover design by Jass Richards
Cover image by Amanda Kelsey and Jass Richards
Formatting and interior book design by Elizabeth Beeton

www.jassrichards.com

Library and Archives Canada Cataloguing in Publication

Richards, Jass, author
This will not look good on my resume / Jass Richards.

Short stories.
Reprint. Originally published: Sundridge, Ontario : Magenta, 2010
ISBN 978-1-926891-48-4 (pbk.)

I. Title.

PS8635.I268T45 2013 C813'.6 C2013-902287-2

with chess

(and Taffi)

(and thanks to Bailey, Lundee, and Buddy)

TABLE OF CONTENTS

1

THE PSYCH HALFWAY HOUSE

My first job was in an office. I hated it. No, that's not true. Actually, I liked the job. It was the people I hated. Thus from the start, I was destined for a long line of jobs in 'the people professions'.

Perhaps most notable of these was my job at 602, a residential program run by the Mental Health Association. Selected patients from the local psych hospital (those with potential!) were transferred, at some point in time, to 602—so called because its address was 602 Bonkers Street (I kid you not)—where the staff would teach the residents life skills, help them find a job and an apartment, and generally provide support during their transition from institutionalized living to independent living. (I highly recommend the program to those who work in an office.) I was hired as a relief worker and mostly covered the midnight shift. Which meant that I helped the residents make the transition from sleeping in a bed to sleeping in a bed.

Which was okay because I would've had trouble teaching life skills. How to buy groceries, how to keep track of your chequing account—these were adults we were dealing with, and I had neither the desire nor the need to infantalize them. After all, people who need people are, well, codependent.

Besides, you want *life* skills? Okay, how about how to deal with the recognition that you're never really going to amount to much. And how to be content nevertheless. And, yes, how to make foil headgear that is durable yet fashionable.

On my first midnight shift, I took Kessie with me, partly thinking of all those sweet and cuddly animal therapy programs, and partly thinking that if I dozed off, she'd be my alarm system, sure to wake up growling the second any crazy with a knife walked into the room. Turned out, she refused to go sleep. I stretched out on the couch and—she sat on my head. All night. At full alert. Apparently ready to scream. The place scared her.

No wonder. All of my coworkers had previous experience with mental illness. First-hand. In fact, I think that was a prerequisite for obtaining a full-time position. A relapse seemed to be the prerequisite for promotion.

Unfortunately, it turned outthat I was hired just in time for the annual staff retreat. I suspected it was an office party disaster waiting to happen. I didn't want to go. But I also didn't want to be reprimanded, yet again, for not being a team player. Damned if I do, damned if I don't.

So Friday evening, six of us piled into Kathy's minivan. We were obviously going to get a head start on the group bonding thing. I asked if that was fair. They smiled indulgently and said, "Oh you just want to drive down on that new Harley of yours instead of being with us." Well yeah. Duh.

We arrived at the retreat site, which was well off the highway, and for a second I was glad I came—it was beautiful. Forest as far as the eye could see, in orange and gold, a sparkling blue lake, a couple canoes on the shore, gentle babbling from a stream that fed the lake . . . We spent the entire next two days inside. Replenishing our inner spirits.

Saturday began with a pre-breakfast yoga session, a breakfast get-to-know-you, two morning sessions, and a lunch mixer. So I was told. I don't get up until noon. (Well, unless I work the midnight shift. Then I don't go to bed until noon. Which means that on any given day, or, well, on any given night I guess—oh never mind.)

At around 1:00 p.m., I found myself being hustled to the first of three afternoon sessions by one of my coworkers, Clara. Who was way too chirpy. Obviously a morning person. I grabbed a carafe of tea and a cup from the lunch table as we passed it, and stuffed some creamers and a plastic-wrapped egg salad sandwich into my pocket. She led me into a roomful of people, and to the corner occupied by the 602 staff.

"Hello again," the session leader at the front of the room said, and beamed. "Wasn't that a fantastic lunch?" she asked, and everyone applauded. Applause? For egg salad? Plastic-wrapped egg salad? I glanced around the room. A lot of people looked suspiciously beatific. Did I miss something spectacular? Were the leaders that charismatic? No wait, I've seen that look—they're fucking all on Prozac! I missed the free samples!

"What we're going to do first this afternoon," she continued as if she were about to present a won-der-ful gift, "is something called 'What Colour are You?'" You've got to be kidding. I had finished my first cup of tea and had poured a second, but was still way too tired to run through my Meyers-Briggs critique, and anyway these people should know better, this is all so old, and lame, "—but with a little twist." Her eyes twinkled. Mine twitched. "I want you to think about what colour each of your coworkers is. Then we'll have you pow-wow in your work groups to share your perceptions. Be open. Be honest. Remember, those are the building blocks of a good team . . . " Yeah right. Like I'm gonna fall for *that* again. (When did you stop hitting your wife?) Director Jean, you're airhead blue. Kathy, you're—oh my god. They're *all* airhead blue.

"I'm going to pass on this one," I said. "I really haven't had time to get to know any of you," I tried to smile. "And I really have to pee," I pointed to the carafe.

When I returned to the room, I discovered that things could indeed get worse. Each session ended with a group hug. I looked around. Surely they don't have enough Academy Awards on hand to cover this performance.

The next session was a 'revitalizer'. Up on our feet, stretch up, that's it, one arm, skyreach, the other arm, skyreach, now climb that ladder into the clouds— I can't believe I'm doing this. I imagined myself presenting these warm-ups to my old track buddies, started to laugh, caught Clara's glance, then imagined myself back at the unemployment office. That's it, now exhale, and blow those clouds away! Good! Now stand on one leg and lift the other, from the hip, that's it, how do you feel?

"Like a dog taking a piss." Oops. Jean gave me a look of disappointment. As did Kathy, Clara, and Lynn.

And then it was time for another group hug.

Shortly after the retreat, we got a new resident, Dave. Dave was what we called a 'high functioning' person. He could tie his own shoelaces. Within a week, he was placed at the local 'sheltered workshop', another MHA program, designed to provide employment opportunities to both the mentally delayed and the mentally ill. (I never did understand why the two were put together. Would *you* put Gomer Pyle and Adolf Hitler in the same treatment program?)

Speaking of 'mentally delayed', what a wonderfully optimistic label. Your train will, some day, pull into the Normal IQ Station, dear. It's just been a little delayed. Delayed, deschmayed. His train was derailed.

As for the workshop, it was a woodworking enterprise that made crafts and furniture which nobody bought. Except the employees of the MHA. At Christmas time. I imagined those at the workshop spending the morning putting round pegs into round holes and the afternoon putting square pegs into square holes.

When Dave came home at the end of his first day, he said the job sucked, and he couldn't stand his boss. He wanted to quit. I congratulated him, telling him that he was certainly on the road to recovery, and if he kept the job for five years, he'd be normal, if not healthy.

One midnight shift, when I had finished *Inside the Mind of a Cat*—which should be required reading for all new staffers, by the way—I started on the house copy of the *Diagnostic and Statistical Manual on Mental Disorders*. Christ, was I sick.

The next night, eager to display what I had learned, I gave my coworker a pop quiz.

"Why did the delusional person cross the road?" Lynn waited expectantly. "Because he *thought* the grass was greener on the other side." We laughed. Okay, I laughed. Lynn disapproved.

"Here's another one. Why did the masochist cross the road? He didn't. *Because* the grass *was* greener on the other side." Yuk yuk.

I held up Sheila's file. "Why did the passive personality cross the road? Because I told her to," I said and giggled.

"No, one more—" Lynn was leaving the office, wringing her hands. I waved Bob's file, our King of Hallucinations, "Why did the schizophrenic cross the road? To follow the chicken!" That one always cracked me up.

It's not that I don't have any sympathy for those who are mentally ill. It's just that I can't figure out which mental illness leaves you with an inability to do your own laundry and a tendency to leave half an inch of iced tea in the pitcher when there are two boxes of mix sitting in the cupboard.

One of the midnight duties was to get the morning meds ready. This meant making sure the right number of pinks and whites and blues and yellows were in the proper dispensers, labelled for whoever got said pinks and whites and blues and yellows. Once I played musical chairs with everyone's meds for a week. Oddly enough, there was no noticeable difference in anyone's behaviour.

So, seeking an alternative to pharmaceutical therapy, and just plain curious, I wondered what would happen if I acted crazier than the residents. One day I served everyone a slice of cake batter. Another day I posted signs written in my own private language.

Regular staff didn't agree, but I say that *did* result in an improvement—if only because of a general increase in self-esteem: I mean, compared to me, they figured they were doing pretty good. They weren't stupid, after all; they were just sick.

Or they were Mary Margaret. She heard a voice in her head. It was God. So the staff thought she was crazy. I thought they were jealous. Or just as crazy. And I told them so at the next staff meeting.

"You all believe in God?" I asked, by way of explanation.

Of course. Nods and murmurs of assent all round.

"And you pray?"

Yes, indeed they did.

"But none of you hears voices, none of you hears God."

No, we do not, of course not.

"So you spend your time—some of you, your life—talking to a god that doesn't ever talk back. And," I continued, "you don't really expect him to."

Mary Margaret lay down naked in the middle of the road one day because God asked her to. She assumed she had been chosen as a sacrifice because at forty, she was still a virgin.

"Why didn't you just go have sex instead?" I asked her, when we were sitting in the tv room one night.

She gave me the oddest look and walked away. Silently. Solemnly.

The next time I was in, I was told she'd been out to the bars every night soliciting men. Apparently she'd had sex with over two dozen in the last week alone. Staff was concerned with this further decline into depravity.

"You know, you only have to do it once to not be a virgin anymore," I told her when, again, we were sitting in the tv room. "I don't think God will choose you to be a sacrifice anymore. Or you can do it with yourself," I added. "That counts."

She looked surprised, confused, relieved, and pleased—though not necessarily in that order.

The following weekend, I was informed that not only had she stopped going out, she had started going to bed rather early. The staff was relieved—and surprised, pleased, and confused.

"So," I plopped myself down on the couch in the tv room. She was sitting in the chair, her chair, across from me. "Heard from God lately?"

"No," she said with some anxiety, "and I'm a bit worried about what He'll ask me to do next."

"Hm." I thought for a moment. "I have a confession to make." She raised her eyebrows. "God talks to me too. But I don't think it's the same god."

Her eyes widened. Clearly she was torn between the possibility that God might speak to someone else and the possibility that there might be another God.

"Every Tuesday at 11:00," I said. "I think that's my appointment time."

Her eyes widened further. "What does he say?" she eventually asked, genuinely interested.

"Oh, lots of stuff," I said casually. "'Be kind.' 'Be happy.' 'Always wear blue.'" Again her eyebrows raised. I pointed to my jeans.

"One time he told me to put my paycheques straight into the bank and only take out so much in cash so I'd always have enough for rent and food. That way I'd always have a safe place of my own, a home. That was real good advice."

Mary Margaret was thinking hard. Very hard.

"But I don't think it's the same god that talks to you," I continued.

"Oh." She seemed sad. "Why?"

"Well he says his name is 'Godd'—he really emphasizes the 'd' at the end, so I think he spells his name G-o-d-d. How does your god spell his name?"

"He's never said." And until now that wasn't a problem.

I nodded. Wisely.

"Why don't you switch?" I asked.

"What?" Wow. Another possibility to ponder.

"Why don't you switch gods?"

"I didn't know you could do that."

"Oh sure. It's like those long-distance carriers, you know, for phone calls. You just have to call and say you'd like to switch."

So we went into the office and I helped her find the number for Bell, or maybe it was Rogers. And she called right then and there. It was 2:00 in the morning. And the customer rep at the other end, bless her, not only let her switch from God with one 'd' to Godd with two 'Ds', but also gave her an appointment time of Fridays at 10:00 p.m.

I saw Mary Margaret at the mall a couple months later. She had moved out of the house and into her own apartment. And she had on the cutest baby blue polyester pantsuit I'd seen since the '70s.

Another time, about two weeks later, I left Gilman's *The Yellow Wallpaper* in the tv room. It and Martha were gone the next week. I heard she left her husband. Plath's *Belljar* disappeared next, with Jill. I heard she left her husband *and* her parents. Vonnegut's *Eden Express* disappeared with Tony. Who took with him 602's entire stock of vitamins. (Well, that and the stereo.) I called it my covert bibliotherapy program. The program ended, unfortunately, when Jean confiscated Szasz's *The Myth of Mental Illness.*

That same night, coincidentally, Bob attacked Lynn with a kitchen knife, shouting "Let's kill the aliens!" over and over. Okay. Point taken. So when I visited her in the hospital, I took her some reading material. A copy of *They Really Are Out To Get You.* She actually called Security. And, apparently, Director Jean.

2

THE O & D

It was a little ironic that she had called Security, because at my other job, I *was* Security. They didn't actually call us that, but that's what we did, or rather, provided. The O & D (Observation & Detention) was another residential program, and, again, I was a relief worker. Again, primarily for the midnight shift. Its purpose was to detain (D) 'young offenders' while they were waiting for a court appearance—for trial, sentencing, or whatever. (So actually we were called Adolescent Workers.) (In reference to our clientele.) While at the O & D, said young offenders would be observed (O), and the log kept by said adolescent workers offered to the court for consideration. This meant, of course, that, as with regular jail, you had innocent kids rooming with guilty kids.

Furthermore, in an odd display of parallelism to the mixed agenda of the MHA's workshop, the O & D also served as a safe house for kids who had been abused—who had not even been charged with anything criminal—while they were waiting for an adoption placement. (Essentially, for trial, sentencing, and whatever). And the interesting thing was, relief workers weren't allowed to read the kids' files. I confess that my behaviour toward a kid who's taken a cigarette lighter to the family gerbil would be different than my behaviour toward a kid who's had a cigarette lighter taken to himself. (So if it was the same kid—as it was likely to be—I was, well, confused.)

And as for my behaviour toward the cigarette-burning parents of such a kid (occasionally, parents came to visit their kid; *very* occasionally, now that I think of it), first, I'd have them both sterilized. That's it. No more kids. Then, since such parents demonstrate arrested moral development and are probably operating at thepre- adolescent stage, understanding morality only in terms of reciprocity, I'd take a cigarette lighter to the both of them.

Now, you might point out that chances are that's already happened—that's *why* they're the parents they are. Right. So not only would I sterilize the parents, I'd also sterilize the kid. The O & D could easily add it to their referral services. It could be a family outing. We're supposed to encourage that sort of thing.

But that's not fair! I know. But one, you're assuming the kid will actually want to *have* kids, and, truth be told, that's probably unlikely. (I say that because, truth be told, *most* people don't actually want to have kids. Whenever people announce to me they're 'expecting', I ask them 'Why?' They usually give me a look, as if I'm sort of slow, and then they say, with a rueful grin, something like 'It was sort of an accident.') (To which I reply something like 'Excuse me? You don't *accidentally* ejaculate into someone's vagina, nor do you *accidentally* catch some sperm with your vulva.') And two, it may be unfair to the kid, but otherwise it's unfair to the kid's kids and all the people who then have to deal with yet another victim of cigarette lighters. And it's especially unfair to gerbils.

Another interesting thing about the job was that staff were expected to psychoanalyze these kids' every move, or failure to move, and none of us were psychoanalysts. Half of us were ex-daycamp leaders, and the other half were cop-wannabes. (And then there was me. I just liked the hours.) Let me just say that if for twenty-four hours/day, seven days/week, *your* every word and action was subjected to intense microscopic examination, by unqualified idiots, you'd have an anger management problem too. (Admittedly, most of us would have such a problem if we were subjected to intense microscopic examination by *qualified* idiots.)

Once, during an evening shift, I was reprimanded because I sat on the couch in the main room, reading. (*Popular Mechanics* or *Car & Driver*, I can't remember.) (Amish porn, in any case.) A mistake. Not *what* I was reading, but *that* I was reading. I was supposed to interact with the kids. Hell, we interacted with the kids more in one day than my own parents interacted with me in a whole year. (Not that instead they ever sat on a couch reading. Or took a cigarette lighter to me. But the only time my parents interacted with us kids—apart from the occasional reminder or query regarding various aspects of the household routine—was during the holidays. On Christmas Day, during that long time between opening the gifts and Christmas dinner,when we didn't have any chores to do, we weren't allowed to do any homework, we especially weren't allowed to watch tv, and there's only so much enthusiasm you can generate for new socks and pyjamas and one or two toys, mom was in the kitchen, of course, making Christmas dinner, which somehow took all day, but dad wouldn't dare escape to his workshop, so he and my brother would have their annual game of chess, and my sister and I would sort of watch. There we go: parent-child interaction. Normal, healthy parent-child interaction.) (Okay, perhaps more normal than healthy, but still—)

So I put the magazine down and reluctantly joined the monopoly game in the kitchen. Another mistake. First, I implemented a sliding scale of payments for those who landed on my property. Then I interrogated prospective buyers: what do you intend to do with the property? 'Cuz if you're going to develop it into one of those super malls, forget it. We don't need more stores. We don't need to 'go shopping' as if it were a leisure activity. We in the so-called 'developed' world have way too much shit as it is. And we keep coercing those in the so-called 'developing' world to make it for us. Part way through my discourse on the sociopolitical evils of supermalls in general, and Walmart and McDonalds in particular, I was kicked out of the game.

Another time, at the end of a midnight shift, I was encouraged to watch tv with the others. Watching tv is interacting with the kids? Okaaaay. As it turns out, it was a Sunday morning and nothing was on but religious programming. Halfway through some evangelist's sermon, I started reciting "Jabberwocky": "'Twas brillig and the slithy toves did gyre and gimble in the wabe, all mimsy were the borogroves . . . " They all yelled at me to shut up. Like they really wanted to hear the sermon.

Then there was a station identification announcement, concluding with the comment that as a religious network, the station did not accept ads for beer, liquor, or feminine hygiene products.

"Well, that makes sense," I said. "I mean, we all know what a good buzz you can get from a tampon." Silence. Not one 'Shut up!'

The next commercial was for guns. I kid you not. 'Course, as a religious network . . .

"I've got a better idea," I said when it was over.

"Yeah?" a kid snorted. I couldn't possibly.

"Yeah, what you do is get a dart gun and load it with a tranquilizer, or an emetic, or an extra-strength laxative. Your guy's not going to be a threat if he's unconscious, puking his guts out, or shitting his shorts, right? And while he's doing that, you can run away!"

"Run away?" He was disgusted.

"Well, you could kick him good first," I suggested.

Okay. That was okay then.

"It achieves the same thing as a real gun," I continued. "But if you get caught, see, it's a lesser charge."

That got the kid's attention.

"And if someone happened to get in the way, well you wouldn't kill anyone by mistake. And that's kind of a good thing, right?"

The kid had to think about that. "Okay," he said, "but what if they shoot back with the same stuff?"

"Well better that than a bullet in the head, no?"

He had to think about that one for quite some time. "Maybe," he finally conceded.

Every now and then, when the O & D pressure cooker got to be too much, sometimes before or after a court appearance or a parental visit, a kid would blow. And we were supposed to restrain him or her. We were taught several restraint holds, one that could be done by one person, another that required two, but they all immobilized the kid's arms and legs while protecting the head (the kid's mostly) (unfortunately). What a stupid idea. As a teenager, whenever I was volcanic, I went for a run. A good hard run. Long too, depending. (I still do that. In fact, shortly after I last spoke with Director Jean, I set a personal best for my ten-mile.)

Instead of holding them down, which to my mind just adds to their rage, we should be letting them go—taking them to the nearest high school and letting them loose on the track or the football field. Escape shouldn't be a problem; there is, or should always be, at least one of us who can outrun a 15-year-old.

'Course there is the chance the kid will run full speed into one of the goalposts. But that needn't be considered a bad thing.

At the end of a week during which I happened to be lucky enough to be staff escort for a trip to the grocery store with the 602s *and* a trip to an outdoor festival with the O & Ds, I had a great idea: why not pair a 602 with an O & D? I imagined a program that was a cross between those that paired juvenile delinquents with dogs and those that paired ex-cons with people in wheelchairs. You know the ones I'm talking about. (Kessie thought it was a great idea. But then she'd somehow gotten the idea that she'd get to go for a car ride in a wheelchair.) So I stayed up late, or early, and presented the idea to each place during the weekly staff meeting.

Surprisingly enough, it was accepted. Any idea proposed by a mere relief worker is usually rejected out-of-hand; actually, that's not quite true—rejection presupposes some degree of consideration. So I figure it was probably that time of the budget year when program directors were told to either 'use it or lose it'—and I suspect that neither the 602 program director nor the O & D program director had proposed anything new in a long while, so they were quite happy to grab the ball and run with it. My ball. Of course I didn't get any credit for it. Not that it would've done me any good—relief workers are simply not on any career ladder, and neither initiative, good work, long service, nor ass-kissing results in advancement.

But that's just as well because the program—'Northerly Hills 602OD'—was pretty much a disaster. Rott (short for Rottweiler), a big kid with hair that was a cross between a Mohawk and an Afro, was a repeat offender for assorted assaults. Actually, one of these was against a coworker who, in a moment of canine confusion, called him Poo (short for Poodle). That was the first time. The second time happened when I dared said coworker to tie a pink ribbon in Rott's hair when he was asleep one night (we had to do bedchecks every half hour). Anyway, Rott was paired with Len, the meekest and mildest of the 602s (who didn't have so much a personality disorder as a personality deficit). The idea was that antagonism would be statistically impossible and hence another assault equally unlikely. Rott beat the crap out of Len at their first meeting.

So then he was paired with George, who was not only physically intimidating, at 6'4" and 240 lbs, butwas also suffering from delusions of questionable grandeur—he thought he was Hulk Hogan. Rott beat the crap out of George too. (The upside is that George no longer believes he's Hulk Hogan.)

Two other pairings are worth mention, both having been reasonably successful. Lily was 602's compulsive shopper. Luann was one of O & D's shoplifters. The three of us headed out to a mall one day, the two of them delighted at discovering in common an enthusiasm for shopping. They made a bee-line for one of those sprawling economy department stores that have everything you could possible imagine but nothing you could actually want. Let alone need. I trailed behind, at a discreet distance that was supposed to make them feel independent, one of such a trip's many purposes.

Lily grabbed a shopping cart and began to fill it at once—with socks, tshirts, scarves, hats, jeans, sweaters, umbrellas—all the while maintaining a chatter that was part auctioneer and part shopping channel spokesperson. Luann followed, recognizing Lily as the perfect decoy, and stealthily secreted various items into various pockets.

By the time they left Ladies' Wear, Lily was onto her second shopping cart. By the time they'd gotten through Kitchenwares, she'd enlisted Luann to push a third. She was in Shoppers' Heaven. She'd never filled *three* shopping carts before.

Luann was feeling aggrieved—it was clear she was outdone. She'd never be able to lift more than Lily was accumulating. So she scored the next item when Lily was watching, and winked at her. Lily was confused for a moment, looking much like a puppy seeing for the first time an older dog calmly walk away with the just delivered pizza box. While stealing clearly had advantages over buying, she realized, as Luann had, that she couldn't possibly take nearly as much that way. So she decided to stick with compulsive shopping. And that made Luann doubly aggrieved. So when Lily put shoehorns into that third cart—six of them, one of each colour—Luann blew.

"YOU DON'T FUCKING NEED ALL THIS SHIT!!" she yelled. So loudly she lost half her loot. Among the many items that fell clattering to the floor was a mini-shoeshine kit. Lily stared at this shoeshine kit. Luann stared at the shoeshine kit. Lily looked at her shoehorns. Luann looked at the shoehorns. I call it 'the shoe moment'.

Then, wordlessly, they both left the scene. Unfortunately for me, through different exits. I eventually found them both, wandering in the parking lot, looking for my car. (I was doing the same thing.) We left the mall and neither one of them went 'shopping' again.

The other interesting pairing involved Shane, whose conversation was pretty much limited to "Fuck this!" and James, who had no conversation—he hadn't spoken in five years. We figured that Shane, having to carry both ends of the conversation, would be compelled to become a little more articulate.Or at least increase his vocabulary. And that's exactly what happened. When he was with James, he was overheard saying things like "Wanna coffee?" and "Gotta piss." Given another ten years, I thought, he might actually engage in the mindless pleasantries that indicate social maturity. (Go figure, but that's how people measure social maturity.)

But the really interesting change occurred in James. One day, sitting alone in his room, he was heard to have quietly said "Fuck this." Now, not only had he uttered words, but there had been a reasonable facsimile of emotional expression in the utterance as well. Whatever, saying those two little words quietly, alone in his room, seemed sufficient to simply dismiss whatever it was he had been obsessed to silence with for all those years.

A little while later, while watching tv with the others, somewhat less catatonically than before, he again said, "Fuck this" and left the room. It was the first display of autonomy the staff had ever seen.

Of course, only one more step remained, which he took a month later. He said, once more, "Fuck this"—and walked out of 602, never to be seen again.

A few weeks after the demise of 602OD, I showed up for a midnight shift at the O & D to discover I'd be working with John. Shit. John is the kind of man who takes himself way too seriously, the corollary being that he takes me, and all women, not at all seriously. We had finished with 'shift change' (an interesting routine in which the outgoing shift read their logs to the incoming shift) (a routine for which we were required to show up fifteen minutes early—unpaid time, of course), and the evening staff had left. John and I were in the upstairs office. I happened to be sitting at The Desk, in the position of Power and Authority; John was sitting in the small chair at the side. The arrangement clearly bothered him. So he stood up, thinking, I guess, that if we were playing basketball, he'd have the height advantage. I ignored him. That clearly bothered him too.

"Why don't you do the logs tonight," he said. Then he added, "You're good at writing"—in a tone implying that writing was a sissy task unworthy of his effort.

"Sure, okay."

In fact, when I first started at the O & D, I found writing the logs to be quite an engaging activity. Witness this gem: "Early in the shift, Matthew seemed to be trembling slightly as he lay sleeping. Thinking he was perhaps cold, I put another blanket over him. However, at the next bedcheck, I discovered he had thrown the blanket onto the floor. Obviously he was resisting even the smallest gesture of kindness that might be offered by others. Or maybe he was too warm.

"He spent most of the night sleeping in a fetal position, which, to my mind, could well indicate a desire to return to a state of infancy rather than accept the challenges of adulthood. However, since he is, after all, only thirteen, and has probably faced too many adult situations already, this is probably a healthy desire. Matthew *should* have a childhood.

"At one point, however, he moved onto his back, arms flung out to either side and feet crossed, suggesting, of course, the crucified Christ. One could easily interpret this posture as indicative of a persecution complex. However, again, since so much has actually happened to Matthew during his young life, this attitude is not necessarily pathological. Nevertheless, we may be wise to realize that perhaps he is reaching a critical threshold with regard to unpleasant things happening to him that interfere with whatever life plan he might, if it were not for this constant 'persecution', develop.

"Towards morning, Matthew's legs were jerking, as if he were running. Given the above observations, it may be that he is planning an escape attempt during tomorrow's outing, and day staff might want to be extra vigilant in this regard. Or maybe he dreamt that he was chasing rabbits."

Shortly after, I was told that I didn't have to be that thorough, and I was advised to look at other midnight shift logs to get an idea of what was required. So I did. The first one said "Slept well." I noticed the difference right away, but read on through several other logs.

"Slept thru the night." "Slept soundly thru the night." "Restless but slept thru the night." "Did not fall asleep until mid-shift. Then slept soundly thru the night." Hm. There's a pattern here.

Why not just use a key? The half dozen variations could be listed and numbered, and then staff could just enter the appropriate numbers in the logs. As I started to prepare such a key, however, I realizedthat we didn't even need a half dozen—two options would suffice. 1 - Slept soundly thru the night. 2 - Did not sleep soundly thru the night. On further thought still, I decided that 'thru the night' was unnecessary. I put my final version of the key at the front of the master log and ever since, my midnight log entries have consisted of simply '1' or '2'.

Now John was probably not aware of this, but it didn't matter. I was still "good at writing" and I was still agreeable to doing the logs for our shift. And he was still standing over me. I guess he was waiting for me to vacate the chair of Power and Authority. After all, the first few times I worked with him, I pretty much did what he told me to do; I had just been hired, and he'd been working at the O & D for a while. But he probably thought I'd been deferring to his Almighty Maleness.

"You can get started on the laundry and the meals, if you like," he said. "I can handle the Security Checks myself," he added, smiling. He actually called them Security Checks. He even had his own flashlight, a rather large and sturdy thing suitable for Arctic Search and Rescue missions. It dangled from his belt loop.

"No, that's okay. If I'm doing the logs, it makes more sense for me to do the bedchecks." After all, the logbook was kept in the office upstairs, which was where the bedrooms were. He continued standing there. Rather dumbly, I thought. So I clarified, "*You* can do the laundry and the cooking tonight." And reached into my knapsack for the book I'd brought to read.

Well that did it. I may as well have castrated him and thrown it into the garbage. He stomped around the small office as I opened my book and started chapter one. Then he stood in the doorway, arms raisedand pressing against the frame. (Be big. Be very big.)

"Why are you being so uncooperative?" he demanded.

"I'm *not* being uncooperative," I said. "I agreed to do the logs and I offered to do the bedchecks."

"But you're supposed to do the laundry and prepare the meals. That's part of the midnight shift duties."

"*I'm* supposed to? Why am I supposed to?"

"Well why do you think they always put one guy and one girl on shift together? The guys take care of Security and the girls do the cooking, cleaning, and stuff."

"Nooo, that's not it," I absently turned a page. "'Cuz we all have the same job description."

He came over to the desk then and leaned on it, *over* it, putting his hands rather far apart. But then found he had nothing to say.

"As for why one of each," I continued, "I suspectthat it's in case a strip search has to be done for a new admission. Though that assumes all our kids are heterosexual. Frankly, if I were a young gay male, I'd rather have me looking him over than you."

Oh that was definitely it. I'd now, somehow, called him gay as well as suggested he do the women's work. He was not, definitely *not* going to stand for this.

"What?" He looked at me as if I was crazy.

Unfortunately, we were not exactly whispering at this point and one of the kids woke up. Told us to shut up. (Damn. Now I'd have to erase '1' and change it to '2'.) Which unfortunately woke up another resident who called out, with some anxiety, "Stop fighting! Please, I didn't do anything!" John was now leaning in the doorway, arms crossed, glaring at me. I got up, brushed past him, and went to the kid's room to tell her it was okay, she was okay, go back to sleep.

When I returned to the office, John was sitting in the big chair at The Desk, smiling smugly. So I took my book, and the log, went downstairs, and made a pot of tea. I did not do the laundry. I did not prepare the meals. I did go upstairs every half hour to do the bedchecks.

First time, he grunted, as if I was a simpleton, that he'd just done them. Second time, he informed me *again* that he'd just done them.

By the fourth time, I think he figured out what I was doing. (The bedchecks.) And then his 'I just did them' got louder and angrier with every passing half hour. At the 5:00 bedcheck, I pointed out, being careful to whisper, that if he didn't start the meals soon (tuna salad sandwiches for lunch and some kind of casserole for dinner), he wouldn't get them done before shift change.

"I'm not doing the fucking cooking, are you dense?!" he exploded. And everyone woke up. Except Matthew, who was chasing rabbits.

Well, the day shift was rather peeved to discover that neither the laundry nor the meals had been done. It was hard enough for two adults to keep tabs on four kids who were restricted to one floor when you *didn't* have anything else to do. Especially when the kids had something new to complain about all day.

When the supervisor spoke to me about that fateful shift, she said things like "If you can't resolve conflicts with your coworkers better than that, well, I'm afraid you're not much of a role model for the kids" and "I'm concerned that you put the kids at risk—who knows what could have happened while you were busy bickering." And I said things like "John has a little flashlight" and "He lacks the capacity to follow a recipe." Then she said something like "What *you* lack is the capacity to get along with people."

So, later that morning, or evening, at around mile seven, it occurred to me that maybe I should look for a job that didn't involve people.

3

MAINTENANCE

In this respect, my next job was an improvement of sorts. I worked on maintenance at a summer camp. It was a beautiful camp, on a lake in Muskoka, with swimming, canoeing, arts and crafts, theatre, waterskiing, tennis, golf, horseback riding, and etiquette for the ruling class. Maintenance was responsible for thegrounds, the docks, and the buildings (dining halls, rec halls, cabins, washrooms/showers, offices, infirmary, sheds, and stables). For a while, I did okay. There was some concern, I admit, when, on the day the kids arrived, I started dancing around, weaving in and out of clusters of mostly wide-eyed and wary kids, taunting "I don't have to deal with you! I don't have to deal with you!" However, since the episode wasn't repeated, everyone pretended it didn't happen. And I went about my business cutting the grass, repairing the docks, painting the cabins, and so on.

But then there was lunch. With the rest of the crew: Jimmy, the youngest member, summer help for three years while getting a forestry diploma, and now full-time; Clyde, a little slow—slow-thinking, slow-moving; Zeke, a wiry guy who would have reminded you of a

World War I marine even if he *didn't* have that tattoo of an anchor on his arm; and Mac, our supervisor. Jackie, summer help like me, wasn't there. She didn't eat lunch. But the others did, and they were talking about going hunting on the weekend.

"I don't understand hunting," I joined in. The look Mac gave me indicated that women were to be seen and not heard. Hm. John's brother? He did have a ridiculously large and sturdy all-in-one wrench thing hooked onto his belt loop.

"I don't understand the desire to kill," I spoke again, loudly.

"It's not that," Zeke said. "It's the excitement, the thrill of stalking an animal that's big and wild and can tear you apart!"

"Yeah right. Like Bambi's cousin's going to tear you apart."

"And it's the challenge!" Clyde added. "Deer are smart, you know!"

I'd say the average deer has an IQ of what, three? So I had to ask, "Smart compared to who?" For example, I understand there were a lot of hunting injuries the year the M-10 Moose Call came onto the market. Well, what do you think's gonna happen when some moron stands in the middle of the forest during mating season and yells out in moose language 'COME FUCK ME NOW!'

"The challenge?" I continued. "Give me a break. You guys hunt in a group, so already it's what, six against one? And you use dogs, and ATVs, and even helicopters, to scare the animals out of the bush. And then you've got some geezer sittin' in a truck parked at the side of the road just waiting to pick off the first fear-frenzied creature that runs across. Oh, the challenge." 'Course then again, since said geezer has probably been chugging beer all afternoon, I guess that *would* be a challenge.

"It's not just all that," Jimmy pitched in. "We like the meat."

"Then why don't you go to a deer farm and just shoot one that's out grazing in the field? Or a cow farm. Hey, I know! Get a job in a slaughterhouse!"

"'Cuz it's gotta be wild," Zeke grinned at Clyde.

"Okay, why don't you just go shoot a skunk?"

"*Big* and wild," he winked. He winked?

"Yeah, about this 'bigger is better' thing," I responded. "It's *completely* illogical. I mean, anyone can shoot a moose that's just standing there. If you really wanna brag, hang a pair of chipmunk ears on your wall." They looked at me with such— What? Had I suggested castration again?

"And the wardrobe," I carried on. "Also highly illogical. I mean we have the—," I adopted the bored and very gay voice of a pretentious British fashion designer, "—matching pants and shirt in camouflage 'I'm hiding' greens and browns. With perhaps a smudge of olive or taupe. While the accessories—vest and cap—are in fluorescent 'I can't help but be seen' orange. The ensemble fairly shouts 'I'm a man.'" By this point, they were ignoring me. Well, eating did require their full attention.

Another time, another lunch, I heard Jimmy and Mac mumbling to each other trying to figure out if Cathy, one of the new kitchen staff, was Chinese or Japanese. Or maybe Korean. Vietnamese even. They asked me what I thought.

"Isn't she Canadian?" I replied innocently.

They glared at me. *Now* what? Oh. I'd broken another rule. The 'Never ever expose our dim-witted prejudices, we take pride in being assholes, we take even greater pride in being ignorant assholes' rule. So I asked her when she next passed by our table.

And with only half the attitude she was entitled to, she answered simply, "Canadian."

Never one to pass up what was coming to me, I said, "See I told you so! Ya bunch of dim-witted prejudiced ignorant assholes." Well, lunch was clearly over.

They all got up, heavily, as if eating was a job well done.

"Tonight then?" Mac looked at Zeke.

"Yup—Clyde's place, right?"

"Right—"

"Who's bringing the beer?" Jimmy asked.

Ah yes, it was Friday. Friday night was poker night.

"Y'know why women can't play poker?" Mac asked, smiling nastily at me, rubbing in the exclusion. "They're no good at bluffing."

Hm. "Guess you've never had sex with a woman then, eh?"

So on my third day of 'firewood duty'—a supposedly punitive assignment that involved being dropped off at the chopping site first thing in the morning and not picked up until the end of the afternoon, leaving one all alone all day long to chop firewood—I figured as far as being on the maintenance crew goes, life doesn't get much better than that—on the third day of chopping wood, I developed my Theory of Man. Frankly, I think it rivals the Theory of Everything for explanatory value regarding life, the universe, and, well, everything.

My theory is this: men have a defective chromosome. The Y was supposed to be an X, but somehow it ended up missing something. Maybe it's a case of stunted growth or arrested development. Whatever, due to this defective chromosome, uniquely characteristic of the male, men are less evolved.

Consider their fascination with movement. They always have to be doing something. They can't sit still. This importance of movement is characteristic of many lower animals. Certainly it's required for flight and fight. (And no other options occur to lower animals.) And for many, movement is a form of posturing—which explains the way men walk, and stand, and sit. On the other hand, such excessive physical activity may simply suggest that the organism's mental activity doesn't provide enough stimulation.

Not only must they be doing something, they must be doing it loudly. Men seem to be inordinately fond of engines, jackhammers, and chainsaws. This desire to make noise is suggestive of the lion's roar—the louder the noise, the greater the threat.

Because, usually, the larger the animal. And of course size is another male obsession. Girth which in a woman would be considered obese and disgusting is carried by men as if it *increases* their value, their authority: they thrust out their gut just as they thrust out their chest. It brings to mind the many other animals that inflate themselves—the blowfish actually doubles its size. Men are concerned not only with physical size—in general and in particular—but also with the size of their paycheques, their houses, and their corporations. Simply put, the bigger, the better.

Closely related to the size thing is the territory thing. Men occupy a lot of space. Again, look at the way they stand and sit. They take up, they occupy, more space than they need—they lean on counters, sprawl on chairs, take over small countries.

Consider also men's obsession with speed. Cars, trains, planes. Sex. Speed is, of course, important for flight, one of the forementioned behaviours favoured by so many lower animals.

Like their sexual response, men's emotional response is, well, uncomplicated. They are easy to please. This lack of complexity is further indication that they are less evolved.

Some say that language is the mark of higher life forms. And, of course, as any grade school teacher will tell you, boys lag behind girls in verbal development. They're just not very good at communicating. I believe the word I'm looking for is 'inarticulate.'

By way of summary, consider dick flicks. Also called 'action movies', there is indeed lots of action. And lots of noise. The heroes are usually big. And they have big things—big guns, usually. The central conflict of a dick flick is almost always territorial. There is little in the way of plot or character development, but there's always at least one high-speed chase. And, understandably, the dialogue in a dick flick consists mostly of short and often incomplete sentences.

Alas, lunch wasn't the only problem. There was also that 'Merger Maniac' thing. Of course, maintenance staff was not supposed to interact with the kids—it goes without saying that we're unqualified to do so. Which is why one kid stopped in his tracks on hearing me, seeing *me*, the *janitor*, take a moment to play some Chopin on the piano in the rec hall I'd just swept. Janitors can't play Chopin. It totally rocked his world view. I'd probably sent him into years of therapy.

Anyway, one bright summer day while doing the washrooms, and pondering the cleaning products I was supposed to use—my rubber gloves were disintegrating—I heard what sounded like an awful lot of kids chanting "More! More! More! More!" Curious, I stepped outside, toilet brush in hand, to see four or five teams of kids on the playing field, each under a huge banner variously proclaiming Microsoft or Monsanto or something. After the chant, they'd huddle in their teams and apparently plan hostile takeovers, because then they'd all run around and, according to rules I still haven't figured out, some won and some lost, and the kid in the corner with a huge stock market ticker tape thing changed some numbers.

At the next scrimmage, I ran onto the field with my pail of water—yes, dirty washroom clean-up water—and doused 'em all. I flicked my rag in the face of each of the camp leaders present, yelling, like Pink Floyd, "Leave the kids alone!"

I tried explaining—to Security, ironically—that I was *not* threatening to throw bricks at anyone, nor did I even *have* any bricks, but the incident went on record nevertheless.

And then there were those little signs on the sanitary receptacles. One sign per receptacle, one receptacle per stall, ten stalls per washroom, five washrooms—that's fifty times a day I'd read "This sanitary receptacle is provided for your convenience. You are requested to co-operate and use it for the purpose intended."

'For our *convenience*?' I suppose the toilet paper is for our convenience too. No doubt some *man* came up with these signs.

'A sanitary receptacle'? That's just wrong. The receptacle may well *be* sanitary, thanks to yours truly, but I think what's meant is 'a sanitary *napkin* receptacle.' 'Course the napkins put into the receptacle aren't very sanitary at that point—'*menstrual* napkin receptacle' would be more accurate. But men do have trouble with such words. (Though they seem to handle 'cunt' easily enough.)

'You are requested to co-operate.' Someone's been watching way too many late night movie interrogation scenes. Really, I think a 'please' would've sufficed. And actually, I don't even think we need a 'please'. I doubt we even need to be asked. I mean, why shouldn't we 'co-operate'? Women are generally inclined to keep things clean. And this was, after all, the girls' washroom, not the boys'. (Twice as much time was allotted for cleaning the boys' washrooms. At first, I thought that was because the men on the crew worked twice as slowly. But then one day *I* was assigned to the boy's washroom. Until then, I'd always thought 'pissing contest' was just a metaphor.)

Lastly, 'for the purpose intended.' What else might we use a 'sanitary receptacle' for? A lunchbox? A weapon? ("And now for tonight's top story: as we speak, gangs of women are roaming the streets armed with sanitary receptacles . . . ")

So I took all the little signs off the receptacles and bolted them to the walls in the boy's washrooms—one above each urinal. Alas, this too went on record.

And then there was that trip to the dump. Jimmy, Jackie, and I were to make a garbage run. Not knowing how long the trip would be, I asked Jackie, who'd gotten into the front seat of the pick-up beside Jimmy, who was already at the wheel, if I could ride up front instead. "I'm very prone to motion sickness." It's true. Ask any one of eight airline attendants. And five train attendants. I even get nauseous working the microfiche machines in the library.

"Oh no, me too," she moaned. She had a crush on Jimmy.

Well, the solution was obvious. "Okay, Jimmy, how about you sit in the back then and one of us'll drive?" He glared at me. Then angrily started the pick-up, jerked it into reverse, and headed out to the road, spinning gravel and bumping recklessly over all the ruts. I guess I was staying in the back. My stomach lurched. What'd I say? I couldn't figure it out. Surely he knew I could drive; in fact, I was driving my van clear across the country 'bout the time he was just getting his license. Halfway to the dump, it dawned on me.

"Oh I get it!" I leaned forward into the front seat. "My truck is my penis!" And then I threw up.

Near the end of the summer, the kids put on a talent show. Curious, I joined the other members of the crew sitting at the back of the main rec hall. Suddenly, everyone stood. What's this, they stand for the Camp Director's grand entrance? I looked around in disbelief. Then everyone—kids, counsellors, staff—started singing the national anthem. They were standing for the anthem. Shit. If I'd known that, I would've shown up late. Mac glowered—down—at me. I'd never actually seen anyone glower before. Glare, yes. Glower, no. Then as soon as it was over and everyone sat back down, he jeered at me, "Too stiff to stand?" (I'd been chopping firewood again.)

"No, I just don't stand for the anthem."

"Why not? You some kind of commie?"

"One question at a time," I kept my voice low, as someone had come onto the stage to introduce the evening's events. "I don't stand for the anthem because first of all, it's a bit arbitrary—why not play the town anthem instead, or the provincial anthem, or the planetary anthem? Second, why even encourage group bonding? I prefer to encourage *individual* identity: it's much less dangerous, not to mention healthier."

He gave me a blank look. You know that look of incomprehension, the look Sultan, Köhler's chimp in that famous experiment, probably had on his face *before* he understood he could pile the crates on top of each other to reach the banana?

"Whenever we divide ourselves into little groups," I continued to explain, against all odds of succeeding, but because the guy was taking a long time to introduce the first act, "there's a good chance we'll get into a hyperemotional, nonrational gang thing. And groups based on territory, such as nationalistic groups, are the worst. If you have a sense of self, you don't need the identity of a group, a gang. As Einstein said, 'Nationalism is an infantile disease.'"

"So you *are* a commie."

"What?" It took me a few seconds to figure out his mistake. "Communism is an *economic* system, not a political system. It's at odds with *capitalism*, not nationalism. And actually, my guess is that communists are quite nationalistic. They probably stand very proudly for their anthem." Was the first act *ever* going to begin?

"You should still show some respect." What a fine upstanding citizen he was. As self-righteous as they come.

"But I *don't* respect—"

"What's your problem?" He cut me off angrily. And a little loudly.

"I don't agree with what the anthem is saying, that's my problem. For example, the line 'I'll stand on guard for thee'—well, I won't—"

"You don't have to sing it, you just have to stand for it." He was getting very impatient with me.

"Well, when I stand for something, I *stand* for it—for what it means."

"Oh quit your nitpicking, it's not really supposed to mean anything!" He was shouting by now, and people were starting to turn around to look at us.

"Then why does my not standing for it upset you so much?"

Amazingly enough, I wasn't fired. I quit. Well I didn't actually quit, I just kind of left early. It was near the end of August, the kids were gone, and we had just begun the summer's-end clean-up. Apparently it would take the better part of a day just to drive around and empty the cabins of all the stuff left behind—clothes, food, you name it. A mere hour into that day, Mac whipped an unopened container of talcum powder into the pick-up from a cabin door. I happened to be standing between him and the pick-up. He looked first, I saw him. Turns out I ducked in time, the container sailed through the open back window, hit the windshield, and exploded. Pink talcum powder filled the interior. With the fresh scent of roses. I figured then was a good time to pick up my paycheque and not say goodbye.

But working with inanimates—the firewood, mops, and so forth, I mean—went so well, I got another maintenance job, this time at a rural recreation complex. And this time I *was* fired. You'd think little could go wrong when you're dealing with inanimates. Not so.

Apparently I wasn't happy enough. It was the second time I was being fired for not being happy enough. Still, it threw me. I mean, it's not enough that I do my job well?

"You don't have lunch with the rest of us," the assistant manager said. "Not even coffee breaks," she complained. "You'd rather play with your dog." Well yeah. (I had been taking Kessie with me on nice days. She amused herself in the bush while I did whatever it was I was supposed to be doing. But at five to ten, five to twelve, and five to two, she'd be sitting outside whatever building I was in, waiting patiently, confidently, her ever-present bright fluorescent green tennis ball at her feet.)

I did spend one break watching the skating practice with the garbanzo guy. (It was a cold and rainy day—Kessie'd stayed at home.)

"Why aren't there any *men's* precision teams?" I asked him.

He looked at me, then back at the skaters.

"Sure, it requires attention to detail and a highly developed spatial sense. But men have those abilities, don't they? I mean, isn't that why, we're told, they dominate science and engineering?"

He looked at me again, but said nothing.

"Maybe it's the degree of cooperation required. Men are capable of cooperation—that's what *team* sports are all about—but in hockey, football, basketball, and the like, there's always room to be a star. Not so in a precision skating team. I betcha that's why there aren't any men's synchronized swimming teams either. There'd be way too many drownings.

"And sure, men are capable of the timing that cooperation entails. Quarterbacks and their receivers demonstrate this all the time. But the perfect synchrony of a precision team performance is achieved not by such *discrete* instances of cooperation, but by *continuous* cooperation. The sport requires ongoing adjustment to others, which requires awareness of and sensitivity to others, not to mention patience, and persistence, with the practice. It's not only about relationships—to the ice, to the music, to each other: it's about *maintaining* those relationships."

He spoke then. "Drill."

Right. "Oh, well, give a man a gun—"

We continued to watch the guys skate around. Then another thought occurred to me. "I know what it is: members of a precision team have to put their arms around each other—that's it, isn't it?"

He exploded at that point, shoving himself back from the boards. "I don't know why you're so hell-bent to get men into it! Let the girls have their synchronized skating. If they played hockey, they'd get hurt." True. They would. Because men have made beating someone senseless *part of the game*. And, in another case, *the game*.

"After all," he added, "you gals're more prone to injury, you gotta admit that." This from the sex that has its reproductive vitals hanging by a thread, at the bull's-eye of the body, with nary half an inch of fat for protection. And competes on the pommel horse, voluntarily.

"You're quiet when the others are chatting on the job," the assistant manager had continued. I'm thinking, I thought.

"You hardly ever smile," she said. That's because of *what* I'm thinking, I thought.

"For minimum wage, the smile's not included," I said. Unsmiling.

"Well, perhaps some day you can go back to school, get a degree, and get a job that pays *more* than minimum wage. I think you can do it," she smiled, encouragingly. And I remembered then that, of course, I'd put only grade 12 on my resume—if I'd listed my degrees, I wouldn't've gotten the job. And it had been either that job or welfare.

"And truth be told," she said, "I wasn't pleased with your little informal pay equity inquiry." I had noticed that there seemed to be a clear division of labour, based on sex, and I had wondered if there was a difference in pay. Aloud. (And yes indeed, people get paid almost twice as much to stack chairs as to clean them.)

"Or your mention of black lung." This was after one of my coworkers had said her whole arm was numb the evening of the day we did the dining hall floor. Said dining hall was as large as a school cafeteria and we had to scrub each tile, on our hands and knees, with a steel wool soap pad thing.

"Numb?" I had asked. "Does that happen a lot? I mean, how often do we have to do that floor?"

"Yeah, why doesn't she just rent a couple of sanders or polishers or something," one of the other women asked.

"You guys ever hear of black lung?" I asked. "Occupational hazard of working in the mines. They eventually got compensation for it, I think. Employers have to provide a safe and healthy workplace. You should say something."

Right. Maybe something like, "When can I pick up my severance pay?"

(I figured the Labour Board would have fun with this one. But of course unless you've worked for three months at the same place, none of the labour laws regarding dismissal apply.) (You'd think I would've remembered that.)

4

THE BUSINESS PROGRAM

So if I had a couple degrees, what was I doing cleaning floors for a living? Good question. I wasn't always so career-challenged.

Oh, hell, yes I was. Career-challenged. *So* always.

In my final year of my first degree, I was hired, as many English Lit students were, to be a marker for Comm101. It was a course that had a lot of written assignments, and it was a course intended for students who couldn't write. An interesting arrangement.

After the third or fourth set of assignments, I was no longer given batches to mark. It avoided the hassle of firing me. The professor of the course said she had received several written complaints about my marking, most of which were disturbing to read.

"So don't read them," I told her. Duh.

One student had complained about one of my comments: beside his sentence, "He was a sick man," I had written, "Avoid redundancy."

Another said he had a problem with my attitude, pointing to my "Hey Shit-for-Brains, use a capital letter at the beginning of a sentence!" remark.

Yet another accused me of being "prejudist" when I said that even Business students should learn how to spell. "That's what secataries are for," he added. "But how will you no if there doing a good job?" I wrote back.

Apart from being shallow, narrow-minded, selfish, and materialistic, business students just aren't very smart. (And yet, they're the ones who are trained to be our supervisors. Another interesting arrangement.) Consider their understanding of profit and loss. I was enlightened on this matter one night at the campus pub. (A couple of my track-mates were Business students, and they had invited me over to their table while I was waiting to shoot some pool. So it was that I became a semi-regular at their table.) (They didn't know I marked their papers.) It was just an ordinary pub night, not the Business Society Pub Night, so they weren't all dressed up as pigs and trying to drink beer through two straws shoved up their nose.

Shouting over the music and pouring myself a glass from one of the many available pitchers, I had asked the table at large, "Why is profit good?"

No one said, "Because it gives me pleasure, it makes me happy, I wanna be a rich sonuvabitch."

Instead, Tom, a serious student and the first to buy an attaché case, said, "Profit is good because it enables you to expand: to hire more people, to establish branches in other cities, to increase production."

"And why is this expansion good?" I asked.

"Well, because then you can make more profit."

"Can you say 'circular'?"

There was a pause in the conversation.

"What?"

"Profit is the purpose of business!" Dick proclaimed with his beer mug. "Why else would you go into business?" He was genuinely puzzled. And a vice-president-in-progress.

"Yeah, we have a *right* to maximize our profit!" Harry added with passion.

"Yeah? On what basis do you have that right?" I asked. "And

doesn't it trump, oh, I don't know, the right to food, water, and shelter?" There was another pause.

"What?"

"We have a *responsibility* to maximize our profit—a responsibility to our shareholders," Tom went for the A+ again.

"Can you say 'pass-the-buck'? What?"

There was another pause. With compound interest.

"Look," Tom was patient with me—after all, artsy fartsies aren't likely to understand this—"if someone invests in your company, giving you money to use, you have an obligation to give them the best return on their money."

"The best?" I repeated. "Why the best? Why not set a *fair* rate of return, and then include that as an expense, rather like the interest on a loan?" Surely Tom must've paused a moment, realizing how easily 'rate of return' came tripping off my tongue. But maybe not. For in that pause, surely I would've identified the phrase as an excellent example of alliteration.

"But why should people invest in your company if they can make more with another company," he said. "They're taking a loss then."

Thus was I introduced to their strange definition of loss. For most of us, loss is the difference between what you have at Time 1 and what you have at Time 2. Yesterday, I had ten marbles; today, I have seven; so I lost a few. Three, to be exact. However, people in business define loss as the difference between what you get and what you might've gotten. The baseline is not an actual amount, but some ideal amount. (And they say business people are realists.) So if they get ten marbles and they think they could've gotten a hundred, they 'suffer a loss' of ninety marbles. (Which means, I'd like to point out, that, by their own reckoning, they've lost quite a few more than I have.)

"Well if they'd stop reproducing like rabbits—hey, Sprintster!" One of my track buddies called me over as I passed by, on my way to the pool table. (I ran the 3,000 and my sprinting capacity was pretty much limited to the last ten metres—and reminiscent of Michael

Collins' slow-motion strides on the moon.) (Or would have been, if he'd bothered, back in 1969, to get out of his command module lazy-boy and go down to the surface.) "If they'd stop reproducing like rabbits, maybe they wouldn't be so poor." I was surprised at the topic of discussion. International Business must be this term.

"Yeah," I grabbed a chair, "it's about time they had tougher rape laws."

"What?"

"Well," I also grabbed a glass, "you don't think all those women *want* to be pregnant for seven or eight years, do you? I mean, do you really think a woman will *consent* to child number four when the other three are still under six? Do you have you any *idea* what it's like to look after three little human beings under six, for twenty-four hours a day? Especially when they're crying because they're so hungry, or they're retarded because they're malnourished—"

"That's just what those women—"

"—were bought for, I know. By their husbands, from their fathers. *Men* are the ones with the obsession for progeny—*their* progeny, *male* progeny." I was moving too fast for them. No doubt some were still considering the notion of tougher rape laws. Or, more likely, just the notion of rape. But I carried on. "And don't forget the violence of war factor. Iraq and Gaza top the chart with birth rates of 6.7 and 8.0 respectively. I wonder what the figures are for Bosnia, Croatia, Serbia—I mean really, do you think that after a hard day of castrating the enemy and raping its women, the Man of the House is going to come home to bed and *ask* first? I don't think so." I took a swallow. "And don't forget, this is war! *We* have to outnumber *them*! Funny," I added, "the Pope comes to mind just now." I saw I *had* lost them. "Though I suppose they wouldn't have to change the rape laws. They could just come up with a male contraceptive, 'the pill' for men. Actually, they did, back in '85."

"Yeah I remember something about that," one of them said. "Reduced your sex drive though."

"Oh. Well. We can't have that." He smiled at my apparent understanding. "HELLO," I raised my voice. "Let me tell you about 'the pill' for women. Side-effects include," I started counting on my fingers—a visual aid, "headaches, nausea, mood changes, yeast infections, loss of vision, high blood pressure, gall bladder disease, liver tumours, skin cancer, strokes, heart attacks, and death. Oh, and I almost forgot, reduced sex drive." I took a long swallow from my glass of beer. "Thing is, and get this—do not pass go until you do—taking the pill is, for many of us, preferable to getting pregnant."

"Yeah, well, you're the ones who get pregnant," he laughed. (Can you say 'non-sequitur'?) He had obviously missed my point. But what was *his* point? I really didn't know. Think. No good. Okay, think like a man. I can't, it hurts. Yes you can, try harder.

"Yeah, maybe you're right. Maybe it's okay that you guys refuse to be responsible for your reproductive capability. You wouldn't remember to take a pill every day anyway. What with your busy life of going to work and coming home again. So we'd end up being responsible for reminding you—perhaps after we pick up the kids on *our* way home from work, and make dinner, and do the dishes, but before we start the laundry, and see that the homework comes before tv. Which would sort of defeat the purpose." I paused. "'Course if it were beef-flavoured and chewable, like, say, the jerky treats my dog scarfs down—and it would have to come in regular and extra-strength so you could boast about your virility—" I switched into my Budweiser voice, "'I need the extra-strength to subdue my guys!' And it would have to be available without a prescription, of course—'Don't need to see no doctor to tell me what *I* can and can't take!' At all hardware stores. And beer st—hey, wait a minute! We could put it *in* the beer!" I raised my glass for a toast, but, sadly, no one joined me. Oh well. Pity.

By the end of the night, the marketing guys were holding the floor. They were trying to determine the best slogan ever.

"'You deserve a break today'," someone suggested. No. Close, but no.

"'Harvey makes a hamburger—" several guys joined in, "a beautiful thing.'" Too long.

"'This Bud's for you!'" someone loudly nominated and burped. And I swear I suddenly saw its genius: it's monosyllabic.

"'Gimme a Golden!'" someone else yelled with enthusiasm, but with dubious comprehension of the point under discussion.

"'Just do it!'" someone shouted. Ah. There we go. Monosyllabic and only three words.

"Hey, Sprintster, what gets your vote?"

I thought for a moment. "White men can't."

Another pub night. Another night of music, pool, and beer. From the entrance, I heard a rowdy "Chugga hugga bugga, Chugga hugga bugga, Chugga hugga bugga—Boo!" coming from one of their tables. Correction. Another night of beer, beer, and beer.

"Who's the occasion?" I asked, as I approached and pulled up a chair.

"Steve. He's going to be a millionaire by the time he's thirty. Just told us his plan."

"Yup. I wanna be a rich sonuvabitch!" Steve shouted, presiding over the table.

"Why?" I shouted back.

"What do you mean?" he sat down.

"Which word don't you understand?"

"What?"

"You don't want to be rich?" Steve asked then, realizing it wasn't a rhetorical question. Or would've, if he knew what a rhetorical question was.

"Not particularly, no."

"Why not?"

"Too much responsibility, figuring out what to do with all that money. Frankly, I'd rather watch *Murphy Brown*."

"Coupla cars, house in the Bahamas, what's to figure out?"

"Oh. You'd spend it on yourself? Even though you didn't deserve it?"

"I'd've *made* it!"

"Yeah, but that doesn't mean you'd've *deserved* it. A million bucks—that's what, thirty times what most people make in a year? There aren't enough hours in a day to have worked thirty times as long. And I can't imagine anything that would be thirty times a hard as what most people do. Would you have made a contribution to society thirty times as valuable? What's your big plan, are you going to manufacture the cure for AIDS? Build plants that can de-radiate nuclear waste?"

Arnie snorted into his beer, and some of the bubbles went up his nose. "Beer straws!" he blurted when he had recovered. And Steve pulled a straw out of his pocket. A very fat straw.

"The prototype," he said, sticking it into his mug, and draining it.

"You get drunk faster," someone explained cheerily. Right. Of course. I got up to shoot some pool.

When I returned to the table, the discussion was about whether there were aliens walking among us. And if so, should we kill them.

"I say kill the mother fuckers!"

"Yeah. And ask questions later!"

"But what if they're here to help us?"

"Help us what? Do we look like we need help?"

I almost sprayed my beer across the table on that one.

"Why would they come if not to take over, make us into slaves?"

"Yeah or take all our resources or something."

"Or use us for food! Arnie'd make a beautiful hamburger!" Arnie acknowledged the comment by raising his mug.

"Hey Sprintster, what do you think?

"Aliens walking among us? Yeah. They're called men." I grinned. "And yeah. Kill the mother fuckers."

Believe it or not, all this led to another job. Which makes me think that even business *students* are schmooze so through and through it leaks out, no, it oozes out, and—a faculty member came by the table one night and vaguely asked if anyone knew anyone who could mark papers for a distance ed course he was teaching.

Well, my track-mates, knowing I was this airy fairy *English* student, immediately volunteered my services. Turns out I didn't even have to say I had experience. Which I did, you'll recall—though the reference letter would've been a problem. I was hired on the spot. And this was the prof who taught HR—the course that covers hiring and firing procedures. (Can I give an example of foreshadowing?)

When I dropped by his office the next day to get the details—and to confirm that he actually remembered hiring me—I found out that the distance ed course he had referred to was for banking professionals seeking certification in various specialties such as—I kid you not—'Wealth Management.' To obtain such certification, said professionals had to complete a number of courses offered through correspondence by university professors.

Since I didn't know anything about wealth management (and would likely never need to), I was a little concerned about my ability to mark the assignments. However, my concern evaporated—or, more accurately, turned into something of a decidedly different nature—when I received my first batch of assignments along with the 'answer key.' Basically, the assignment questions required short answers of one or two sentences, which essentially could be copied from the course text. Pretty much everyone got 100% except for the few who missed a question or two. I was amazed. And indignant. University credit—an A+ no less—for copying sentences from a book? (I suddenly understood the vehemence that had often accompanied the Comm101 complaints about my "excessively high marking standards".) I wrote in the margin of the first few of these assignments, "Try to put your answers in your own words instead of copying verbatim from the book," but when I realized that such a comment was warranted on all 134 papers, well, I confess to inconsistency with regard to the provision of feedback.

Before I figured out whether and how to express my concern to the professor, he asked me to come to his office to discuss another project. Turns out he was writing a revolutionary book called *Power Training!* He showed me the outline: two neatly formatted pages with five columns, headed Motivation, Readiness (carefully subdivided into Psychological and Intellectual), Content Acquisition, Content Application, and Feedback. The first two columns were in green and supra-headed Pre-Put; the next, Content Acquisition, was in blue and supra-headed Input; then Content Application was in orange, Output; and finally the Feedback column was in red and supra-headed Post-Put. In each column, there were some phrases—'target questions', 'key examples', and so on. He was excited, pacing around me as I scanned the two pages, waiting for my response to this master plan.

"Well?" he asked eagerly, eyes shining.

"It's pretty" came to mind. I had not yet developed the meagre diplomatic skills that would, in any case, have been inadequate. Fortunately, I was still a little stunned, and a little confused as to my role. "It's . . . "

Never underestimate the power of arrogance to overestimate. "Yes, isn't it great?" he gushed. "See, most people in business, in the real world, who train employees don't really know what they're doing. They're given a content manual, but they know nothing about actually *teaching* the skills they expect their employees to have by the end of the training. This book will fill that gap! See—*Power Training!* This book will train the trainers!" He was very excited. Perhaps he was easily excited. In any case, I could tell he was the kind of person who calls an idea—one idea—a 'brainstorm.'

"And . . . " I still didn't know what I was doing there.

"And I'd like you to help. I need someone with good English, good writing skills."

Ah. "Oh, so you want me to proofread, or edit—" I was on firmer ground now, and I looked around for a manuscript.

"Well—yes. See, if you could just write it up—you'll need to develop the ideas a bit—then I could take a look at it—"

I held the two sheets of paper in my hand. And then realized that that was all he had. And then demonstrated beyond a doubt the absence of forementioned diplomatic skills. "You want me to write your book for you."

"Well—*I'd* still be the author, see they're *my* ideas," he said kindly. I looked at the sheets again: motivation, readiness, acquisition, application, feedback. *His* ideas. It suddenly occurred to me that university professors have no teacher training. (I can give an example of irony.)

He continued, “My project grant can cover wages for a research assistant for four months.” Is this how you people do things? Is this what you call ‘delegating’?

“You’ll get the usual undergraduate student stipend,” he added. Which was a little over minimum wage. He was hiring me to write his book for minimum wage. Tell you what. *You’re* the author. *You* write the book. *You* ‘develop the ideas a bit’. Put them into, oh, I don’t know, sentences. And paragraphs. And chapters. Then if you want me to check your spelling and grammar, well, maybe. Call me.

“And if you need any guidance with the research, let me know,” he smiled. (A really good example.)

So a month later, mostly because I could use the money, I presented a first chapter. It was from a little book I’d been using to prepare for my Piano Teachers’ Associate exam about the principles involved in teaching piano. I had turned to the section on motivating children and had pretty much copied it, verbatim. So I expected an A+. And got it. He was very impressed.

“Excellent! This is great!” he said, skimming the pages. “This is perfect for professionals already in the field! Just the right level, the right tone.” He beamed. “I look forward to the next chapter!”

Well. It was too easy. And way too much fun. So I carried on. Chapter two came from a manual used at the Training Center for Subversive Warfare. I had to make a few changes—for example, ‘Interrogation Techniques’ became ‘Pre-Quizzes’—but it was surprising how easily ‘free America’ could be replaced with ‘free enterprise’ . . . (Nevertheless, I had to delete altogether the section on ‘Advanced Torture’.) Again, he loved it.

The big test was chapter three. Content Acquisition. The content in question was to be HR-related. I knew next to nothing about HR. So I took most of it from the text he was using for his course. He didn’t recognize any of it.

At our next meeting, two months in, he was brimming with

pride—he'd sent the first three chapters to the publisher as an interim progress report. Apparently this was standard procedure. I didn't know that.

So, in lieu of chapter four, I presented him with the original material used for the first three chapters, along with the page from the university's calendar that defined plagiarism.

Actually, I didn't exactly present it to him. I sort of left it in his mailbox one night. Well, one pub night. And in good spirits—in very good spirits—I had written across the top—in green, blue, orange, and red—"Chugga hugga bugga—Boo!"

As for marking his distance ed assignments, well, I was going to quit anyway.

5

NANNY (NOT.)

Right after that first degree (and I want to emphasize that it was a *double* Honours, in English Lit *and Philosophy*— because most people seem to be in some sort of denial about the existence, let alone the value, of the latter discipline) (referring, as it does, basically, to thinking about stuff), right after that first degree, I got a job out in B.C. It was absolutely incredible. I was hired by a married-with-two-kids couple who lived on a lake. So I lived on the lake too. Talk about too good to be true. May, June, July, and August stretched lazily before me, glistening in the sun on the water, the mountains in the distance . . . I could dive into that clear cool water morning, noon, and night, I could wander along the stream that fed the lake, I could hike through the forest . . .

I lived in a room above the garage and while they apologized for it being apart from the main house, I thought the solitude was, again, too good to be true. A room of my own. In the garage was a little Kawasaki I was welcome to use (and I thought going *up* the mountain was a rush . . .). In the house was a piano I was also welcome to use (which was great because I still had half of my Associate exam to take), as well as a pool table (my minor, you'll recall). And if all of that weren't enough, they were water ski enthusiasts. Yee-haw!

My *job* was part cook, part maid, part babysitter, part tutor, part groundskeeper, part chauffeur, and for two or three days a week when I accompanied the husband to his office in Vancouver, part executive assistant, part researcher, part gopher supreme. No nine to five routine here, this was the best!

I got fired from half of the job after two weeks. The best half. The lake half. You have to wonder how, with all those fringe benefits, I fucked up. You *do. I* do.

"You don't seem happy," the wife said, as she lounged in her padded chair by the lake, drink in hand. (This particular observation was obviously a recurring leitmotif in the history of my employment.)

Well, being on call twenty-four hours a day to an aggressive workaholic and a passive perfectionist and therefore seldom having more than half an hour at a time to enjoy all those fringe benefits does rock the cruise ship a bit. These people actually got up at six in the morning to go skiing. I was expected to spot. Sure, I could ski too, but at six in the morning, I generally have trouble walking.

"And the kids don't feel comfortable coming to you with their problems," she added, vaguely gesturing.

It's true. I consistently fail the National Nanny Test. "Well, why should they?" I asked. "They don't even know me. *You're* their mom. Besides," I added, "I don't like them." I mean hey, kids are *by definition* immature.

She stared at me, horrified. Why is it that so many people, I wondered, expect everyone to put children first? Especially *their* children. Whenever I did my chauffeur bit, I routinely adjusted the mirrors, checked the oil, and then ripped off the 'Baby-on-Board!' sign.

First, Jenny and Todd weren't babies anymore. Second, even if they were, I think they have as much right as anyone to be fatally injured in a rear-end collision. Why should *I* be expected to go through life giving right of way to *your* offspring?

People replicate themselves, for the most part rather thoughtlessly, even recklessly, and then demand the results be treated with the utmost respect. Why should I act any more responsibly toward the product than you did toward the process? It's not like you obtained my permission—but now you expect my participation.

(Interestingly, we have the same irrational attitude to the newly dead. Like the newly born, they are imbued with some sort of purity. Never mind that in between, they're just ordinary, unremarkable assholes who don't much give a damn for anyone but themselves.)

Well, apparently my attitude sucked. (This was also to become a recurring leitmotif.) So she fired me.

I suspect she was just pissed about the dinner party. They had a lot of day-long dinner party things, for which we spent much of the previous day preparing. I 'took care of' the vegetables. Interesting how flexible the definitional limits of that phrase are. On the first of such preparation days, I washed the piles she had put on the counter: potatoes, carrots, celery, tomatoes, other red things, white things, and a bunch of green stuff I didn't recognize. Then I thought I was through. The look she gave me indicated otherwise.

"You may as well peel them now," she said, tactfully, as if I had planned to peel them later. Right. As if.

So, remembering my mother's manufactured obsession with white, I peeled the brown skins off the potatoes. There went the vitamins. Next—I glanced over, the She-Bitch-Wife was still supervising me from the other end of the large kitchen—were the carrots. Beets too had to be peeled. Who knew? I'd spent the previous year living on potatoes (unpeeled) (and raw), apples (ditto) (ditto), canned beans, and Shreddies. (I could say that that was due to the lack of a fridge and a hotplate. But I'd be lying.) When I started on the celery, I got another look. The tomatoes too were spared. Okay, *now* I'm done. I rinsed my hands and dried them on a towel.

"Slice and dice!" she said sweetly—though really I'm just guessing about that—as I moved toward the door.

Why would you slice and dice, for example, carrots? They're much harder to eat that way. A fork is required. Mindful of the hours of practice I still needed if I was to pass my exam, I handled this slice and dice task with the greatest of concentration.

Then she showed me how to make 'radish roses'. At first I thought anyone who carves radishes into roses has *way* too much time on their hands. But then I got into what I started to call 'raw sculpture'. I discovered a thing that makes melon balls. And I discovered a melon. I started putting poppy seed happy faces on my little melon balls. Then sad faces, and stern faces, and winks. Recalling the balloon toys of someone's childhood, I joined orange and green melon balls with toothpicks and made a centipede. A happy centipede. Hours passed. Then I remembered Mr. Potato Head! She stopped me when I started dressing my melon creations with Jenny's doll clothes.

In the meantime, she took care of marinating the meat. She put it into a pan, poured some stuff over it, and then watched it. An hour after I'd left the kitchen, she was still there, sherry in hand, watching the meat soak. (Perhaps it was a metaphor.)

Anyway, at the dinner party in question—I noticed a dish of cucumber cubes beside the dish of radish roses—she had obviously discovered what I'd done with the cucumber, complete with a cute little sailor hat, and had sliced and diced it. (No doubt *that* was a metaphor.) At the dinner party in question—they always assumed I'd look after the guests' kids, as well as Jenny and Todd—one kid was pre-linguistic but ambulatory. (That's just wrong, by the way. Kids should learn how to talk *before* they start moving around.) And yes, I did notice she wasn't quite house-trained. But I didn't know how to change a diaper. Seriously. (Why do people assume such knowledge is genetically encoded with the X chromosome?) (Okay, true, even if I did know . . .) Somehow my apparent incompetence made the She-Bitch-Wife look bad, like a tarnished trophy.

As did my apparent competence. Later in the evening, when everyone had 'retired' to the spacious 'piano parlour' and she had left for a moment, one of her guests asked me to play something (I can't remember how they found out I could play). So I did. I played one of the pieces I was working on for my exam, the Mozart. And I must say, that piece, at least, was definitely performance-ready. When she returned, she also played something. Unfortunately, it was the very same piece (what are the odds?), and comparison was all too easy.

So I figured she was just pissed about the dinner party. Well, that and Todd's birthday party. Todd, a quiet boy, didn't have enough friends for a game of checkers, let alone a birthday party, so from the start the party had the effect of accentuating his social inadequacies. But his mom insisted that her little boy would have a birthday party. He was turning six. So she invited all these other boys—she'd probably put up an ad at the Seven-Eleven—who were aged anywhere from, well, seven to eleven, it turned out. Todd didn't know most of them. And he didn't like any of them. And he was afraid of some of them.

Now, I don't know anything about doing a kid's birthday party. They didn't ask about that at the interview. They asked if I had a drivers' licence, they asked about my hobbies, and they were very impressed with the fact that I was university-educated. But I hadn't taken Birthday Parties 101. I hadn't even taken Child Psych. (I had taken Criminal Psych. So if Todd, or Jenny, had had a criminal record, *that* I would've been able to handle . . .) (And I'd taken Abnormal Psych. Which, actually, turned out to be—oh never mind.)

I did, however, bake him a birthday cake. Sort of. Turned out I invented a pudding-in-the-middle cake. And if I had patented it, years before Betty Crocker or Duncan Hines did so, I could've been a rich sonuvabitch by now. (Where was Steve when I needed him?)

Anyway, the boys wanted to play cops and robbers or cowboys and indians or missionaries and natives, but whenever I hear gunshot sounds, I imagine people dying. Go figure. So I said no and suggested they listen to a piano concert instead. My Bach needed work.

Well, no one but Todd wanted to do that. So I kept the birthday boy happy, oddly enough, by playing one bar at a time of Bach's second Prelude over and over . . .

The other boys went swimming and, apparently, two of them drowned. As I later explained to Todd, that was an excellent example of natural selection. If people who can't swim are stupid enough to jump off a dock, well, what happened was a good thing. Especially since, as young boys, they hadn't yet replicated their stupidity.

Todd mutely nodded his agreement, having been tossed into the lake at three years of age by his He-Man-Dad, a strong advocate of the 'Sink or Swim' school of thought. (Todd had promptly discovered a third option, 'Flail about in Terror', thus demonstrating the false dichotomy error of reasoning. And so, though he hasn't spoken above a whisper since, he will have an advantage over his classmates in Critical Thinking 101.)

Ah well. So long, and thanks for all the granola. As I packed my stuff, it occurred to me that another factor might have been the Wrist-Master Moment. While driving to work one day—in the pre-SUV minivan—not the Mazeratti, or the pick-up—and we never took the big Kawasaki of course (this guy was intent on being a man—he just couldn't decide which one)—the He-Man-Husband started to do repeat contractions with this hand-exerciser wrist-master thing, explaining, between grunts of exertion, how good it was not only, grunt, for his slalom time, grunt, but also, grunt, for his tennis game. He invited me to try it. Well. I pinched the thing together like it was a clothespin. He almost went off the road. Hey, He-Man-Dickhead, four hours a day at the keyboard for fifteen years, a solid half hour of which is Hanons and octaves—hello: pianists are *not* the limp-wristed fags you like to think they are. (It sure wasn't technique that got me second place in the I-dare-you arm-wrestling competition one night at the pub . . .)

And, okay, that dance class might have also been a factor. One day, while I was watching Jenny's kinderdance class from the back of the studio, perched on a small chair with the rest of the mothers or mother-substitutes, the teacher had to suddenly leave.

"Would you take over for a moment, please?" she said to me, rushing out. Serves me right for sitting closest to the door.

Okay. Sure. How hard can this be? I stood in front of the class.

"All right, let's try a simple step-together-step-touch," I said, demonstrating, moving to the right, and then to the left. And forgetting for the moment that they had probably just learned how to walk. Forward. I was now expecting them to dance. Sideways.

A glance in the mirror tipped me off. One went down. Then another. And a third. Ohhh, that had to hurt. The fourth watched speculatively, chubby legs planted firmly, thumb in her mouth. It refused to try the step. It was destined for great things in life.

Okay, I thought, I'm no Bob Fosse, I'm not obsessed with that particular step, my choreography can do without it.

"Good," I said after the three casualties had regained an erect posture, "Very good." (I knew the importance of positive feedback—it was in *Power Training!* after all.) "How about just a step-touch, step-touch, step-touch," I exaggerated the step, moving from side to side.

Interestingly, all of them got it almost immediately. Well, the step part anyway. They weren't having anything to do with the touch part. They all just started rocking stiff-legged from side to side. A few glanced with furtive pride to the back—Look Ma, I'm a dancin' fool!

'Course, none of them were in time with the music. Well then, let's work on our rhythm. I put on what would become one of Kessie's favourites, "Dead Skunk in the Middle of the Road."

"Let's all clap in time to the music," I said with enthusiasm, clapping in time to the music. They tried. It sounded like an erratic echo chamber. One loud clap—mine—on beat one, and a bunch of tiny echo claps scattered haphazardly among the microbeats of the rest of the bar. Quite a neat effect, actually.

I then noticed that a few had hands that kept missing each other. Coordination! Of course! I'm sure that's also in the lesson plan! So when they had tired of clapping, fourteen seconds into the song, I said, "Okay, everyone, let's try something else. Put your arms out straight. Now close your eyes and touch your nose with the second finger of your right hand."

Drunks, the whole lot of them. Especially the few who fell down as soon as they had closed their eyes.

"All right, good try. This might be easier. Open your eyes. Now turn to the person beside you and try to touch *their* nose with your finger!"

I did not say 'run'. I did not say it was a new game of tag. I swear I did not. But suddenly they were all screeching with glee, zooming around with both arms outstretched, fingers pointing, aiming for someone's nose. Of course, the nose is rather next to the eyes.

"Okay, everyone," I clapped my hands for attention, "Come sit in a circle! That's it—help those who have been recently blinded—help them find the circle, that's it, over here, a little to your left . . . no, your other left . . . "

6

RECREATION DIRECTOR

So what was next? Exactly what you might expect for an ex-track team member, an avid athlete. I became a Recreation Director. At an old age home.

Okay, so I wouldn't be organizing squash tournaments or high impact aerobics classes. But surely they'd be able to handle shuffleboard and line dancing.

Or not. Apparently somewhere around eighty, one leaves the golden years and enters immediately into the rust years. Not only do things fall apart, they disintegrate. Flesh, bones. Brains.

The manager of the home, my supervisor, was Mrs. Sloane. She was a young woman in her early seventies. And, like many of the residents, she had Alzheimer's and no short-term memory whatsoever. (There was a similarity here, now that I think of it, to the 'must have first hand experience' requirement at the mental health home.) (Who trained these HR people?) (Oh, I bet I know . . .)

"Good morning, Mrs. Sloane," I said on Monday.

"Who are you?"

"I'm Brett Laramie. I'm the Recreation Director."

She nodded and walked away.

"Good morning, Mrs. Sloane," I said on Tuesday.

"Who are you?"

"I'm Brett Laramie. I'm the Recreation Director."

She nodded and walked away.

They say that people with Alzheimer's do have lucid times. In fact, hearings to determine mental competence are scheduled for exactly such times. Mrs. Sloane's lucid time was obviously not morning.

Nor was it late afternoon.

"Goodbye, Mrs. Sloane, see you tomorrow."

"Who are you?"

Insofar as a hefty chunk of what we call 'self' is memory, those with extensive loss of memory can be expected to have, as well, extensive loss of self. This is not to say, however, that there weren't any colorful characters at Parkdale. There were. Most notable of these was Mr. Flynn.

First day on the job, I heard him say, from somewhere behind me, "Hello, luv!"

"I'm not—," I turned to deck him one, "—nearly as colorful as you," I finished lamely. He was wearing orange pants and a turquoise-and-yellow-splashed shirt.

The day after, he was in purple striped pants and a fuchsia shirt.

The day after that, he was in emerald green plaid pants and a lime green shirt.

"I've spent my entire life wearing black, grey, brown, and navy," he explained. "With white shirts. And I'm sick of it!" He stamped his cane for emphasis. "Who said straight men have to stick to black, grey, brown, and navy? What kind of a stupid rule is that?"

I shrugged. It *was* a stupid rule.

"So I decided I'm not going to wear black, grey, brown, or navy ever again. I'm going to wear orange, and red, and yellow, and turquoise, and pink, and mauve, and—" he ran out of breath, "and I have to sit down." I helped him to one of the many chairs that seemed to be all over the place. Now I knew why.

"Good for you!" I said. "I mean, what does color have to do with—anything?"

A few days later, amazed at yet another get-up—he never wore the same thing twice—I asked him where he got all his lively clothes.

"Second-hand shops," he said. "You know, where people donate stuff that doesn't fit anymore, stuff they don't want anymore," he lowered his voice, "stuff that belonged to people who have passed on."

"Really?" I was surprised. Not that people donated the clothing of the deceased to second-hand shops, but that that was where he got his clothes. Either there are a lot of dead gay men out there—well, actually, I guess there are—or there are a lot of dead straight men who had secret closets full of colorful clothes.

A week or so later, I happened to drive him to such a second-hand shop. I figured day trips were well within my job description. They were, after all, recreational. If not for him, certainly for me.

As soon as he entered the store, he made a bee line for the women's section. Of course. And why not? For years, I've been buying half of my clothes in the men's department.

That's not to say there weren't any boring residents. There were. Mr. Cooper, for example. The only other man at Parkdale. (That's right. Sixty residents, fifty-eight women. Yay us?) I joined him for lunch one day, as he was always sitting alone.

"Bobby Orr is the greatest damned hockey player there ever was!" He told me angrily.

I nodded noncommittally.

"And you've got no business trying to tell me otherwise!" He glared at me, threatening.

"I'm not," I said. Defensively. I couldn't help it.

"He's got the best stick handling, he's got the speed, he's got more assists, and more goals than *anyone* in the league! I'm telling you!" He was red-faced by now. Intimidation is such hard work.

"Okay, okay," I said. Now *I* was getting angry. "I'm not disagreeing with you!"

No wonder he was always sitting alone. He was always—still—at ninety-three—fighting. Whether or not anyone was fighting back. Geez, what was this guy's problem?

Too bad *he* didn't get Alzheimer's. It could wipe the slate clean and he could start over. 'Course, by the time your experiences shape your personality, it probably doesn't matter whether you remember them or not.

One day as I was wandering around looking for something to do—most of the residents seemed quite able to amuse themselves, what with watching television and listening to the radio—I saw Mrs. Plume standing at a hallway T-junction that was barricaded with ribbon.

"Hallway's closed," she told me with a happy officiousness. "Go-cart race."

"Go-carts." I was doubtful, it's true.

"Well, no, not really go-carts," she admitted. "We use our chairs. Some of those new powered ones can really go!"

Well, I had to see this.

"Do you need any help? Is the entire course cordoned off already?"

Before Mrs. Plume could respond, the sound of a horn in the distance made her jump. Well, sort of.

"They're off!" she shouted (well, sort of) and fixed her sights on the corner at the end of the hall. "Here they come!" she said excitedly and stared down the hall with intense anticipation.

I looked down the hall. Nothing. A minute went by.

"Here they come!" she cried out again.

Two minutes went by.

"Go Edna!" she called out. "You can do it!"

Just as I was beginning to think Mrs. Plume was living in her own little world (which was fine, by the way), I saw Edna—Mrs. Hartley—edge around the corner in her wheelchair. Though from the manic glint in her eye, you'd think she was moving at breakneck speed. Actually, given the brittle state of her bones, she really *was* moving at breakneck speed: anything faster than stationary and she could easily break her neck.

A full half of her wheelchair was visible by now.

"Go Edna!" Mrs. Plume was practically jumping up and down. Physically impossible, of course, but she was flexing her knees just the tiniest little bit, and jabbing her arm in the air. Well, waving it feebly.

"Go Mrs. Hartley!" I yelled. Then Mrs. Austin rounded the corner. And right behind her, someone whose name I didn't know.

"Go Mrs. Austin! Go Mrs. Whoever-you-are!" It wouldn't do for the recreation director to play favorites. We watched them as they made their way toward us, and shouted encouragement every five minutes.

"Vroom, vroom!"

"Grrrrrh!"

What the—they were providing their own sound effects.

Mrs. Austin pulled ahead as, I suspect, Mrs. Hartley's finger fell off the power button. But she recovered as they passed us and re-gained the lead.

"Vroom, vroom!" They were having a riot, an absolute riot, as they raced (well, sort of) around the next corner and disappeared from our sight.

Just as they did so, we heard a whistle.

"She's stuck! That's Edna's whistle!" Mrs. Plume took off. "Gotta go! I'm her pit crew!"

As I hurried—well, no, I just sort of strolled along beside her—we heard a, a kazoo?

"It's a pile-up!" she shouted. Okay, spoke a little more loudly. And she upped the pace. "Come on!" she urged. Herself, since I was already ahead of her. Mrs. Bronner entered the track from the next side hall and pulled alongside Mrs. Plume. She was Mrs. Austin's pit crew, no doubt, since Mrs. Plume started elbowing her aside to gain an advantage. Either that or she kept losing her balance.

Then I heard a—what was that? It sounded familiar, but I couldn't quite place—a pitch-pipe! It was one of those round plastic pitch-pipe things that my grade three teacher had used way back when. Mrs. Willerby. I did the math. It could *be* Mrs. Willerby!

I rounded the corner then and saw that it was indeed a pile-up. A three-chair pile-up. A recurring three-chair pile-up, as all three of them were backing up then ramming into each other over and over. Road rage? Not by a long shot. They were all cackling with delight. Laughing their fool heads off. I gathered that none of them had been allowed to go go-cart racing when they were young. Or ride in the bumper cars. Note to self: it's never too late to make up for lost time.

Mrs. Plume and Mrs. Bronner finally arrived at the scene, and Mrs. Gardenia, from the other direction. The pit crew personnel extricated the racers from each other, and they continued on their way.

"Go Edna!"

"Go Alma!"

"Go Gladys!"

Fifteen minutes later, they rounded the next corner and were into the straightaway. There in the distance was Mrs. Shanty, waving a checkered flag.

"Come on!" she yelled, waving them on, "Come on!" She had a stopwatch. Was someone about to set a record? Zowee, what excitement!

"Go Edna!"

"Go—" Mrs. Bronner had obviously forgotten Alma's name. No matter. Alma had forgotten the race.

"Go Gladys!

Edna and Gladys approached the finish line neck in neck. Just as Mrs. Shanty fell down and broke her hip.

Inspired, I decided to organize the Parkdale Olympics. We held the event in the back by the shuffleboard court. Actually, we held it *on* the shuffleboard court. Given the nature of our two events, it was more than sufficient. The spectators sat in the lawn chairs, and the kitchen staff provided lemonade—Gatorade for the competitors. Mrs. Plume had helped set up the finish line with her ribbon, and Mrs. Shanty had agreed to officiate as starter with her horn. It was something she could do from her bed. It had wheels.

I called the first event, the 10M. Instead of the men's and the women's, we had the free-standings, the canes, and the walkers. There were five competitors in the free-standings race, and Mrs. Juvenal won by a full minute. Hardly fair, though, as she was a full decade younger than the other four.

The canes race caused quite a stir. Unbelievably, Mr. Cooper knocked Mrs. Sheffer's cane out from under her about three metres from the finish line. What was wrong with this guy? Amazingly, she kept her feet. Which, given the state of her knees and her persistent dizziness, was like landing an aerial on the balance beam. We all applauded. She took a bow. Well, a nod. A few minutes later Mr. Cooper broke the tape at the finish line, and actually threw up his arms in victory, to no one's cheers but his own. That movement made him lose his balance, and he went down. To everybody's cheers but his own.

The walkers race turned into a free-for-all relay, mostly because everybody ran out of patience. I'm happy to say that not one exchange ended in the disaster I anticipated when I saw old person after old person get up, shoo a racer away from her walker, and take over.

Our second event was the broomstick throw. I probably could have gotten my hands on a javelin, but, to be honest, I didn't want to. Not with Mr. Cooper around. I don't know where the six brooms came from, since maintenance was responsible for cleaning the residents' rooms, but each of the women entered in the event brought her own broom. One by one they stepped up to the line and, in a weird ritual they all seemed to have agreed on, they swished their broom back and forth on the ground in front of them, then heaved it as far as they could. Which was actually quite far, given the relatively poor aerodynamics of a broom. The longest toss was—well, the one that went the furthest. We didn't bother measuring, since we could tell at a glance which one had been thrown the furthest, once they were all lying there in a pile. Two passers-by who had elected not to attend or participate in the Olympics (or, more likely, had forgotten it was taking place) saw the event in progress, and, not fully understanding what was going on, returned with dustpans, which they enthusiastically threw into the pile of brooms. Then again, perhaps it was me who didn't fully understand what was going on.

Our Olympics stimulated enough interest to start a rudimentary calisthenics class. Very rudimentary. But it turned out to take a lot more energy to go through the motions in slow motion, very slow motion, than to do them at the usual speed, so I ended up just giving directions from a chair.

"Left. One.   Two.   Right. One.
Okay, good, class is over, see you tomorrow!"

Watching tv with them one afternoon (fortunately, it was not a Sunday), I decided to solicit suggestions.

"What would you like to do?" I asked them. "What recreational events or activities would you like me to organize?"

"I'd like to try snowboarding," Mrs. Bennett said.

"Whitewater rafting," Mrs. Joule suggested.

Hm. But why not? I mean, isn't that the best way to go? In the middle of doing something you really want to do? Compared to dying there, in an old age home. Or worse, in some hospital room. I'd be providing support for their transition from institutionalized living to—no, that wouldn't be recreation, by any definition.

And even if I could—even if I started going on all these day trips and coming back with an empty car, someone would put two and two together (well, two minus one) and, well, I'm sure *that* would be grounds for dismissal.

I thought a nice contrast to all that physical activity would be some entertainment. So I called the local high school and invited the drama club to come perform their current show for us. The drama teacher was delighted. They were preparing for a festival and dress rehearsals were all very well, but there was nothing like having a live audience. (Well, sort of, I told her.)

So they arrived one Tuesday afternoon, all young and eager. They cleared a performance space by moving all the dining room chairs into rows, which were occupied immediately by Parkdale's finest. They didn't want to miss a thing. The students carried on with great concentration, the tech students setting up some rudimentary lighting, the music students tuning up, the designated costume and make-up students making last minute adjustments. By the time they were ready to begin, most of the audience was exhausted. And asleep.

Me too, I'm ashamed to admit. Well, not right away. But a few minutes into Act One. But geez, it was Gilbert and Sullivan. *H.M.S. Pinafore*. Why oh why do high schools insist on having their students perform those tired old musicals? My god the thing's over a hundred years old. Can the school not afford a set of scripts for something new? I doubt the students even know, or care, what a pinafore is.

Feeling rather bad about how that turned out, I contacted the teacher the week after with an exciting proposal.

"You know how business students and tech students have co-op programs? They work in an office or a garage for a couple weeks, for credit? Well, humanities students don't have that opportunity, do they? I mean, there aren't any co-op programs for English or Music or Drama students. We know nothing about the real world when we graduate. We are totally useless. Humanities students should have the chance to be, like, interns at a publishing company or assistants to symphony orchestras."

"Oh, I agree," the teacher said. "Completely. But there aren't any publishing companies or symphony orchestras here."

"No. But there's Parkdale."

"I don't follow."

"I propose that we start a drama co-op program."

"Doing what? I mean, what would the students do there that would enhance their dramatic skills?"

"They could pretend to be the family members of residents who don't get visitors. Have your students come once a week. I'll assign each student to a resident, one with memory loss, who'll never know the difference. The students can pretend to be their great-grand-daughter or whoever. I'll take care of the matchmaking and have their assignments ready when they arrive. I'll provide a bit of a back story, but they'll have to improvise from there. All in all, they'll get a unique acting experience." I paused. "Okay, they'll still be useless when they get out into the real world, but hey, it's a start."

She loved it. We started that same week.

"Okay," I said to Jessica, shy mousey Jessica who didn't seem at all the drama club type, "you can be Mrs. Matthews' great-grand-daughter. Down the hall on your right, Room 16. Mrs. Matthews used to be an accomplished pianist. It would delight her to no end if she knew her great-grand-daughter was studying the piano."

"But what if she asks me to play?" Jessica asked, worriedly.

"Improvise! You're a drama student after all, right?" She looked doubtful.

"You can do it!" She headed off down the hall. "Shine!" I called out after her.

"And Ryan," I looked up at a throwback to the 60s, "you can be Mrs. Devreau's great-grand-son, from—" I consulted my files "—Jamaica."

"Okay, mon'," he smoothly slipped into a Jamaican accent. That was half British. Or maybe Norwegian. "But I left me ganja at home. Can I—?" He decided not to finish the question. "We be happy anyway." He lilted away, down the hall, and I swear I could feel the sun on my face . . . Too bad about the ganja.

"Sara." Sara was riotgrrl extraordinaire. "You can be Mrs. Lewis' grand-daughter. She works in a bank."

"Aw, can't I work in a pizza joint instead?" I caught a flash of her pierced tongue.

"I don't know. Why don't you run that by your grand-mother and see what she thinks."

I finished assigning the remaining students to various residents, then starting walking around, standing outside the rooms of those residents with 'visitors', briefly listening in to make sure things were going smoothly. They were! My co-op program was working beautifully!

Then I saw Jessica being pulled along to the living room by an enthusiastic Mrs. Matthews. Oh no. There was a piano in the living room. I started to follow at a discreet distance, then stopped, then started again—do I really want to witness this? Too late, I was already at the doorway.

Well. Jessica give a magnificent performance! It was showy, it was passionate, it was sensitive. It was *dramatic*! And it was an awful cacophony, nothing but dissonance after dissonance, please make it stop . . . She leaned into the keyboard and swooshed from end to end with what would have been a sparkling cascade of arpeggios if she'd managed to hit the notes of any known chord. After that flourish of a finish, Mrs. Matthews burst into applause, beaming with pride. I had to applaud as well. It was, after all, a stunning performance.

"Bravo!" I called out, as I walked toward them. Jessica beamed. It was a moment. It was the moment she became an actor. A brilliant actor. And she was launched into an encore. I grabbed her wrist with a steely grip.

"Mrs. Matthews is stone cold deaf," I said. "Please. I am not."

By the fourth week, the students were clearly bored with being good little great-grand-daughters and -sons. Especially since they'd discovered old people aren't necessarily nice people. So I said they could create their own characters for the following week.

Sara showed up as a vampire. "Someone with Type AB, I think," she deadpanned at me. I obliged.

Squeaky clean and annoyingly preppie Jason was a prison inmate. He had the bright orange coveralls (didn't find those in the high school costume collection, I bet) (I hope) and a scruffy look.

"Can I visit Mrs. Esson?" He also had the flat voice—of a sociopath. "I want that bitch to see the apple doesn't fall far from the tree. What goes around comes around. She never should've had kids."

Oh my.

Frankly, I shared his view of Mrs. Esson. But, "Don't you think she'll notice you're—black?"

His impressively dull eyes just looked at me.

"Tell me you're not in for murder."

An ever-so-brief moment passed. "I'm not in for murder."

"Room 38," I said.

And Kyle, handsome Kyle, smart Kyle, Kyle who was going to have an amazing life, I just knew it—Kyle was all nervous in a pink shirt. "Mr. Flynn, I presume?"

"No, Mr. Cooper, please."

I raised my eyebrows. "Dress rehearsal?" I asked, after a moment.

He nodded anxiously.

"Okay, Mr. Cooper it is," I said. "Down the hall on your left." He headed off. "Good for you!" I called out after him. Though in retrospect, that probably should have been "Good luck!"

And Ryan, God bless him, Ryan was Jesus Christ. He had the robe, the sandals, the oh-so-beatific expression. Hm.

"Mrs. Stornaway has been a little low in self-esteem this week," I said. "Why don't you visit her? Tell her you're her son."

Two weeks later, I decided it was time for something a bit more active. It was time for a field trip! I found out what was playing in Toronto, asked around as to preferences, and decided we'd go see *Cats*. I'd always wanted to see *Cats*. It was bound to be better than *H.M.S. Pinafore*. So I scheduled a bus and arranged for the purchase of a block of tickets. We'd leave in the morning, then somewhere along the way, pull over for an early lunch. It was a matinée performance, and on the way back, we'd stop for a quick dinner. All set!

So, on the morning of our big trip, we were all gathered outside in the parking lot eagerly awaiting our bus. When it came into view, we cheered. We were a cheerful group. We were going to see *Cats*! The bus pulled to a stop, and the driver opened the door. Oops. While I'd remembered to book one with an on-board washroom, I neglected to ask that it have an automated lift. None of them could make the steps.

Oh well, I had fun anyway.

As planned, the bus returned around seven o'clock. It pulled into the parking lot, and I got out. Mrs. Sloane was there waiting.

"Hello Mrs. Sloane!" I said cheerfully. "I'm—"

"I know who you are. You're Brett Laramie. You're the Recreation Director. And—oh my god—the bus is empty! You've come back with an empty bus! What have you done?" She was horrified.

Apparently the evening was Mrs. Sloane's lucid time. Sort of.

7

TRAVEL WRITER

So when I was on campus one day—I'd decided to stay in Vancouver (it didn't have much sun, but it did have sand) (and ganja) (so I'd heard) and spend some time taking courses I hadn't had room for when I was doing the double English Lit and Philosophy thing (am I an over-achiever or what), I saw an interesting ad.

"Can't afford to travel to Europe?" Why, no. I can't. I can't afford to pay my rent. "Write your own ticket!" You can do that? "We're looking for university students who have never been to Europe to write about their experiences there!" Um. If they've never been to Europe, how can they write about their experiences there? "Call us for more information about this fantastic opportunity!!" Well, that writing about non-experiences bit did seem rather fantastic, so, what the hell, why not.

Especially since my courses weren't going too well. I'd been kicked out of Music Composition when I'd said that I thought Bartok's endings were cop-outs. I mean, he did all this weird and wonderful off-the-wall stuff in his pieces and then ended with the standard V—I cadence. Despite having asked us what we thought, the professor became absolutely livid when I expressed my opinion. Truth be told, though, I think my comment was just the last straw. My very presence in class was, apparently, disruptive. Perhaps he couldn't deal with a woman who wanted to be a composer, or, since I showed up in jeans, leather jacket, and construction boots—

The construction boots were from my brief stint as a litter picker back in between my first and second year. University students who were hired to work in the City's recreation programs during July and August were hired for May and June to form litter crews. Armed with a burlap bag and a litter pick—essentially a sawed-off broom with a four-inch nail stuck in the end—which was why steel-toed construction boots were mandatory—a very good idea, by the way—bunches of us would be let off at a park in the morning, and then picked up late afternoon, with the expectation that the park would be litter-free by then. One day, we—okay, I—organized the Litter Crew Olympics. The empty litter bag race was a hoot, and the full litter bag toss was also fun—though the appeal seemed to be not so much the length of the tosses as the exploding litter bags—but the litter pick spear throw went horribly wrong . . .

—and carrying my motorcycle helmet, perhaps the esteemed professor couldn't deal with a motorcyclist who wanted to be a composer. Or maybe the problem was a woman who drove a motorcycle. In any case, my opinion of Bartok's endings sent him over the edge. And shortly after that, I quit the Studio Fine Arts class—I'd gotten into an accident at an intersection and broken my arm. I couldn't draw worth a damn with my right hand; trying with my left was a complete waste of time.

So, as my arm was pretty much healed, and my bike was still at the shop, I decided to call about this Europe thing. Turns out it was a travel magazine catering to university and college students, and they were looking for people who had never been to Europe, to go. They'd pay fifty bucks for each 'travel report' sent back to be published in their magazine. Why the 'never been before'? Partly, they wanted a fresh, first-time feel, and partly, they figured first-timers wouldn't take anything for granted—they'd say what experienced travelers might omit, assuming it to be common knowledge. So the reports were to have practical value (they were supposed to be helpful for first-time travelers) as well as marketing value (see how much fun this person is having, you should go too!).

So a few days later, I was on my way to the airport. Terminal One.

Okay, first of all, a terminal is not terminal. It goes on forever. You can get lost in it for days. In fact, I did.

And a gate is not a gate. It's a waiting area. It's a bunch of chairs, with a counter, and a door. There is no gate.

Having searched the terminal for two days looking for a gate that didn't exist, I decided to hop on one of those conveyor belts that, presumably, get you from point A to point B more quickly. Well, this one did not. It just kept going around and around. And every now and then it went through one of those carwash curtains. Only it wasn't a carwash. I could have used a spray of cold water. Especially since so many people were staring at me. I'm sure that by the fifth time around, I wasn't looking my best.

Then, since I'd already passed through security a dozen times, it finally dawned on me that the curtain meant I was going through the security thing. Okay, cool. When I thought I'd received enough x-rays to have become sterile—I figured it would save me a lot of money in birth control pills—I jumped off. 'Course by then I'd gone around so many times, I was dizzy. I toppled as soon as I hit the floor. Then Security showed up. Most confusing.

So another two days later, I was finally on the plane to Sweden. *Travel Tip #1: If you have never traveled by air before, arrive at the airport at least six months before your plane is scheduled to depart.*

At least I thought I was on the plane to Sweden. I hoped I was on the plane to Sweden. Because I had reservations at a bed and breakfast in Stockholm. No, wait, that was for the four days that had just passed. Hmm.

*One of the things I don't understand about air travel is 'Business Class'. It makes no sense at all to give the luxuries to those on business trips. If they're uncomfortable and annoyed and get a headache, well, hey, they're on the job! It's when you're on a vacation—*we're *the ones should be getting the free drinks, the extra leg room, the good movies, and so on. After all, if someone on a business trip gets a bit of bad luck with regard to seating, well, better luck next time. But if it's your first and once-in-a-lifetime trip, there will be no next time. Especially for the three-year-old who kicks the back of your seat for six whole hours.*

Then it dawned on me. It's not really about comfort. It's about status. People in business class need to feel important. *They need to feel* special. *So they get to board* ahead *of us. Along with the rest of the infants and small children.*

It's really irritating though, because most people won't get that. All they'll see is that business gets priority. The message is that as long as you're doing something for money, you, and whatever it is you're doing, are considered important. Such a stupid message. Such a dangerous message. Because some things are actually more important than money. On what basis should your pursuit of money get priority over my pursuit of pleasure? Let alone my pursuit of the betterment of society. (Should I decide, one day, to pursue that.)

And of course it's no coincidence that business class is predominantly male. Whatever men do is important. It's axiomatic. They have a way of making everything they do seem important. Even when it's getting on a plane to attend a bimonthly meeting of electric toothbrush sellers in order to pat on the back and shake hands with the guy who has sold the most electric toothbrushes in the last two months.

So when I arrived in Sweden, I was directed to the admissions counter, or greeting center, I don't know what it was called. I just know I had to get in line and answer some questions. At least that's what everyone else was doing. 'Course there were so many lines at the airport, it was really a crap shoot as to which one I was supposed to be in.

"Are you traveling alone?"

Hmm. I looked to my right. No one there. I looked to my left. No one there either. "No, I'm traveling with my invisible friend."

You gotta love translation: "And did your blind companion pack his own bag?"

Hmm. Did my *blind* companion *pack his own bag*. I would guess not. "No."

"Can I see it?"

"No." Duh. It's invisible.

So, six hours later, when that guy's shift was over, I tried again.

"Are you traveling alone?"

"Yes, sir, I am. Traveling alone. I have no friends. No friends at all."

"And what is the purpose of your travel?"

"Well, I'm visiting Sweden to investigate the gender parity. I mean, a woman prime minister. That's something. And I wonder whether it trickles down or whether it trickled up—I suspect the latter. In any case, I'd like to spend some time in a country where women are not second-class citizens. I imagine it'll be—pleasant. And I suppose I'm visiting Norway and Denmark for somewhat the same reason—the whole Scandinavian society thing. Not just the gender thing, but the socialist thing too.

"Then Amsterdam. Well. I am *so* intrigued. What kind of country makes marijuana, prostitution, *and* euthanasia legal? I mean what are the people like?

"Paris, that's for the art. They say you can get lost in the Louvre for days. And I'm sure I will.

"Italy, the art, again, and the architecture. I've chosen Florence though. No way, Rome. Wouldn't want to be burned at the stake.

"Greece is for the climate. I've never been to the Mediterranean before. I want to experience the climate. The clear blues and greens of the Mediterranean sea, the dry heat, the magical Greek light.

"Austria, I confess, was a last minute addition—it was too expensive to fly to Australia and, well, they're spelled almost the same."

He sort of stared at me. Wrong answer?

"And," I added, somewhat desperately, "they say travel is good. Broadens one's horizons and all that. Pushes you over the brink with first-world guilt. Creates an existential crisis wherein one must constantly face the possibility that one is not authentic, that one is living in bad faith, and the *nausea*—let me tell you about the relationship between travel and nausea—"

"Business or pleasure?" he interrupted.

"Oh. Um." I would be getting paid for my travel pieces, which makes it business, I guess, but a trip to Europe, surely that's pleasure. In any case, it was a false dichotomy: it could be both business *and* pleasure, or *neither* business *nor* pleasure—"I don't know."

I sort of wandered away again, and in case the next person on shift was given a heads up, I changed clothing. Good idea in any case, since I'd lived in my current outfit for what, five days now?

One can tell a lot from the size of a country's public garbage bins. In Sweden, they're small, discreet, chrome canisters, about two feet high and ten inches across. Very unlike our own huge barrels. I can't remember how to calculate volume of a cylinder, but it seems to me ours are about ten times the size of theirs. Yay us.

Bicycles are also revealing. In Sweden, they have large, padded seats. As if the rider is expected to actually sit down while riding. Which one does unless one is racing. What is it with this obsession with competition we have? No, sorry, not 'we'—men.

And there's so much walking space! The sidewalks are wider, and there are promenades and plazas everywhere, with places to sit! I'll bet 'loitering' isn't a crime here! Gee, with a layout like this, who *needs* a car?

The men in Sweden don't wear ties. Any country in which the men don't *walk around wearing little nooses gets my vote. Then again, given that most countries come nowhere near Sweden's 43% with regard to women in government—hell, they've had a woman prime minister for years—well, the noose thing does provide a certain—convenience.*

And in general, the men seemed a little less driven, a little less insecure, a little less volatile, a little less . . . what's the word . . . immature.

And this—this really blew me away: I was riding on the train and there was a man and a boy, maybe about eleven, and they showed interest in a baby. They actually smiled at it! See, back home, men of all ages ignore babies. In an almost contemptuous way. They certainly wouldn't smile at one.

('Course they don't smile at anything.) (Except a sports victory.) (Not their *sports victory, mind you, someone else's—someone else with whom they identify, despite having nothing in common except a penis.)*

Another young man, a teenager really, was sitting on the train reading. A book. There's something else you don't see back home. Real *men don't read.*

One of the things I was looking forward to in my travels was food. New food. Different food. I was tired of orange juice and peanut butter and strawberry jam, metaphorically speaking. So I went into a grocery store and put dragonfruit pear juice into my basket, and cashew butter, and lingenberry jam. And rhubarb yogurt, and cloudberry pastries, and half a dozen other things I'd never tasted before. Put them through, let the cashier help herself to my money—I couldn't tell a nickel from a dime—probably because in Sweden they have neither—and then I noticed everyone was looking at me. Waiting to see how I could carry all those items in just two hands. Silly fool. To go shopping and not take a bag! Did you think all your purchases would walk behind you, levitating a couple feet off the ground? So I set out, juggling my purchases, determined to get to where I was going with all of my stuff. And then I got lost.

Not one to make the same mistake twice—well, except for getting lost—I managed to do that considerably more than twice—even on the same route—I took a bag with me when I went to the mall a couple days later. Unlike other people, shoppers are the same all over the world. I may as well have been in the Walmart mall back home. I found a store that had really neat marbles, though. Shiny ones, iridescent ones, cool ones called 'oily', and hot ones called 'electric'. So I bought a bunch and put them in my bag. *Travel Tip #2: It is always wise to purchase heavy objects at the* beginning *of a long trip.*

On the train to Norway, an American lawyer happened to be sitting beside me. When he found out I was Canadian, he informed me how disappointed 'they' were at 'our' decision not to support them in whatever war they were fighting at the time.

"We did consider taking certain action, in revenge, like we did against France, but we sort of consider Canada our little brother, you know?" Revenge for not supporting them? *Who's* the little brother?

In explaining why we should have come to their aid, he said, "I mean, we protect you, right? You benefit from our defence."

We benefit from their defence. Yeah right. Like the safest place to be is standing right beside the jerk who's mouthing off and waving a big fat gun, the asshole everyone wants to sit down and shut up.

"Europe is full of intellectuals. We do. Whereas they think." He said it like it was a bad thing.

In Norway, I decided to go on a fjord cruise. When is a fjord just a bunch of water? When the sides are too far apart to see.

The cruise let us off in front of the palace, and we happened to see the palace guard change. After their performance, I led several like-minded travelers in the Monty Python version, throwing in a few extra dipsies. We got more applause.

I also decided, in Norway, to find a used bookstore since I'd already read the single paperback I'd brought with me. But there were no phone books. No yellow pages. So what does one do, wander around aimlessly? But I'd been doing that. For days. In the rain. *Travel Tip #3: It's important to have a rainy day plan. Such as sitting in your room all day and watching tv.*

What I did find was a McDonalds. Out of perverse curiosity, I went in and ordered a McToast. I got a grilled cheese and ham sandwich. (In Paris, it would be called a "Croque Monsieur".) It was quite good, actually. I discovered that in Norway, sandwiches are always on grilled bread. They usually have a slice of some sort of cheese inside, and then whatever else you usually order on a sandwich.

The weather report on tv in Norway was really interesting. A young guy in his 20s wearing jeans and a long-sleeved shirt stood in front of a map of Norway, which had the relevant region in color, said, "It'll rain tonight over most of the area. But it'll probably stop in the morning. And it'll be a bit colder tomorrow."

He seemed almost embarrassed to be *announcing* the weather forecast. It'll rain tomorrow. What's the big deal? Is that really worth a public announcement?

In Norway, weather reports are not presented with grand gesticulations, action thriller voice modulations, and implications of great significance. They don't feel the need to make the weather an exciting and theatrical clash of opposing atmospheric forces, a drama unfolding from setup, through conflict, to climax, and resolution, with dashed hopes and incipient depression or self-righteous exultation and communal celebration. Why do we?

When you're travelling in different countries and people don't necessarily speak the language you do, you quickly realize it doesn't really matter whether you say "Thank you" or "Tousen takk" or

"Merci" or "Danke schoen"—as long as you say something and smile, your gratitude will be appreciated and the other person will smile back.

So when I got off the bus at the stop for the train station kindly indicated by the driver to whom I'd shown my Eurail pass and then gestured helplessly out at the streets, I smiled at him and said "Your children have fleas." And sure enough, he smiled back, nodding happily.

Unlike bus drivers, train station ticket clerks must be bilingual, I guess. Because three days later, I disembarked to find myself looking out at the Arctic Ocean.

When I finally got to Denmark, I had just enough time to buy a danish. A Danish danish. This amused me for some reason.

When I got on the train, again, I had to pass through a border station or entry checkpoint or something. I have no idea. I showed my seat reservation, then I showed my actual ticket. Proudly. It had taken me two hours to find the ticket counter at the train station. "Do you need to see my passport?"

"No, you are from Canada, yes?"

"Yes."

"Prove it," he said.

What? So I started singing our national anthem. (I figured this qualified as an exception to my rule.) "'O Canada, our home and native land'—though that should be 'our home *on* native land'—at least if land ownership depends on who was there first. Which is not as defensible a position as you might think.

"'True patriot love in all thy sons command'—and it's really about time our daughters were included, seeing as women are now people too, have been since 1929 when what's-her-name, Emily Murphy, took the issue to court. I learned that from one of those Canadian Heritage Moments on tv.

"'With glowing hearts, we see thee rise'—oh, please, we're not particularly patriotic, this is the first time I've ever even *worn* a Canadian flag and that's just so people don't mistake me for being an American—"

"Enough," he said. "You—are—Canadian!" And he mimicked raising a bottle of beer. Right. Should've just done that.

While on the train, I read the Amsterdam section in *Let's Go Travel* and was delighted to discover that the hostel at which I had a reservation was pretty much in the red light district. *Let's Go* says *Let's Not*. "Do not go to this area at night until you have locked your bags at the station or the hostel." Not helpful since I had to walk *from* the station *to* the hostel *with* my bags *at night*.

As a general observation, Europe just doesn't have the junk food we do. I had a heck of a time finding Doritos. Especially in, of all places, Amsterdam.

It does have a lot of street musicians though. I saw one just clapping—in time, I guess, but I have no idea to what.

I also happened to see another palace guard. No ceremonial changing of the guard. No tourists taking pictures. Just one guard standing, well, on guard. So sober and serious. I made faces at him to make him laugh. He remained stone-faced. Poor man, couldn't laugh. Then I gave him the finger to make him mad. That he could do. Unfortunately I had forgotten that he was holding a rifle at the time. Turns out it's loaded. Turns out he really *is* guarding the palace. *Travel Tip #4: Don't taunt the palace guards.*

When I was released from the hospital—the bullet had just grazed, well, my head—I started walking to my first art museum. And got lost. I found it before it closed, though, and saw that famous shipwreck painting, the one with the central figure dramatically draped over crates and sails on the beach, the epitome of utter despair and exhaustion, and I thought 'Oh get a grip.' I am so ready for the Louvre.

Amsterdam is not as liberated as it thinks. Not one man was on display with services for sale in the red light district.

But I did see a huge Rottweiler cheerfully trotting along with, in its mouth, a huge—dildo. A very well-chewed dildo. Street patrol? Good girl! That'll—make 'em think twice.

In Europe, every train station has pigeons—not just out on the platforms, but actually inside the station buildings. They very thoroughly, and considerately, pick up every little scrap of food, no matter how cruddy. Wouldn't it be cool to breed them to eat cigarette butts?

I saw this one pigeon actually ride the escalator: it flew up off the floor to avoid being stepped on, landed on the escalator handrail, and then just—took the ride.

Another figured out that if it hung around the station musicians—and I use that word loosely—one accordion player was obviously self-taught—unsuccessfully so—he sort of randomly pushed and pulled the accordion, and pressed a button or a key to sort of make a chord every now and then—he sang too, in a Leonard Cohen sort of way—one of the pigeons figured out that if it hung around the station musicians, it could get *a lot* of crumbs: people typically nibbled on something as they stood around and listened.

I saw the bird two days later. It had its own act doing aerial manoeuvres. I don't know where it got the hat, or the sign saying "Cruddy chunks of food much appreciated," but it beat the hell out of the accordion guy.

Not only were musicians at the stations, they were also on the trains. One day one of them must have gotten up off the floor to avoid being stepped on, ended up inside the train, and then just—took the ride. In any case, these musicians would walk up and down the aisles, hoping for—and not moving until they received—payment. And they wouldn't accept cruddy food. So when the accordion player stopped at my seat, squeezing his accordion in and out, in my ear, given that he was standing in the aisle and I was sitting in my seat, I casually reached over and squeezed as well. The Albanian folk-song suddenly got transposed up an octave or two, and he moved on.

When you get off the train in your destination city, you should call your bed and breakfast or hotel to confirm your reservation and get directions. At most public phones, you can use either the correct coin-age or your credit card. It doesn't really matter. Figuring out which coins are from which country will be impossible, as will be figuring out the amount of each coin. Figuring out then how many of each you need is easier—but obviously irrelevant. And your credit card will never work, no matter how imaginative you get about how to insert it into the slot. In any case, you will find that your bed and breakfast or hotel doesn't exist.

One of the first things I did in Paris was visit the famous opera building. And wow, talk about opulent: marble columns and gold everywhere, and chandeliers and plush red velvet seats and brocade wallpaper. And I kept thinking, standing there in my khaki shorts and tshirt, "Boy, am I underdressed."

The ceilings, in particular, were incredibly beautiful. What we need, I thought, staring up at one, is a lounge chair rental service. Mobile lounge chairs. You could rent one when you walked in, have a lay-down, then motor all over the place—and truly enjoy the ceil-ings without getting a cramp in your neck. I wonder if the artists back then charged time and a half for ceiling work. Must have been hell to paint. Unless, of course, they had mobile lounge chairs.

Copenhagen is made *for pedestrians. It has lots of pedestrian-only spaces, the streets have these* wide *sidewalks, and in Copenhagen, pedestrians* always *have the right of way. You can be crossing the street* anywhere *and the cars will stop for you.*

They'll do that in Amsterdam too. Though that could be because you're apt to be crossing the street backwards and up the middle. Giggling.

But in Paris, cars *always have the right of way. Even if the little green man in the light says it's okay to cross. Actually in Paris the little green man says "Okay—you can* try*—"*

Walking along the famous Champs-Élysées was—unpleasant. Mainly because of the traffic whizzing by; there must've been four lanes in each direction. The trees lining each side were cool though—an especially nice view from the middle of the street. Which is where you get to stand if you don't turn into Marian Jones when the light changes. There was this one small group of tourists stranded on a concrete island divider at a corner—I don't know how they got there, but they couldn't get off; they couldn't cross the street in any direction because cars kept coming, really fast, and none of them slowed down. The drivers didn't even seem to notice that there were people standing there, trying to cross. Well, except for the guy who looked out his window at us and started laughing. I think maybe he might've noticed. Eventually they had to send out some street-crossing officer to get us. But by then we were so dehydrated, and a little disoriented, that a few of us refused to leave our little island—it had become safe, you see . . .

One of the shops on the Champs-Élysées is a travel agency for Iran Air—"The Airline of the Islamic Republic of Iran". I'll bet they're not doing much business these days. Given the tendency of Islamic pilots to fly *into* buildings.

I noticed there were no garbage cans along the Champs-Élysées. Absolutely none. And I thought "Well, *that's* wishful thinking." I mean it's nonstop tourists. A block later, having been almost run over a couple times, while *on the sidewalk*, I might point out, I realized they'd just said "The hell with it," given a woman a go-cart (not Edna, alas), put a vacuum cleaner on it, and made it a full-time job.

Even before I got to France and Italy—in fact, as soon as I got to Sweden and saw huge outdoor flower pots at the airport terminal and then sculptures and art videos in the subway stations—I realized just how much 'the aesthetic' simply does not count back home. It has no value whatsoever.

*'Course you can't really blame us. DaVinci and Michelangelo—*those *guys didn't bring their talent, their vision, to the New World. No, we got the guy with the accordion. Not only that, we got the one who thought it might be more profitable to play on a ship than on a train—a ship full of people who'd just spent their last penny on passage.*

While in Paris, I also went to the Rodin museum, and the Orsay museum, and the Monet museum—mostly because I got lost trying to find the Louvre.

As a species, we are so in love with ourselves: almost every single one of the sculptures and paintings I saw featured *human* subjects. I saw a few horses, a rabbit or two, and an antelope, but they were usually dead. Or dying a very horrible death. 'Course it could just be that animals won't sit still long enough. That could also explain why they're usually dead.

There was one painter though, Descamps, who seemed to like dogs: beagles and Bassett hounds, at least. No Shi Tzus—though they really aren't dogs.

And there is a cute little terrier in Rubens' *The Birth of Louis XIII*. It's looking up at little Louis with an expression on its face more intelligent than that on any of the people in the picture who by comparison look positively vacant. You can actually see the dog working through what's happened: "Everybody's fawning over the *baby* now . . . "

Although I did eventually find the Louvre, *and* its main entrance, I didn't actually see the *Mona Lisa*. Partly, because I couldn't stand standing in line, because every second person had a cell phone. "Hi—yeah—I'm at the Louvre—I don't know—Rubens, I think—or Renoir—somebody with an R—yeah—McDonalds, okay—I think there's one here actually—"

And partly, because I wouldn't've been able to ever get to the front of the line, because everyone kept taking photographs. People took photographs of everything. *Travel Tip #5: How to wreck a perfectly good picture of any one of a thousand works of art: put your mother or boyfriend in it.* I swear I saw people taking photographs of the postcards in the souvenir shop. 'Course, why not—they always look better than the real thing.

And partly, no surprise, because I kept getting lost. About an hour before closing, I had gotten lost for the eighth and final time. About a half hour after closing, they found me, sitting with the beagles and the Bassett hounds, a silly grin on my face, eating a Caramilk bar.

While walking through all the famous art museums, I was struck by how few of the women were able to keep their clothes on. From peasants to goddesses, every one of them was sporting not just an off-the-shoulder look, but a pulled-down-to-the-waist look. Breast after breast after breast was bared—in the most inappropriate contexts. For example, The Sacrifice of Iphigenia *by—somebody—there are lots of them—apparently it's a common theme, women getting sacrificed—Iphigenia is "sacrificed" in order to make the wind blow in the right direction so her father can get to his precious little war. Okay. But why the hell is she topless at the moment of her death?*

Later, at some famous theatre in Vienna I think, I noticed, at first with delight, that the walls were covered with women. But then I noticed that every one of them had that negligee-half-off look. And then I noticed they were always in pairs. A pair of half-naked women, then the sculpted head of some distinguished man, then another pair of half-naked women, then another distinguished man. What is this?

Eventually, it dawned on me. One day I was in Amsterdam's red light district looking at all the men gawking at the famous window displays, and the next day I was in the Rijksmuseum looking at a painting called The Drawing Room—*in which a bunch of men are gawking at a nude model. I suddenly understood: being an artist was just an excuse to see women's naked bodies; the drawing room legitimized voyeurism. So the masters are just peeping toms, art is little more than thinly veiled porn, and the history of art, like everything else, boils down to the history of men dismissing women by identifying them as sex objects.*

I also went to the Versailles Castle. It felt like I was on a tour of the mansions of the rich and famous. The fireplace in one room was all set and ready to go with three logs in it—each seven feet long, ten inches thick. That'd take a lot of lighter fluid.

And the huge wall-to-wall murals of battle scenes—the 17th century version of Terminator on Imax, I guess.

And the Hall of Mirrors. Guess the King didn't use Windex. Oh, what am I saying! Not the King, his legions of domestic servants!

And the beds—canopies, embroidery, feathers, gold , and a four-foot-high platform. Talk about pressure to perform.

The description said the castle was actually King Louis' hunting lodge "enlarged" by his son. I'll say.

I wondered if they had chandelier insurance: if one of *those* things should happen to fall—well, there'd be 99 chandeliers left, but—

Travel Tip #6: Oddly enough, it is difficult to find a croissant in Paris. Had the best cup of hot chocolate ever in Paris though. I swear they must have used table cream. Not half-and-half, but 100% table cream, undiluted, and oh, I don't know, a couple squares of Baker's semi-sweet chocolate.

So after Paris, I thought it'd be nice to stay for a bit in some quaint village in Provence, maybe stroll through the vineyards, so I decided to take a train to the south of France. Which meant that first I had to find the bus stop for the bus that would take me to the train station. And then another bus stop for the bus that would take me to the train station I missed because I didn't get off at the right stop when I was on the first bus. Then, once I was at the train station, I had to find the ticket office. The right ticket office. There are several. And most of them are the wrong ticket office. Then I had to find the right platform. There are several. And—it was not a clue that at many of them, the train was facing the wrong way. Because I had no idea which way the train I wanted should be facing. Plus, they just as often travel backwards as forwards.

The train to Provence dropped me off in the middle of highways. A shuttle bus took me to the middle of a city, Aix-en-Provence. I found the tourist information center, which was across the street (no, not that street), stood in line for three hours, then told the clerk I'd like to stay somewhere in the south of France, in some quaint little countryside village, maybe stroll through the vineyards . . . The harried clerk gave me a list of accommodations in the area, but she couldn't say which ones were near vineyards. In any case, I needed a car to get to all of them. So I stood in another line for two hours and was told there were no cars available. I could rent a bicycle though, which was fine by me, actually. I was given a map of highways. Can I bike on the highways here? Well, no, not really. So I stood in the first line again and asked for a list of accommodations one could get to without a car. There was a hostel one could get to by bus. But I needed a reservation. Did I have a reservation? Hm. Would I be standing in line asking about accommodations if I had a reservation? Never mind, I wouldn't have found the right bus by the time it left anyway. So while I stood outside the center, exactly where I'd arrived seven hours earlier, I saw the shuttle bus to the train station just about to leave. I got on. Didn't even get lost on the way.

Over the next two days, as the train traveled to Marseille and then over through Toulon, Cannes, and Nice, I saw the south of

France. I saw lots of rolling hills, old mountains, and greenish milky water. I'll bet I even saw a few vineyards. But when I asked others on the train, "Is *that* a vineyard?" and "Is *that* a vineyard?" they couldn't say. They were laughing too hard.

At Nice, we (the occupants of the train, I mean—I was traveling alone, remember, except for my invisible friend) (who was blind) (so he didn't see any vineyards either), at Nice, we were herded off the train in the middle of the night and onto a bus that would, someone assured us, take us the rest of the way to the border, to Italy, because there was a problem with the track. This is how the holocaust happened, I thought.

But everyone else got on the train, so I did too. This is how the holocaust happened, I thought.

Then I was put onto a train which would, overnight, get me to Venice, from where I could take the three day ferry to Greece. Or so I thought. Some kind attendant on the train who spoke English understood that my goal was Greece, not Venice, and told me to get off in Padua because otherwise I wouldn't make the ferry connection in Ancona in time. What can I say? I got off the train when he told me to.

So, having disembarked in Spain, I have to say it's true that when you travel, your horizons do get broadened. *Travel Tip #7: It's important to not get on the wrong train. And it's impossible to know which is the right train.*

But metaphorically speaking as well, your horizons do get broadened. There was a person sitting across from me at one point who was reading the *Proceedings* from some conference. I thought history maybe, or sociology. Turns out it was the *Proceedings of the Fifth Annual International Congress on Boar Semen Preservation*. They have congresses on boar semen preservation. See, I didn't know that before.

Travel would be so much easier if we could just beam ourselves from point A to point B. You could be sitting in your living room and think 'Gee, I'd like to go to New York'—and then just beam yourself there. 'Course we'd need traffic conductors to avoid beam collisions. What if your beam crossed the beam of a dog on the way to Chicago. You could arrive in New York half-Pekinese.

Eventually—and I use that word loosely—I was on the ferry heading to Greece. I went through the boarding process okay and was given a card saying A2, which was supposedly where my room was. After an hour, I was sure I was in the right place, but the floor said 9 and the wall said F. The porter had said the door to my room would open with a key, and I saw a key hole, but all I had was the card. It took another hour to find someone to help me. Turned out, though, he couldn't. It took another hour after that to get back to where I was, and this time the door opened with my card. Couldn't quite figure that one out.

Inside the room, or crypt, I saw six berths, each with a thin mattress and just enough vertical space to slide in, then not to be able to turn over. You had to lie flat, staring at the berth above just inches from your face as it got closer and closer until it crushed you to death unless you clawed at it and screamed to get out. Which would wake the others.

The ferry landed in Patras, which meant another train trip, across to Athens. From which point I hoped to take a ferry to some fabulous Greek island on which I would stay. Possibly forever.

Athens has changed since Socrates' time. For one thing, you can't stand on the street corner and converse with passers-by. You'd get knocked about and then hit by a moped.

Once I was released from the hospital (just a lot of bruising), I found a nice hotel in Athens. Unfortunately, I had to walk up a very steep hill to get to it. Fortunately, it had a beautiful view of the Parthenon. Unfortunately, I was awakened at six a.m. by the loud open market just outside my hotel window. Fortunately, that gave me lots of time to catch the ferry from Athens.

I even had time to sit in the plaka and eat my tiropita (a delicious feta cheese pastry thing that I was becoming addicted to). While being attacked by pigeons who flew in from as far as London, it occurred to me that sculptors should make statues with their arms outstretched. It'd be interactive art, then, instead of insult, when the pigeons landed on it. Though I must confess that seeing a pigeon sit on the head of some distinguished military figure looks very right. More so when it drops a, a dropping.

Once on the ferry, I decided not to bother looking for my room. I just stowed my backpack in a locker, wandered around for a bit, watched the glorious sunset, then slept on a chair. Unfortunately I couldn't find the storage locker in the morning and therefore missed my island. Fortunately, the ferry headed on to another island rather than back to Athens, and by the next stop, I'd found the locker and gotten my backpack.

But then I couldn't find the exit or off ramp or whatever. Lots of people were moving so I decided to just get in line. (I know, this is how—) Turned out the line I'd gotten in was heading to the upper level to stand at the rail and wave goodbye to those who had gotten off. I considered jumping. I really did. But, instead, I stood there with the others. Waving goodbye to those who had gotten off . . .

I then resumed looking for the right door, and when I finally found it, I sat down with my backpack, determined not to move until the next island stop. Which was two days later.

So it looked like I'd be spending a week on Syros, not Paros or Naxos. I didn't have a reservation for accommodations on Syros. But then I didn't have one for Paros or Naxos either. I'd been told that there would be people with rooms to rent waiting at each port, greeting the people who disembark, competing with each other to get the tourists to stay at their villa or whatever. They'd even come with a car or a van. Yeah right.

Well, yeah, right! One guy approached me, told me about his four-apartment villa in a tiny fishing village, yes, very quiet, yes, I'd have my own bathroom, and there was also a kitchenette in each apartment, and yes, I'd be able to see the sea from my own private balcony. All for 20 Euros a night. He gestured to his waiting car. I would have said yes even if it were 100 Euros a night and there was blood dripping from the car's trunk.

But, dream come true, it was just as he said. I showered, twice, then slept. I even turned over from time to time. I was not kept awake by the sound of a motor large enough to power an intercontinental train or an oceanic ship. I was not awakened by the sound of people shouting about figs and olives.

When I did finally wake up, it was still light, so I headed down to the village store. And did not get lost! 'Course, it was only a hundred meters away, but still. I bought a tiropita, a package of tea, and a carton of cream. And, will wonders never cease, a few used paperbacks, in English, from a box in the corner. I headed back to my villa apartment, made a very strong cup of tea, then took it, my tiropita, and a book out to the balcony to watch the sun set over the Mediterranean. Aah, life doesn't get—eew. I made another quick trip to the store because—I hadn't really noticed until now—all dairy cartons look rather the same. *Travel Tip #9: Whipping cream goes better in tea than sour cream.*

A few days later, I rented a moped to get from my little fishing village into town. Some officials can be *so* unhelpful. While I was in town, I stopped at the ferry office to find out when ferries went from Syros to Santorini. There was a schedule posted outside, but that route wasn't listed. So I went inside and asked the ferry office person whether, and when, a ferry went from Syros to Santorini. She directed me to the posted schedule.

So I went back outside and read it again, and again, looking carefully at each of thirty different trips for three different ferries on seven different days leaving at six different times. Nothing from Syros to Santorini. I went back inside.

"Is that the schedule for *all* ferries?" I asked. Yes.

"Does the schedule change from week to week?" No.

"Does the schedule list all islands stopped at on the way?" Yes.

Finally, the question I eventually asked—which wasn't among my first twenty—was "Is there another name for Santorini?" Sure enough, there was. And the ferry went from Syros to *Thera* on Mondays, Wednesdays, and Fridays, at 7:00 a.m.

I got lost, of course, looking for more tiropita, and so it was night when I drove back. On the narrow winding road with hairpin turns to get all the way up the mountain and then all the way down.

Not only do the Greeks not have streetlights, they don't really use guard rails to keep you from driving off the mountains and plummeting to a certain death with dismemberment along the way. At the really scary sections, they might have a few posts. No cable connecting the posts, mind you, just the posts. Set sufficiently far apart as to allow most vehicles and all mopeds to pass between. Occasionally, a section will have a low stone wall that you might think could act like a barrier. Apparently other people have thought the same thing. They have left smashed gaps in the wall indicating just that.

The ferry trip from Syros to Santorini was awful. Desperate to escape the many annoyances, I spent most of the time tucked beside a huge throbbing generator on the cold side. Inside, there were screaming kids, crying kids, blaring televisions, and loud conversations among the twenty members of each of ten extended families. Outside, people would come and stand right beside me and make a call on their cell phone and shout into it. Bad enough I had to listen to conversations of people who were there. I had to listen to conversations of people who weren't there too? So I held an invisible cell phone to my ear. "Hey!" I screamed to my invisible friend. "Yeah. Well I was going to do that but—yeah. I'm on the ferry now. It's in the water. Yeah, it's moving. Through the water. Yeah."

Then someone would come and stand right beside me and light up a cigarette. Oblivious to the dirty look I'd give them. So I'd move again. Found a spot at the end with chairs, and people there seemed to be rather quietly enjoying the view. I sighed with relief and sat down. Then a damned clicker sat down right beside me.

You know how some men used to jingle coins in their pocket? "Look at me! I'm rich! I have a bunch of nickels and dimes in my pocket!" And then it became cool to carry around a lot of jangling keys. "Look at me! I'm important! I can open lots of doors!" Well, now there's something new. At least for Greek men who've seen Lethal Weapon III, *where the guy walks around flipping a pair of prayer beads or worry beads that's actually a garrote wire. Click-click. Click-click. They flip their wrist and the marble at one end of a string hits the marble at the other end, causing it to rebound and hit again. Click-click. Click-click. "Look at me! I'm dangerous! I can strangle you!" Click-click. Click-click. It can be heard a hundred yards away. Click-click. Click-click. And it's annoying as hell. Click-click. Click-click. Click-click. Prayer beads? Worry beads? I just call them balls-on-a-string. Teeny eensy weensy balls-on-a-string.*

I considered swimming. It'd be peaceful. Quiet. Beautiful. While it lasted. So instead I grabbed the marbles in mid-click and click-clicked them against his temple sort of with a slingshot motion. He crumpled. And was quiet. Beautiful.

When I arrived on Santorini, I ended up staying at Mr. Kosta's Villa. As soon as I entered my room, I heard this huge chain being dragged across the roof just above me. Curious, I poked my head out the window and looked up—and saw two huge heads looking down at me: a Rottweiler head and a Doberman head. Why there should be a Rottweiler and a Doberman chained to the roof of a villa on a Greek island, I don't know. (Oh yes I do. Click-click. Click-click.)

Next day, I headed down to the beach. And just where I wanted to lay down my towel—midway between the bickering couple on the left and the shrieking kids on the right—there were four small rocks. Just four—so I picked them up and tossed them. (No, not at the bickering couple.) (Or the shrieking kids.) I lay down my towel and immediately the wind whipped it up. I smoothed it down again, and the wind whipped it up again. And again. I'd get two corners down and half the towel smoothed out, and then as soon as I got the other two corners down, the first two'd get blown up. Eventually I thought, "Hey—I need something to hold down the corners. I know! Rocks! Four small ones!"

Why is it that people who in their normal lives wouldn't venture to walk around the block decide, when on holiday, to sign up for an excursion climb up a volcano—and show up wearing flipflops, sandals, and heels. Normally, I wouldn't object—everyone has the right to be an idiot.

But not when it means the thirty-eight people behind you on the single-file path have to stop in the hot sun while you negotiate a ten inch step up from one rock to another.

I mean, it's not like you were caught by surprise and thus ill-prepared—if you sign up for "an excursion climb up a volcano" you should know it will involve climbing up a volcano.

And then there's the guy who has the right footwear—heavy duty basketball shoes—but he's so cool he hasn't done up the laces. Watch how cool I am when he turns his ankle and asks for help getting back down.

And there's the other guy who's mistaken the excursion for a race and attempts to pass everyone—at great risk not only to himself, which doesn't bother me—I repeat, everyone has the right to be an idiot—but also to everyone he passes. When he finds himself behind a small group of women, well, you'd think he'd never been so insulted in his life, to see the look on his face and the determination with which he passes them. I almost bump him off. But the volcano wasn't active at the time.

The ferry from Santorini back to Athens arrived in Athens at 12:05 a.m. Buses and subways stopped running at 12:00 a.m. My *Let's Go Travel* said taxis cost only 5 Euros, so I approached one that was sitting there at the port. 25 Euros. I moved to another one. 38 Euros. But hey, since I didn't know where to take a taxi to, it didn't really matter. I figured the up side of spending the night in the train station would be that I wouldn't miss my train. Yeah, right.

I have to say that the train ride from Athens to Patras was *really* annoying. For five hours. Not only because of the steady drone and rattle—that's *two different* annoying sounds by the way—but also because of the almost continuous blowing of the horn. Up to twenty-seven times a minute. I swear the conductor blew the horn even when we were nowhere near an intersection with a road. I figure he must've been one of those kids who wanted to be a train conductor when he grew up. (Either that or—click-click.)

Eventually, recalling my moped nightride from hell, I realized it's the Greek custom to honk every time you approach a curve—which makes sense when everyone drives in the middle of the road—which they do because the roads aren't wide enough for you to drive on one side—unless you're driving a donkey. I'm not sure what the train conductor thought might be coming at us from around each curve that needed warning—and frankly I was afraid to ask.

Once I got to Patras, I took a ferry to another island, Kefalonia. And while there, I decided one day to go for a walk to see a cave that had apparently amazing stalactites and stalagmites. It was September, so the temperature was about 40 degrees—Celsius. That's about 100 Fahrenheit. What can I say, I felt like going for a walk.

Actually, I felt like going for a run, but I'm not stupid.

So I started out on the 5 km walk, about 3 miles, at about the time all good Greeks start their mid-afternoon siesta—the heat stroke time of day.

That Greek guy who ran the first marathon and then dropped dead? I always figured he died of a heart attack or something. Uh-uh. He died of embarrassment, what with all the locals laughing at him for even *attempting* such a thing.

Did I wear sunscreen? Not me, I tan, I don't burn.

Did I take water? Nope. I regularly run 10 miles without a water stop.

I *did* wear white. Which is a good thing. Because it makes you more noticeable to passing motorists when you've collapsed at the side of the road.

As a philosophy student, I'd always wanted to see olive groves, perhaps walk among them deep in thought. Well, at least walk among them. So, I thought with some satisfaction, as I walked along the road on this Greek island, I have now seen olive trees. At least, trees with what are almost certainly olives-to-be, olives-in-progress—potential olives. Whether I've seen olive *groves*, however, depends on how many trees constitute a grove. And I'll bet *that's* a question Plato didn't consider while walking through the forementioned olive groves.

The cave—I did get there—was actually well worth the walk. It was huge. Well, I don't know if it was *huge*, but it was big enough for the Batmobile. That came to mind because there was a bat, a rather fat bat, doing its bat thing up amidst all the incredible rock icicle things. I'd never seen anything like it. The cave, I mean.

Though I'd never seen a fat bat before either. I've seen a cute little baby bat that was hibernating tucked all cozy, dry and snug, between the plastic I'd put over my windows and the wood siding. And I've seen an injured bat that tore its wing—I tried to fix it with scotch tape. (That didn't work, by the way.) But I've never seen a fat bat before. And there it was fluttering around and occasionally hanging upside down on one of those rock icicle things.

On the way back from the cave, I saw some trees, evergreens of some kind, that were oddly cone-shaped, rising straight up out of the ground. Rather like copycat stalagmites now that I think of it. Which is interesting, because the trees wouldn't've ever *seen* the stalagmites.

I also saw a sign outside a small Greek hotel named Virgina. The sign said "Virgina—Vacantly."

A little later on my walk, I heard jingling clunker bells and I suddenly realized there were one, two, no, four little goats, babies with little nubby horns, grazing on the—well, I don't actually know what they were doing there, there was nothing to graze on, but they were cute, so I stopped and talked to them, in baby talk. There was a sign there, but since it was in Greek, I had no idea what it said. Then Papa Goat came rushing at me out of nowhere. Papa Goat had very well and fully developed horns. That Greek guy who ran the first marathon? Probably did it in under two hours. *Travel Tip #9: "φυλάσσομαι από—αίγα βάρδια" says "Beware—Guard Goat!"*

You know, when you walk, you see a lot more than when you drive. A little later, I saw a rat. I'd never actually seen a rat before. Mice, yes—cute little Mickey Mouse deer mice, and the other kind with the brown fur. But not a rat. Well, there was the white rat we were supposed to dissect in science class, but that wasn't a real out-and-about *rat* rat. 'Course, this one wasn't really out-and-about either. Well it was out, but since it was dead, it wasn't really about.

When I finally got back to my hotel, I figured a swim would be nice. People should really be more careful about how they use words. When I asked where the nearest beach was, I was directed to a stretch of water with rocks. They called it a pebble beach. I called it a shoreline.

So when I asked the next person, I specified *sandy* beach. Though that wasn't likely to be any better, since the famous 'black sand' beach on Santorini wasn't sand, it was grit. And just for the record, it was more grey than black.

And then I went to Florence. And, you know, I really can't remember getting there. They say serious trauma can cause amnesia . . .

Florence is rather like Paris in its attitude toward pedestrians, because in Italy there are no sidewalks at all. Well, there are*—but apparently they're for the cars.*

I tried to go to several art museums. But, of course, I got lost.

It's a marvel that any wars at all occurred in Europe. It seems to me that most soldiers would've gotten lost trying to find the battlefield. I suspect what happened was that small groups of primed, angry, young men headed out, got lost, became more angry, got more lost, became even more angry, and so on, until they just picked a fight with the next group of people they saw.

And I suspect the reason everyone was looking for the New World was so they could lay down the streets in a neat and tidy grid, with each and every street running either parallel or perpendicular to each and every other street.

I did, however, get to see some of Michelangelo's stuff. The phrase 'buns of steel' comes to mind.

An interesting thing about Italy is that the street people don't ask you for money exactly—they pray for it. Literally: they kneel on the sidewalk with their little cup in front of them and pray, hands pressed together, eyes closed, the whole bit. So when you give them money, you're validating their belief in—no, wait a minute, that was me *who put the dollar in your cup, not God! Thanks be to* me*!* I'm *God!*

From Italy, I traveled to Austria. When I registered at the negative two star hotel in Vienna (my own shower and sink, but the toilet was down the hall), I was asked for my passport. Apparently, the hotel manager intended to keep it as collateral, like a driver's licence, until I checked out. Said it was routine. Yeah, right, I thought as I handed it over. What's the worst that could happen? He could say I never gave it to him, and I could spend the rest of my life looking for the Canadian Embassy in Vienna.

When I was sitting in a restaurant in Vienna, I saw a waiter take three dead fish on a plate to some people at one of his tables, I guess so they could choose which one they wanted. At first I thought "Ugh!" But then I thought, well, people choose which lobster they want from a bunch swimming around in a tank.

So okay, let's at least be consistent then—next time someone orders wiener schnitzel, let's bring out all the little baby calves to frolic around the table.

('Course if they're gonna be wiener schnitzel, they've been kept too weak to frolic . . .)

I think the highlight of my visit to Vienna was going to see Wagner's *Der Ring des Nibelungen* at the famous, and beautifully lush, Staatsoper. I bought a standing room ticket for a mere 2 Euros. My place was in the second side balcony. On my way up, and up, I had to stop—for a nosebleed.

Then as I continued, I noticed a lot of fire extinguishers on the way. And I thought, of course: a fire here would be a *big* problem. A little later, a little higher, it occurred to me that what I saw could have been oxygen tanks.

The view from the stage must've been magnificent. The view from where I was, however—well, you could see only part of the stage.

Unless you leaned out, over the balcony.

Which was what the guy in front of me kept doing.

Just as I was about to whisper, soon after the opera began, "Sir, would you please sit down, don't do that, you're making me nervous," I was distracted by the brass section (we had a great view of the orchestra pit). The horn players were placing bets with each other. I didn't know on what, I just figured okay, I'm not the only one who's bored with Wagner after five minutes. Then suddenly the guy in front of me *did* lean out too far. He went over, down I don't know how many hundred feet. And half the horn section let out a cheer.

I think I was especially bored because I didn't know what was going on. I missed the English translation on the little screen about the ring thing, what the ring was all about. I did catch the bit about Brünnhilde, whose horse, Grane, who she was giving to Siegfried, had lost all its strength when she rode it. Well, she's a big woman. I have nothing against big women, but there are some things large people shouldn't do, and ride horses is probably one of them.

After a while I gave up my place at the railing and sat on the floor. The next thing I knew, Siegfried was giving Grane to someone else. Poor horse, kept being given away. And when Siegfried was asked if he took anything from the treasure he'd found, he said—well he sang it, of course—"Only this scrap of net, it's not worth much, you can have it." And the other guy sang back, "Oh that's Nibelung's work, it's magic, when you wear it, you can change shape." And Siegfried sang back, "Oh don't I feel stupid."

When I reclaimed my place at the railing, I noticed that the two harp players—both women—who were sitting behind the horn section and who had taken off for a cup of tea as soon as their bit in the overture was done—had returned. In good spirits apparently (okay, perhaps it hadn't been for tea), because they proceeded to provide visual commentary to the opera. "I have lost my way," one guy sang, and the first harp player put her hands to her cheeks, "Oh no!" And when the old guy said to Siegfried "Take this"—I don't know what it was, a horse maybe, probably Grane—"and you can have the woman too," they both gave him the finger.

And that was pretty much the end of my trip to Europe. Next day, I flew home from the Vienna airport. Where they have a drug-sniffing dog. I'd never seen one of those before. This one was really happy doing its job. Every time it completed a circuit of the passenger waiting room, it got a red ball to play with. Yippee!! I think we should all get a red ball to play with when we've done our jobs!

Speaking of which, it turns out that when I was in France—or Italy—or Spain, the magazine fired me. My pieces weren't helpful, they said. Nor encouraging to their readership of potential travelers. Unfortunately, they couldn't find me to let me know. Apparently I was never where I was supposed to be. Well, duh.

8

SUBSTITUTE TEACHER FROM HELL

"Good morning, my name is—could you please be quiet—people—we need quiet before—Class, please be quiet—Excuse me, class—I'd like to begin—Class, Quiet, Please!—Cla-a-ass! SHUT THE FUCK UP!"

Having found my way back from Europe and acquired a degree in Education, my next job was teaching high school. Since regular teaching jobs were scarce, I was what they call a substitute or supply teacher. I supplied a thoughtful critique of the education system.

Let me share with you my carefully considered analysis of 'attendance'. It sucks. Up to the age of sixteen, attendance is compulsory. But as anyone who's taken Psych101 can tell you, the first thing a kid will do when told he or she *has* to do something is *not* want to do it.

It's not that what we teach is irrelevant. In fact, there's more relevant stuff in the curriculum today than when I went to school: in math, students can learn how much it costs to own and operate a second-hand car; in physics, they can learn about mass, velocity, and force of impact; in health, they can learn First Aid—how to treat lacerations, crushed limbs, and impacted steering columns. (And in law, they can learn how to get legal aid.)

And it's not the cafeteria food. 'Cuz they eat at McDonalds.

No, our failure to educate is due to the fact that they *have* to come. Consequently, school has such a bad rep, *anything* that happens there *must* be useless. In other cultures, going to school is a privilege; here, it's a punishment.

'But if we don't make attendance compulsory, we'll have an entire generation of uneducated people!' Hello—we already have an entire generation of uneducated people. Allow me to introduce Willy the Wasteland, the class rep.

First and foremost, Willy the Wasteland is bored. He is especially and chronically bored at school because he can't change channels. He has to watch the same program for a whole hour. The program has only one main actor. With no costume changes. It has only one set. The camera uses only one angle. (Unless you get up out of your seat and move around.) (Which Willy does.) (A lot.) There is no soundtrack. And things happen in real time: in one hour, only one hour passes by.

This state of affairs is a problem for Willy because he can't concentrate under these conditions. (Though it's quite possible he can't concentrate under any conditions.) On the radio, there's a different song every three minutes, and in between, a different voice advertising a different product every fifteen or thirty seconds; the deejay changes pitch more often in one sentence than most of us do in a whole day. Newspapers (should Willy be able to read) are similarly disjointed, presenting material in bits and pieces seldom longer than two or three hundred words, with individual sentences no longer than seven or eight words. So poor Willy doesn't get to—doesn't have to—can't—maintain a fixed focus for very long. And on tv—especially in commercials and music videos—the image changes every two seconds. So unless it moves, Willy doesn't see it. (It is my belief that Willy is turning into a frog.)

Or perhaps Willy's bored because the prerequisite for interest is care, and Willy just doesn't care. About anything. After all, to care about X when you can have no effect on X is to set yourself up for no small degree of frustration. Perhaps Willy is simply exhibiting the healthy response, the logical response to, perceived powerlessness.

Second, Willy doesn't know what to do about his boredom. He can't amuse himself, he can't entertain himself, he can't imagine. He can't think. (Probably because he can't maintain a fixed focus long enough to do so.) His internal landscape is, well, not. (Though on good days, it's the colour of hospital bedsheets.)

So Willy tells his teachers that it's their fault, it's their responsibility, they're supposed to entertain him. Most principals, being only one step ahead of Willy, on any evolutionary scale, agree: teachers should make the class interesting. Forget encouraging delayed gratification (that rite of passage out of infancy). Forget questioning the premise that everything should be interesting. (Chances are your job will be boring—but since it provides you with a paycheque, you'll accept it.) (Then again, as long as you insist that everything be interesting, you'll quit, go on unemployment, and *I'll* provide you with a paycheque.)

But to get back to mandatory attendance: have we so little faith in the value of education that unless coerced, people won't want it? No one forced us to learn how to speak, yet we did it. (Well, most of us.) *And* we did it without the bribe of marks or the threat of detention. And apparently learning to speak is the most difficult thing we'll do in our entire lives. (So as far as skills acquisition is concerned, it's all downhill once you hit four.)

Nevertheless, I did at one time take attendance. A little known Murphy's Law states that in every class, there will be at least one student with a multiple personality disorder. This student will answer "Here!" to every name that's called. You will, therefore, have to pass a sheet of paper around the class for signatures. It will be necessary to escort the sheet of paper, however, because otherwise the students will sign each other's names. Except for those with delusions of grandeur who will simply sign "God". (I do make it clear to those chosen few that they are not God. I am.) (A street person in Italy proved it, after all.) Escorting the list around the room will take at least ten minutes, because half of the students will not have anything to write with and half will not know their names. And it's never the same half.

I solved the problem one day by taking a snapshot of the class. Unfortunately, word got out and the next time I tried that, I ended up with a photograph of thirty-one bare asses. None of which I could identify. Shortly after this Kodak moment, when the vice-principal requested my attendance records, I submitted said photograph.

So, at the next school that hired me, when confronted with the same request, I said, "Since mandatory attendance is an administrative rule, not a pedagogical one, taking attendance is your responsibility, not mine."

"But," the vice-principal said, "if a student gets a borderline mark, attendance records are used to determine pass or fail."

"Why not just flip a coin?" I asked. (Better yet, flip the student. If he lands on his head—) "If you're not sure a student has mastered the material, wouldn't it make more sense to re-test than to count the number of times he was sitting in class?"

"And anyway," I reminded him, "you already have a policy for dealing with borderline marks: 'All marks in the 40s shall receive a 50.'" The rest of that policy says 'No student shall receive a mark lower than 35' and 'No more than 20% of the students in any one class shall fail.' I'm serious. I discovered that policy when 45% of my class failed.

"Certainly I can justify my figures," I had said, to yet another vice-principal. "Twenty-nine of the thirty-six students who failed did not hand in at least half of the required assignments. Another one did hand in everything, but with only his name on it. Misspelled. As well, all failing students were absent at least fifteen days during the term—that's three weeks of missed classes. I offered to send work home with a friend—sometimes they knew in advance if they'd be away, remember that Genetically Modified Nose concert?—but they laughed.

I offered a make-up test where applicable and they laughed harder—they insisted that if they weren't here for a test, they couldn't possibly fail it." I had pointed out that if they weren't here for a test, they couldn't possibly pass it either. But they weren't interested in anything I had to say. Ever. "And," I had continued, "the end-of-course questionnaires revealed that 65% of the students had never done *any* of the homework and 70% hadn't tried very hard."

"Well, would raising all of the marks by 15% bring the failure rate down?"

What? "Yes, it would." Duh. "It would also give six students a mark of 105% or better."

"Oh, we can't have that."

"No, 'percent' means—"

"The computer can only handle two digits."

This kind of thing is as common as it is illogical. I mean, if a 42 is a 50, then shouldn't an 82 be at least 90? (And Darlington is a safe nuclear power plant.) Wonder no more how someone can get to university and not know how to spell 'university.' Look at any school's records. How many students got a 50 in any subject in any given year? Now what are the odds of getting a 50? (One in a hundred.) (Did *you* get a 50 in math?)

But then logic has never been any school's strong suit. Consider the all-too-common 'No Swearing' rule. I collided with this one after I supplied for an English teacher one day who had left the following instructions: "Have the students rewrite one of two scenes from *Romeo and Juliet*—either the balcony scene or the fight scene—into contemporary English."

"Okay," I said, "this can be lots of fun, let's take a look. Open your books to the fight scene, please, and imagine it: you have these guys raging at each other, and they've been doing it for years; they're gonna fight now, and they're gonna fight so bad, a couple of 'em end up stabbed to death. Now instead of saying 'Thou wretched boy that didst consort with him shalt with him hence,' today Tybalt would say it differently, he'd say maybe 'You fuckin' bastard, I'm gonna kill you!' Got the picture? Okay, go to it!"

And so they did! Enthusiasm in the classroom is a rare thing. So much so, it was worth mention at many a dinner table that evening. And in my mailbox the next morning.

"Why did you take it upon yourself to introduce vulgarities into a lesson?" this principal asked at our after-school meeting.

"I didn't 'introduce' anything—the assignment left by Mr. Aberson instructed the students to rewrite a scene into contemporary English. Unless you live with the Waltons, 'contemporary English' includes 'vulgarities'. As does Elizabethan, and in particular Shakespearean, English."

What amazed me the most throughout the long and tortured 'discussion' that followed was the principal's inability to differentiate between swearing and quoting a character who is swearing. Philosophers refer to it as the 'use - mention' distinction. Most other people call it the difference between reality and make-believe. I really thought I had made some headway after an hour or so, but then the principal said, "Will you at least promise never again to swear in class?"

I crawled back to square one and said, "No—to do that would imply that I have already sworn in class, and I haven't. The best I'll do," I said, "is promise never again to quote a character who swears, in class. But that's a lot," I assured him, and tried to explain the fundamentals of censorship as they apply to education. To no avail.

"To quote a character swearing gives the impression that you condone swearing," he insisted.

"But last year's major play had a murder in it," I said—and saw that I needed to finish the point—"and I don't think anyone thought the school therefore condoned murder." Clearly, I was talking to another Sultan. Pre-banana.

"You're a role model," he insisted.

"Yeah right. If my students saw me as a role model, they wouldn't be throwing their books across the room, they wouldn't be coming to class unprepared, they wouldn't be absent more often than not. And they wouldn't be listening to country music."

To add to the confusion, apparently the students had said that I had said that it *was* okay to swear. This is simply not the case. (As it happens, I *do* think it's okay to swear. It was just an oversight that I didn't say so in class.) (Words are not intrinsically good or bad. It's how we use them that makes them so.)

I explained to the principal, however, that I do think swearing is appropriate if the character and/or the scene warrants it. *Not* to include swear words in the verbal exchange between two hot-headed male adolescents involved in a gang fight so impassioned that one *kills* the other would be, to my mind, unrealistic, and, further, would reveal an incomplete understanding of character. Further still, as I had mentioned earlier, Shakespeare himself used vulgarities all the time. Three times in the preceding scene, I said, one of the characters screams 'A plague upon your houses!'—well, that's a curse, isn't it? And there's much 'biting of the thumb' at each other. He asked what that was. I explained that it was an Elizabethan gesture of contempt, perhaps the equivalent of—and I gave him the finger.

Things began well enough at the next school. "Good morning, your regular teacher isn't here today, so I'm doing her—" I paused to look at the assignment sheet, "—sex-ed class. Aha—sex-ed. Have you read the results of that survey—wait, how old are you?" I looked out at the all-girls class.

"Sixteen," one called out.

"Seventeen," another said.

"Okay, good. An interesting survey was conducted recently, you'll want to hear this. Over a thousand boys aged 15 to 19 were asked a couple questions. First question. Is it okay to tell a girl you love her so you can have sex with her?" I started walking around the room. "And the answer is?" I raised my eyebrows as the girls pondered their predictions. "Yes! *Seven* out of ten said Yes! Lie to get sex! That's okay!" They exchanged looks.

"Second question. Should a guy use contraception whenever possible? And the answer is? What do you think—what did they say?"

"No!" they shouted with obvious anger.

"You're right! *Eight* out of ten, of 1,000 guys, said No, don't bother with a condom! Are you crazy? It's not our problem!" They exchanged free clinic phone numbers.

"Third question. If you get a girl pregnant, would you want her to have an abortion? And the answer is?" They weren't sure about this one. "*Nine* out of ten said—No! It's wrong! No abortions!" They exchanged plans to maim and mutilate.

"Knowing this," I continued circulating, "knowing that seven out of ten times they're lying to you, eight out of ten times they won't take responsibility for not making a zygote, and nine out of ten times they won't agree to abort it before it turns into a baby—knowing this, and then adding AIDS to the picture, I ask you," I paused at front and centre, "What idiot would ever agree to have sex with these people?"

I was later called to the principal's office and introduced to another logic-defying rule. He held up my announcement for a discussion club, wherein I had listed abortion as a possible topic.

"Nothing Controversial," he informed me. At first I was relieved. I had thought he was going to say 'Nothing Sexual.'

But then I thought, what does that mean—'Nothing Controversial'? 'Controversial' simply means 'subject to differing opinions.' So to discuss nothing controversial means to discuss nothing subject to opinion, for surely anything subject to opinion is subject to *differing* opinion. Only a fool (or a principal) would believe there's never dissent on matters of opinion.

(It's ironic, therefore, to hear the students insist, defending their irrationality, "Everyone's entitled to their own opinion." At a school where nothing controversial is to be discussed, obviously *no one's* entitled to their own opinion.)

Could it be that those who forbid controversy, who thus forbid opinions, *know* that some opinions are better, more valid, than others? Could it be they know that their own opinions aren't worth much—held as they are, more often than not, on the basis of inheritance rather than reason? No, that would presuppose an IQ of—well, an IQ.

So I deleted the word 'abortion' from my announcement. And put it in extra-big letters on all the signs I later posted throughout the school. Pity I wasn't able to see how many students showed up for the discussion club's first meeting.

At the next school, I unwittingly set a personal best, committing three violations in a row before the first class even started. During homeroom, I did not stand for the national anthem, nor for the prayer, and to the student who tried to politely point out my transgressions—"Miss—", I said "Please don't refer to me as an Unmarried Female."

I was read *The Education Act*. "Teachers are duty-bound," the principal glared at me, "to inculcate by precept and example," he glared at me again, "respect for religion, and the principles of Judaeo-Christian morality, the highest regard for truth—"

"Well, see," I interrupted, "there's a contradiction right off the bat—one can't respect both religion *and* truth."

He continued as if I wasn't serious, "—justice, loyalty, love of country—"

"But it's *because* I love my country that I don't want to see its young people caught up in the fervour of nationalism and joining the killing corps. Standing for the anthem is not the only, nor even the best, way to inculcate love of country."

Again, he ignored me, "—humanity—"

"There's *another* contradiction—'highest regard for humanity' necessarily excludes 'love of country'."

"—benevolence, sobriety, industry, frugality—"

"Yeah right, do you know how much paper this school wastes?"

"—purity—"

"What the hell is purity?"

"—temperance, and all other virtues." He put the book down.

"I guess 'all other virtues' includes hypocrisy, huh? I mean, teachers aren't required to stand for the anthem in the staffroom."

"*And* you will insist the students call you 'Miss', 'Mrs.', or 'Ms.'"

"But neither my marital status nor my sex is important enough to me to be part of my name."

"We encourage our students to show respect to their teachers."

"I fail to see how 'Unmarried Female' or 'Female Person' is a token of respect. Furthermore," I picked up the 300-page book, "*The Education Act* forbids sexist materials and policies." I thumbed through to find the relevant chapter and verse. "'Sexist' means 'differentiating on the basis of sex'. 'Ms.' and 'Mr.' are titles that differentiate on the basis of sex." Can *you* put the crates on top of each other to get to the banana?

So the next day—it was a long-term placement and the paperwork for dismissal took a while—I wore a see-through shirt. I figured that if my sex was important enough to be revealed by my *name*, it should surely be revealed by my attire as well. But no. Such attire was 'unprofessional'.

And so it was that I came to put on a fashion show for that particular principal. I was trying to discover what, exactly, was "professional"—"appropriate, then"—"all right, acceptable"—"well, there's a certain standard"—"an expectation." It took him all of twenty seconds to get from the intriguing 'professional' to the disappointing 'expected'. No matter. According to *The Education Act*, the principal has the right "to set the tone of the school." (Why he should attempt to do this by paying attention to what people wear scares me.) (But then, so do image consultants.)

Jeans and a pink sweatshirt? Not okay. Is it the denim? Apparently not, because a denim skirt was okay. Ah, so as long as my legs are showing? No, because shorts were not acceptable. Grey cotton pants styled rather like jeans. No. Am I getting warmer? How about a polyester pantsuit? Yes. Oh dear. (Though I knew where I could get a cute baby blue one.) Back to tops, was it the colour or the fabric that was problematic? How about a pink sweater? Okay. And what about this turquoise thing, cotton fleece, I believe, like a sweatshirt, but ribbed and beaded, like, well no, not like a sweater, but—would a straightjacket be okay? How about a donkey tail?

And is any of this really relevant to the quality of education? Hell, yes! We should teach the students *not* to judge a book by its cover! We should teach them to distinguish between pretence and substance, form and content, appearance and reality! When a colleague of mine confessed that he was very grateful for his suitcoat and tie during his first years of teaching because they gave him the authority and respect he needed to control the class, I wondered which was more pathetic, the teacher or the class? (And of course, when *I* wore a suitcoat and tie, well, that was the day the paperwork came through.)

At the next school, I had a class in a portable. And the students were coming in and out and in and out, talking, shouting, laughing, totally ignoring my requests for attention, for quiet, for collective cardiac arrest, and there I am trying to take attendance, and they're in and out, and then I'm trying to explain what they were to work on, and they're still in and out and in and out and finally I said "Look—make up your mind: if you want to come to class, then come, and stay in; and if you don't, then please stay out."

But they continued to act like I didn't exist and kept on going in and out. One went out and got a can of pop then came back in, then one went out for a smoke, came back and asked a friend, calling from the door to the other side of the room, "Do you have a light?", and then two others called across the room to each other and decided to go out to see something . . .

So. When everyone was out but two—there were two (2) students who were co-operating and working on the assignment—I locked the door. Well. You should've heard them!

"Fuckin' bitch locked us out!"

"She can't do that!"

"How are we supposed to learn if we can't get into class?!"

"You can't do this, we have a right to an education!"

And then eventually someone threw a crushed can at the window. "We're going to the principal to complain!"

(And no, I'm not the only one. I once counted sixty-three gummy bears, those jelly jujube things, plastered to the wall of Barbara's drama class. I guess it's a variation on spit balls. I wonder if she's having fun yet.)

Anyway, so then the principal came to me to complain. (About the students who had gone to him to complain.) "You can't lock the students out," he told me. "They have a right to an education."

"They weren't *interested* in an education."

"Still, they have that right."

"Okay then, how would *you* have handled the situation: you've got students talking and going in and out with total disregard—"

"Well if you expect them to be quiet, they will." What? WHAT? If I expected them to be quiet, I'd be insane; sane people adjust their expectations to fit reality. "And if they're not," he blithely continued, "just ask them to please be quiet and be seated." Oh gee why didn't I think of that.

"Well," I said, "suppose—I mean, I know this is a long shot and probably would *never ever* happen, but just suppose—they didn't. Suppose they didn't do what you asked them to do. Then what?"

"Well, I would talk to them, ask them why they were behaving in such a fashion."

"Okay, but suppose they wouldn't tell you, suppose they refused to discuss the problem with you." Suppose they couldn't hear you ask.

"Then I think the best thing to do would be to ignore the behaviour. I think you'll find that when you stop giving them the attention they seek, they will eventually stop their attention-seeking behaviour."

"Okay, and suppose while you were busy ignoring their bad behaviour in order to eliminate it, suppose it just got worse."

"Well, then, I guess you'd just have to send the troublemakers to me."

"I see. Okay suppose I did that—sent the 'troublemakers' to you. Suppose they didn't go."

"Well you could always just give me their names."

"But I don't know their names. They wouldn't tell me."

"Didn't their teacher leave a seating plan?"

"Um—I don't think they were sitting in their assigned seats." How clueless can this guy be?

"Perhaps then you could call me and if it were truly urgent, I could come out," he sighs at my incompetence.

"Okay, suppose I called and asked you to come escort them to your office—all twenty of them. Suppose they don't all follow you back to your office."

"Well, I'd know who they were."

"Okay, suppose you *do* recall all twenty faces and recognize them in the student card file, then what?"

"Well, I suppose the next course of action would be to suspend them."

"You'd suspend them? *Suspend* them? And deny them their right to an education?!"

Clearly, I had to give some thought to classroom management. It was, after all, what we did. (And you thought we taught.) Because at the next school, in the middle of a very engaging discussion, a student raised his hand and asked if he could leave. I said certainly. So he did. So did all the other twenty-seven students. (In fact, I'll bet more students walk out of my class than any other class in Canada.)

When I was interrogated about this incident, in yet another after-school meeting with yet another principal, this one flanked by his two VPs, I explained that when I said 'certainly', I was merely stating the obvious.

"But they thought you were giving permission."

"No," I said slowly, "they thought they could get away with telling you that's what they thought." Because you are such an idiot. A school is really only as good as its administrators. And, well, its metal detectors.

Perhaps my problem is that I watched *To Sir With Love* too many times in my formative years. And I realize now that the turning point for Sidney Poitier was that boxing match. If he tried that today, he'd be decertified by the Ministry faster than, well, faster than me.

I actually tried the authoritative approach, as suggested by a drill-sergeant-become-principal, and put the students' desks in rows. But of course they simply shouted across the room to have conversations with their friends. We also tried putting the desks in a circle. (For this I was called a revolutionary.) Everyone made faces at each other. For a whole week. (What a revolution.) When I tried teacher-centred learning, they complained that the course was boring; and when I tried student-centred learning, they said they couldn't come up with anything they wanted to learn, and besides, it was boring. I also tried dog biscuits. When the bell rang at the end of that class, Willy salivated. Well, drooled, actually. My biggest success was hypnosis. Using that approach, I was able to maintain a great deal of order and discipline. (I suspect I was also able to successfully teach the intricate steps of "The Bird Dance".) (We'll find out the next time someone says the words "Dance you motherfuckers dance!")

Have I taken care of the special needs students, the principal asked, still pondering my classroom management difficulties. You mean the ones who pick up their desks and throw them at other students, while aiming for me? Well, yes, I've referred to 'Resource and Withdrawal' the maximum allowed by any one teacher. Yes, I have spoken to the students individually, in class, in the hall, and at lunch. Yes, I did that too, but apparently they don't keep their appointments with Student Services. I've done that as well—one kid has three hundred and sixteen detentions to serve. Did that too—one came back, after seeing you, told me to go to hell, and threw his books on the floor. Every five minutes. For seventy-five minutes.

"Perhaps the trouble is you're too radical," the principal suggested. Too radical? Expecting the senior students to act like young adults instead of like two-year-olds? How extreme! (One time a student raised his hand just after the ten-minute between-class break. "Can I go to the washroom?" he asked. "No, if you really had to go, you would've gone during the break." "But I didn't know *then*, I have to go *now*," he whined. *High* school. I was a *high school* teacher. "Do you *really* have to go?" I asked. He nodded most forlornly. "Then piss on the floor!") And talking about recycling in class? Unimaginably too soon, wait a few more years! Demanding the students come prepared with pen and paper? Shocking! Assigning homework to basic level students? They're basic students, they don't *need* homework! (People say education is the key to social change. People also say an umlaut is a Finnish coffeecake.) Radical? I thought I was being reasonable. (So we agree then. Because in the school system, the voice of reason *is* radical.)

"You're too rigid," one of the VPs said.

"You're too flexible," the other one said.

"You seem to have a certain philosophy of education—" Well, that *is* a problem, isn't it.

The principal reached for his copy of *The Education Act*.

I sighed. "Yes, I am aware that *The Education Act* says it's my *duty* to 'maintain proper order and discipline in the classroom'. Section 235. *The Education Act* also says it's the *duty* of *pupils* to 'be diligent in attempting to master their studies, to exercise self-discipline, and to be courteous to fellow pupils and obedient and courteous to teachers.' Section 23. So," I said to him, "if *they* don't fulfill *their* part of the contract, I figure *I'm* released from *mine*." He assured me I was.

Then one fine day—one fine after-lunch actually, after a not-so-fine morning—while pulling into the next school's parking lot, and swerving to miss Willy, who was just standing there, I noticed a sign on the entrance gate: "It is illegal to enter these premises with intent contrary to *The Education Act*." So I called the police and had the students arrested. Every last one of them. Except two (2). And, since Section 236 requires the principal to 'maintain proper order and discipline in the school', I had him arrested as well.

9

CRISIS HOTLINE (PLEASE HOLD.)

So, as part of my community service, I was required to put in ten hours a week at a crisis hotline centre. Which meant that I gained the distinction of being fired from a volunteer job. Well, given the circumstances, it wasn't exactly a 'volunteer' job. And, of course, 'fired' isn't quite right because that implies I was 'hired' which implies I was 'paid'. Perhaps 'barred from the premises' is more accurate.

I really think we should define 'crisis', I said to my trainer after yet another call from someone who was just lonely and wanted to talk.

"But that's what people like us are for," I was told when I hung up on one such caller.

"No, that's what park benches are for. Occupied or not."

And when it wasn't some lonely person calling, it was Willy.

"I don't know what to do today," he whined. Well, okay, to be fair to Sartre, that could qualify as a crisis.

"Have you considered suicide?" I asked.

But when you think about it, who in their right mind—in the middle of a *crisis*—a *real* crisis—would actually decide make a phone call? I mean to us. Wouldn't you just dial 911? Who'd have time to talk? Well, women apparently. Most of our callers were women.

At first glance, that seems to defy the stereotype, since calling is such an active thing. As opposed to being called. Which is, I then realized, what men seem to thrive on. Hm. Then it made sense after all! Men think being called all the time shows how *important* they are.

One operator at the hotline, a man of course, actually convinced the administration to use call forwarding so he could get crisis calls on his cell phone. No doubt it was a big ego trip for him to be constantly interrupted by people threatening to kill themselves. Apparently one night he even answered his phone while making love with his wife. Surprise, it was his wife. Threatening to kill herself.

Women think otherwise. Women who are called all the time yank the damn phone out of the wall. (After, of course, calling the crisis hotline.) That's because women are expected to actually *do* something as a result of a phone call. Calls to them are demands on their time and energy. Calls to men are mostly just FYIs. And any demands on *their* time and energy are simply ignored. (Or passed on to whatever woman is unlucky enough to be in their speed dial.)

Too, I think the hotline gets more calls from women because calling us is asking for help. And of course men can't do that. They'd rather die. And they do. Which, rather like Todd's little friends, is another neat example of natural selection.

We at the hotline, however, generally received calls rather than made them. Apparently that's a policy, by the way. I had once spent a whole afternoon making calls to a telemarketing center. I asked whoever answered the phone if they were satisfied with their banking service provider. I also asked if they were satisfied with their long distance carrier. I asked how many jars of applesauce they had purchased in the last six months and whether they were planning to go on a trip in the next twelve months. I asked them where. And told them terrible things were going to happen there.

As I said, generally we were the ones called rather than the ones calling, but even so, most of the hotline operators were women. Probably because we can talk. We can communicate. In words. And we care. Well, *I* don't—

—And unfortunately that was discovered during a special training session on how to handle calls from people with AIDS. Apparently, I didn't "share the objectives of the organization." Well, no. I guess I don't. I think AIDS is a good thing.

I mean, if we need 'a die off', if we need a major decrease in the human population in order for the planet (the human species included) to survive, then AIDS gets my vote.

War would do it. But, whether biochemical or nuclear, war would also destroy a lot of the environment. Which kind of defeats the purpose. Furthermore, a lot of innocent people tend to die in wars.

And that's the problem with another contender, environmental catastrophe. Sure, a few more droughts would do the trick, but again, a lot of innocent people would die.

There are diseases other than AIDS which, in epidemic proportions, would work quite nicely. Tuberculosis, the Ebola virus, and the bubonic plague, for instance. But see, here's where the beauty of AIDS comes in: those other diseases can be caught accidentally, because they're airborne or spread through very casual contact; to get AIDS, however, you have to do something pretty definite, pretty intentional. Except for in utero transmission, blood transfusion, and rape, getting AIDS can never be called accidental; getting AIDS is generally voluntary.

And, well, that makes for yet another neat self-selection thing: I mean, if you're the kind of person who's stupid enough not to know that having sex can cause AIDS—or even stupider, to think that having sex is worth dying for—then frankly, you're the kind of person we can do without.

Plus, AIDS is the best thing that's happened to women in a long time: it can make rape the equivalent of murder. And the significance of that lies in the law regarding self-defence: the *Criminal Code* excuses killing in self-defence as long as you have reasonable grounds for thinking your life is in danger and it's the only way you can save yourself.

Well, how do you know your rapist-wannabe isn't HIV-positive? Remember Lucas Barker? The guy tested positive for the virus and threatened to take all the women with him that he could; by that point, he'd already been charged with four counts of 'assault with a deadly weapon'. A neat twist on 'This is my penis, this is my gun', but they clearly charged him with the wrong crime—it should've been 'attempted murder'.

In any case, it's reasonable to assume that your would-be rapist has a sexual history of both multiple partners and rough sex. And it's reasonable to assume that it's not a condom he's reaching for. So, it's reasonable to assume that any rape could turn out to be murder. (Consider it death by lethal injection.) So, thanks to AIDS, I now have legal licence to kill the sonuvabitch.

The training session was well-timed, as we soon started getting calls from people concerned about AIDS.

"Crisis Hotline, how can I help you?"

"You know this AIDS thing? It's disgusting. Queers are disgusting, man. Men touching other men, that's really sick." Why did *I* always get the few men who call?

"And a certain cable television program manager would agree with you," I said. "He says that scenes of men kissing and caressing each other are offensive and in bad taste."

"Right on!"

"But men hitting each other, and men killing each other, spattering blood and guts with bullets and knives—that's what, *good* taste?"

"I'd beat 'em up. Whenever I see a bunch of fags—"

"You'd beat 'em up. You'd get real close and touch 'em all over."

"What?"

"Maybe split a lip and, hopefully—oh so hopefully—exchange a few bodily fluids."

"What?"

"And they say men are the logical ones."

I logged the call and took another.

"Crisis Hotline, how can I help you?"

"I think AIDS is just a conspiracy, you know?"

"Yeah. So's the ozone thing."

Silence.

"Well, who's at risk of skin cancer? Talk about your black power." I logged the call.

"Crisis Hotline, how can I help you?"

"Will I get AIDS if I use a condom?"

"Well, it's possible—are you using condoms from before or after the recall?"

"What recall?"

"Some company—Gladiator or Minute Man or Teeny Weeny, I can't remember—they recalled their condoms. Apparently, the old condoms didn't meet the new standards; they felt 'a certain social responsibility' to improve their product."

"Improve the condoms?"

"Yeah. Before, when a defective condom could fuck up a woman's life, well, that was okay. That was an acceptable risk, apparently. But *now*, now that a *man's* quality of life is at stake, now the condoms have to be better."

"I see. Well that makes sense."

"Yeah, as much sense as a judge ordering female sex workers to be tested for AIDS, but not their male clients."

"But now they're using new standards?" he asked.

"Yeah. New, but still double," I reply. Call logged.

Actually it'd be kinda cool to have AIDS. You'd be a lethal weapon. Without all those karate lessons.

And it'd be a great 'go away' line: "Hi, don't I know you?" "No, I'm positive." Then you slit your wrists and bleed all over the place. (Hey, if you're gonna die, you may as well be a little theatrical about it. See, most people couldn't do that.) (Well they could, but it might turn out they were a little premature and then wouldn't *they* feel foolish.) (Well, no they wouldn't, 'cuz they'd be dead.)

Once, during a slow afternoon—crises seldom happen during the afternoon—I reprogrammed the automated answering thing. Instead of just "Please hold"—which was just *wrong*—for a *hot*line—we now had "Press 1 for information. Press 2 for counselling. Press 3 if you have *no* short term memory *whatsoever*." I also reprogrammed the Muzak. With Bobby McFerrin's "Don't worry, be happy . . . " and Wang Chung's "Everybody have fun tonight."

Unfortunately, I was reprimanded for this little funny.

"Hey, I'm a volunteer," I reminded my supervisor. "You can't reprimand me unless you pay me!" Which, now that I think of it, sounded a lot like a rule from the local S & M service.

A couple weeks later, we had another special training session, this one on how to handle calls from 'battered women'.

"See, that's why a pregnancy vaccine is such a good idea." Eight heads swivelled to rivet on me. "What?" I said in response. "I mean, why doesn't the woman just move? Get in her car, and drive to, oh I don't know, there must be apartments for rent in, say, Edmonton."

"She hasn't got a car," someone said.

"She hasn't got first and last month's rent," someone else said.

"Exactly," I said back. "And why? Because she hasn't got a job."

"She's been raising her two kids!" someone protested.

"Q.E.D." I said. Silence. "That's my point," I added. "Case closed."

"But that *is* a job," someone said. "She just doesn't get paid for it."

"Yeah, *that's* the problem," someone else said. "If she got—what would we pay someone who's responsible for a little human being—for its physical, emotional, and social development—twenty-four hours a day, seven days a week?"

"Enough to get to Edmonton with first and last month's rent."

"Yeah, but you gotta admit a lot of the parenting we see out there is unskilled labour. Minimum wage stuff."

I jumped in, "See that's why needing a license to parent is another good idea." Eight heads swivelled again. "What?"

"And a university degree to get the license, I suppose?" the high school dropout asked.

"No, I think you could cover the basics—Child Development, Health and Nutrition, First Aid—in a year or two. A diploma should do it."

"And anyone with a diploma will be a good parent?" someone said doubtfully.

"No, anyone *without* a diploma will *not* be a good parent. You're confusing necessary and sufficient conditions." Silence. "A diploma is *necessary* to be a good parent, but it's not *sufficient*." Still silence. "You need other stuff," I added. Then, "Didn't *any* of you take *any* logic at university?" The high school drop-out glared at me.

"Where can you get that pregnancy vaccine you mentioned?" someone then asked.

"Oh, there isn't one," I said. "The money went instead to research on Viagra and patterns of male balding." Silence again. "You know, some men bald from the front up through the middle like a wheat field with a swath ploughed out of it, while others have a little thin spot on top that gets bigger and bigger like the ozone hole. But hey," I added, as, apparently, the training session was over, "you can always get spayed. Kessie and I did!"

Alas, it was another well-timed session, because we started to get calls from women who'd been beaten up by the men they were living with.

On my first call, the woman and I chatted about the new hairdresser in town, about whether we were going to get any more snow, and about how horse tranquilizers were available from the local vet without a prescription. Soluble and tasteless, I volunteered. After all, I was a volunteer.

On my second call, and my third call, we pretty much talked about the same three things.

Then there was another set of similar calls.

"But he *needs* me!"

"For what exactly?" A punching bag?

"But he *needs* me!"

"So?" Why is it that women around the world feel duty-bound to meet men's needs?

"But he *needs* me!"

"Are you sure it's not the other way around?" And what exactly do you think you need him for?

"Deep down, he really loves me, I *know* it!"

"Being loved incurs no obligation." Say, to love back. Or, um, to take the kind of shit you've apparently been taking.

"But I love him!"

"Why?" No, really, list ten loveable things about him.

By the middle of the week, the local women's shelter was full. By the end of the week, all the shelters in the region were full. Women were leaving their husbands in droves. Even *before* they got beaten up. Graffiti appeared at bus stops, on newspaper boxes, in public washrooms: "But he needs me!—For what exactly?" "But he needs me!—So?" I saw my words written on the subway walls: "Being loved incurs no obligation." It was spray-painted in huge pink letters at several stops. Two Saturdays later, there was a mass exodus: women were walking down Main Street, leaving. It was a veritable parade. Complete with several horses. That were very nicely decorated, I might add.

On top of all that, at the next meeting of the Hotline volunteers, I received the Hotline's Volunteer-of-the-Month Award.

"Oh, my, I'm so happy I could cry," I gushed, doing my Miss America imitation, as they handed me the cheap plastic plaque.

"Why her?" Miss Congeniality asked.

"Well, between the calls made to our administrative offices and the letters sent to our post office box, she received the most death threats this month."

Hm. "How do you know they were for me?" I asked, with some unease. After all, I didn't want to accept an undeserved award.

"You're the only 'Bitch' we have on our lines at one in the morning." Hm.

As the meeting faded into a get-together, the supervisor stood up to leave, turning to me on her way out.

"Could I see you in my office for a moment?"

"Sure," I followed her, clutching my plaque. Might there be a part-time position opening up? Had the Hotline received more funding, now that Viagra was firmly on the market?

She sat down. I sat down. And then I heard the 'It doesn't matter whether or not you actually *are* a bitch, the fact that you're *perceived* as one suggests you're not really right for this job' argument. That's how it becomes all about appearances, I thought.

"So it's all about appearances," I said.

"Well, how we're perceived does affect how we're received—and that affects our success."

"Even if the perception is unreasonable, unfounded—" Have you ever heard of rumour? False allegation?

She nodded. "Even if it's not true, you have to ask why people would even say that about you—and that's a concern to us."

"You do understand it's not the callers who called me a bitch, but their husbands—men who beat people up."

"But why would they think that? There must be something that—"

"Well yeah. I'm a woman. By definition, I'm a bitch."

And that's when she asked for my key.

"You know what I heard?" I said to one of the other volunteers on my way out.

"What?"

"I heard the supervisor has been cooking the books and taking home an extra couple thousand a month. Just a rumour, you understand . . . "

10

LET'S GET ROCKED!

Inspired by the little fun I had with McFerrin and Wang Chung, I became a deejay for parties. And just pretended the people weren't there. It worked. I'd show up, plug in my equipment, and start playing music—whatever I felt like dancing to: pop, rock, reggae, big band, 50s, 60s—and "Achy Breaky Heart" by the Chipmunks. At the end of the night, I got paid. People paid me to have my own private party. Life doesn't get—

Okay, it was the weddings. I made the weddings—memorable. How could I not, given my previous position. (Not quite a 'job', you'll recall.) Besides, how often does one say 'till-death-do-us-part? Twice, maybe three times?

I especially made memorable those weddings that began immediately to snuff out the woman. The weddings at which the couple asked me to introduce them as Mr. and Mrs. Robert Smith or whatever. I'd comply—"Ladies and Gentlemen, Mr. and Mrs. Robert Smith"—but then I'd add on a bit: "Now, according to recent statistics, Sarah—Sarah Jones—has a one in four chance of being severely beaten by Robert during the course of their marriage. So let's all wish them good luck, shall we?" And I'd start clapping. God help us, the guests would always join in. And, God help us, ninety-four percent of all women get married. Only ninety-two percent of all lemmings go over the cliff.

I didn't always use that introduction. Sometimes I'd open with "Doesn't the bride look beautiful in white?" Then amid all the teary-eyed smiles of assent, I'd point out it's the colour of surrender.

On one rather long-winded evening, I picked up my mic and said, "Usually one begins by congratulating the bride and groom." The two of them snuggled and beamed at each other. "But why?" I carried on. "I mean, is it a *good* thing? Half of all married couples end up divorced. The other half just couldn't be bothered." The guests were still plastered with politeness. "Is it an achievement? How *can* it be? There are no skills required, no special qualifications to be met." I turned to the newlyweds. "So you're entering into a legal contract with another person. Whippee. Bet you haven't even read the contract. So you went to a church for some obscure sacrament. Bet the minister didn't recognize either of you." Some of the guests became restless at this point, so I continued, to see if it was the attentive ones or the inattentive ones.

"I mean, what's getting married really about? Proof that you're all grown up, gonna settle down, maybe start a family? As if being a parent means you're no longer a kid. Any fourteen-year-old can have sex. Proof that someone somewhere somehow found you loveable long enough to agree to marry you? Yeah right. Whatever." I pressed the play button, and slowly increased the volume.

"So this first dance is a special one, for Catherine and Heathcliff, Antony and Cleopatra, Tweedledee and Tweedledum . . . " I faded out as Aaron Neville faded in . . . "Everybody Plays the Fool . . . " Cameras flashed.

At some point during the evening, I'd put on a favourite set of mine, "I'll Be There" (Jackson Five), "I Am Here" (Grapes of Wrath), "Here I Am" (UB40), and "What Am I Doing Here?" (Blue Rodeo). Eventually, someone would ask for some Stones. So I'd play "I Can't Get No Satisfaction" followed by "You Can't Always Get What You

Want". Being a deejay was so much fun.

But I refused to MC the bouquet and garter. Instead, I'd get on the mic and ask for a volunteer. Invariably, the best man would lurch up to my table. I'd give him the mic and step back.

"All right, all you luscious available babes—onto the floor!" The best man laughed and took a swig of his beer. "And Marie, are you out there? Got your bouquet? Oh that's pretty." The crowd loved it. "Now I'm gonna count to three—"

"Think you can?" The guests laughed at this challenge from the floor.

"Who said that? 'Course I can. Ready? Okay. Here we go. Ready? Are you ready? Okay. No, wait." He waved the mic. "I'm gonna count *backwards* okay?" Applause. "Ready? Okay? Here we go. Three—Two—One!"

On 'One!' I took the mic, and in my best Monty Python, shouted "Run away! Run away!" The forementioned available babes paused in confusion and the bouquet hit one of them in the head. Cameras flashed.

Once I put a stick of dynamite in the bouquet and when some Juliet caught it, it blew up in her face. (Just kidding. That kind of behaviour would be—aberrant.)

I was expected, of course, to play "The Stripper" during the garter bit. But not once have I seen a bride really comfortable with that. And no wonder. I mean, she doesn't get to crawl her fingers down his chest, opening his shirt, lower, and lower, to the cheering of her friends. For a while, I played the Troggs' "Wild Thing". It was a bit better. Then, God love her, Deana Carter came out with "Did I Shave My Legs For This?" It became my garter standard.

A couple times I was asked to announce 'a money dance'. This is when, one by one, each man at the reception tosses some change into a jar, then gets in line to dance with the bride. I'd put on John Michael Montgomery's "Sold!" and follow the bride with my red spotlight. One night the bulb burnt out during my set-up test. An ordinary deejay might have panicked, but I was professionally trained to handle such equipment failures. So, I got on the mic and said, "We're going to do away with the facade tonight. Instead of the money dance as you all know it, the groom's just gonna haul the bride off to Room 206 a little later, that's 2-0-6, and everyone can have a go at her. Be generous. I suggest $200 a shot—it's her wedding night, after all!"

Most people are surprised to hear that deejays are professionally trained. Indeed we are. Not all of us, of course. There are many imposters out there with their rec room stereos and their K-Tel collections. But in order to become a *licensed* deejay, you have to go through intensive training for two whole weekends.

Three of the four days are spent discussing equipment—the basics, the add-ons, set-up (i.e., how to plug stuff in) (the male goes into the female) (yes, even electrical connectors are sexual) (heterosexual), troubleshooting, emergency repair, and maintenance.

On the third day, we were tested. We were put in groups of four, and each group was assigned a set of equipment that had been sabotaged in some way. One group electrocuted itself. They failed. Another group had a loose connection. Couldn't figure it out. A third group had been supplied with a mono jack instead of a stereo one. So no, it wasn't the speaker. Our group had to build an amplifier with just a piece of string, some bubblegum, a toaster oven, and an instruction manual translated from Japanese. I alone succeeded. Bob, Sam, and Marty refused to read the manual.

During lunch, we had fun with the strobe light and the disco ball. Well, except for Arthur. He had an epileptic seizure. (Good to know. For the Epileptic Association's Dinner and Dance.)

Then we discovered the karaoke machine. I love music, and I love to dance, but I cannot sing. So when it was my turn, recalling Sid Vicious' version of "My Way", I screamed out the words with frenzied urgency: "*I left my heart in San Francisco!*"

Then some guy did a great Frankie Valli with "Walk Like a Man". While leaving the stage, he tripped over some power cords.

The last day focussed on music—styles, tempos, and how to put together a set—and stereotyping—how to make generalizations about what kind of music people like based on their age, sex, clothing, and food preferences.

"So you mean my seventy-year-old grandmother can't possibly like Offspring's 'Why Don't You Get a Job?'" I asked.

Our trainer, Mr. Music Please, said, "No, she'll like Tommy Dorsey. For her, you would play 'I'll Be Seeing You'."

"Would not."

I borrowed the guy-next-to-me's cell phone.

"Hey Grandma! It's me! Do you like Tommy Dorsey? 'I'll Be Seeing You'?

"Yeah, there's this guy here saying that seventy-year-old grandmothers like Tommy Dorsey. That's right. 'I'll Be Seeing You'.

"Yeah. I know. All right. I will. Yeah.

"Right now? Okay."

I turned, grinning, from the phone to Mr. Music Please. "She says to tell the asshole she'd rather hear AC/DC.

"Yeah. Love you too, Grandma. Bye." I handed the phone back to the guy-next-to-me. "Thanks."

Mr. Music Please blinked, cleared his throat, consulted his clipboard, and moved on. "What would you play at a 25th wedding anniversary?"

I saw my fellow deejays-in-training engage in quick calculations: married at 20-25, for 25 years, makes them late 40s, maybe early 50s, and if they're having a party with a deejay, middle-class . . .

"Don't forget," he gave us a hint, "people like the most the music that was popular in their early 20s."

More calculations: that'd be about late 60s . . .

"Where's the event?" someone asked.

"Good question." The Hilton makes them a Beatles party. If it's at the Legion, play Conway Twitty.

Sure enough, someone calls out, "'Michelle'."

"Good choice. What else?"

"Righteous Brothers, um, what's that one, 'Chain of Love'?"

"'Unchained Melody'. Another good possibility."

"Steppenwolf," I called out. "'Born to be Wild'." Everyone looked at me. "What? Twenty-five years of marriage, presumably to the same person, the kids are finally gone, you don't think she's thinking of buying a Harley?" There was silence.

"Ricky Martin," I added. "Same line of reasoning."

The all-time best parties I ever did were the year-end 'Round-Ups' for the local branch of Alcoholics Anonymous. A.A. parties are always good. I think it's because they know better than anyone how to act like drunken idiots. And a sober drunken idiot is ten times more fun than a drunk drunken idiot. When I play "The Hokey Pokey" at an A.A. party, *everyone* gets onto the floor.

Also, A.A. people are usually single—their spouses left them long ago. So everyone dances with everyone, there's not that dreary coupling thing you get at other parties.

Nor is there any pretence. Recovering drunks aren't allowed to pretend to be anything but recovering drunks. Step number something.

One particular A.A. party was a few days after I had finally run my first, and last, marathon. And I had succeeded at all my goals (run it, run it in under four hours, run it at under 9 minutes a mile)—plus one: if I were Jamaican, I'd now have the national record. So I too was celebrating. Not only the achievement of my marathon goals, but also—three days later—the return of my ability to walk, and even dance, sort of.

(I had planned, once I had crossed my finish line—I set up my own course, a round trip from my house—to walk the length of the short dead-end road I lived on to cool down, relax, and bask in my victory, but after a few steps, I changed my mind and decided the length of the driveway would do. Apparently, at around mile 15, I'd turned into a cement mixer: as long as I kept moving, I was okay, relatively speaking of course, but as soon as I stopped, every muscle in my body hardened instantly. Anyway, once I made it the length of my driveway, and into my small house, I discovered I couldn't bend over to open Kessie's doggy door. So I got down on my hands and knees to do so—and then discovered it was just *so* much easier to stay that way for a while. I may not have actually had a choice, but I didn't try to find out. I just crawled around on my hands and knees for an hour until I thought I could climb into the bathtub, blessedly full of hot water, without drowning myself.)

Anyway, the guest speaker did his thing, and while Hi-my-name-is-Al-and-I'm-an-alcoholic told his sad and sordid tale, I kept the music going, providing a background soundtrack, if you will: "You Can Call Me Al", "Bottle of Wine", "Red Red Wine", "Wine-Colored Roses", "Tequila", "There's a Tear in My Beer", and "I've Got Friends in Low Places"; then as he moved into chapter two, "I'm Sorry", "Sorry Seems to be the Hardest Word", and "I'm Sorry" again—and again, two more times; I didn't have "Day by Day" for chapter three—so instead I put on "Short People".

As soon as he sat down, everyone at this particular A.A. event was ready to dance. *Really* ready. Not only was "The Hokey Pokey" child's play to them, but so too was "The Macarena". And "Time Warp". These people could do "Thriller". Every step. It was great!

When someone requested "Maniac", a dozen women parodied the "Flashdance" workout scene. It was hilarious. Especially since I too could most definitely not touch my toes. When someone requested "YMCA", six guys claimed the floor. In costume. The twist, the jitterbug, the polka, the cha-cha, these people could do it all. It was amazing.

Then someone asked for "Dirty Dancing". After The Contours' classic, "Do You Love Me?" I put on the final track, "I've Had the Time of My Life". And of course a few people tried the part where she flies through the air and he catches her. Or not.

After the ambulance left, I decided to put on something nice and slow. Celine Dion, the hit from *Titanic*, "My Heart Will Go On". But then someone leaned too far out the window . . .

After the second ambulance left, I thought long and hard about my next selection. I put on Tommy Dorsey. "I'll Be Seeing You".

In addition to the Saturday special events, I got a gig in a basement bar for a while. Regular, Friday nights. I'd been told by the previous guy, who was moving on, to a real job, that it'd be a piece of cake.

"You won't get any requests, they keep the jukebox on in the other room, and they all watch the game or shoot pool. Hardly anyone shows up to dance until midnight. No one'll really care what you play, you're pretty much on your own." Great. My kind of gig.

So Bartender #1 told me, before I'd even begun, to play Seger's "Old Time Rock 'n' Roll", Brooks and Dunn's "Boot Scootin' Boogie", and "Dance Mix". Gee, none of those would've occurred to me, thanks.

Bartender #2 passed me a list with seven songs on it. Then went back to the other room and watched the game.

After about an hour, some guy wandered in from the other room—must have been half-time—and came up to my table to chat.

"So, are you Mike's little helper?"

I stared at him. "No, but I'll bet *you* are, aren't you?"

"Is that all you've got?" Another guy wandered up to my table and gestured at my set-up, my small speakers.

"No, I've got a 14-inch penis too, but I left it in the car." Kim Stockwood's "Jerk" was next.

Sure enough, a little before midnight, people started showing up. I started putting on the dance-able stuff. And I started getting requests for dance-able stuff. What is it with all these 'requests'—do I have 'NOVICE' written on my forehead? Shortly after midnight, another guy came up to me. "Play some rock, this stuff is shit."

Right. "This shit was requested, but sure I'll put on some more rock." And I did so within two songs.

He came up again, and this time sat himself down in my chair, behind my table. "Do we have a problem with territory?" I asked.

"I've been drinking since 2:00," he said.

"Are you going to piss on my table leg?"

"Since 1:00," he changed his mind. He thought he was bragging. "Play some rock," he said, again.

"I've *been* playing rock—what specifically do you want to hear? What do you mean when you say 'rock'?"

"*Any* rock," he got angry at me. "Anyone knows what rock is!"

He came up a third time. "I've taken a survey and no one wants to hear this shit."

"You must've missed some people." The two dozen on the floor maybe.

"Play some rock and roll!" He was getting really aggravated. But tough shit. I'd already played Seger, Springsteen, the Stones, Cochrane, and Adams; I'd played Tragically Hip and Pearl Jam; I'd played Hootie and I'd played the Smashing Pumpkins. This was one drunken asshole I was not going to be able to please.

So the fourth time he came up, I hauled back and decked him one. He went down. No one noticed. Time for Queen, "Another One Bites the Dust". And, because I was feeling so good, "We are the Champions!"

Around 12:30, someone came up and said to me, "I don't think this is gonna go over too well, you should play something faster." I looked at him. He was about twenty.

"Do you think your being male and my being female gives you the right to give advice to someone almost twice your age. *Unsolicited* advice? *Unnecessary* advice?" I pointed to the floor, which was filling with slow-dancing couples.

"I'm only trying to help," he was genuinely confused. It was very troubling.

Three songs later (mid, mid, and fast), an older guy, fifty-something, approached the table, and said oh-so-helpfully and oh-so-gently, "You can't please everyone, but just try something a bit slower."

"Fuck off!" I replied.

At 1:00, sharp, I cut the power and started packing my stuff. At 1:15, I was outta there. Apparently for good.

11

REPORTING THE NEWS

And, like Mike whose little helper I was not, I moved onto, alas, a real job. Not casual work. No more sticking pins in voodoo dolls and casting spells for five-car crash-ups so I could get someone else's shift.

Not seasonal. No more okay-I'll-put-up-with-this-shit-but-only-because-it's-just-for-the-summer.

And not part-time. Alas, no more mid-afternoon star treks with Jean-Luc Picard.

This meant not only a regular income—a guaranteed amount of money every two weeks (wow)—but also (oh my) benefits: a check-up at the dentist, and the optometrist, paid sick days, paid holidays, and a pension plan (or at least eligibility for unemployment insurance). It also meant respect—for my suggestions, my abilities, my work, and my paycheque. (Murphy's Law #246: the more you need your paycheque—i.e., the smaller it is and/or the rarer it is—the more likely it will have been 'deferred to the next pay period'.)

By the way, whose bright idea was that, dividing work into

'full-time' and 'part-time'? It's actually 'too-much-time' and 'not-enough-time': working 40 hrs/wk means you have enough money to do stuff, but not enough time to do it, and working 20 hrs/wk means you've got the time, but you can't afford to do anything. A simple redistribution (say, 30 hrs/wk for everyone) would, I should think, make a lot of people happy, but the last time I suggested such an equitable job-sharing program, I was reprimanded for being insubordinate. Of course. I was also given a few stone-eyed stares that were an intriguing mix of incomprehension and hatred.

My guess is that this strict division between full-time and part-time, based as it is on a quantitative difference, was established by men. And it is, therefore, completely illogical. Is the lawyer who works 40 hrs/wk really less competent, less dedicated, and less deserving than the lawyer who works 60 hrs/wk? Then why is the check-out clerk who works 20 hrs/wk considered less competent, less dedicated, and less deserving than the one who works 40 hrs/wk? Quantity and quality are not necessarily related. (How many times do we have to say it? Bigger is *not* necessarily better.)

So Monday morning, *early* Monday *morning*, I arrived, bleary-eyed and scraggly-tailed, at my new job: I was now a reporter for the local paper.

The editor led me to my desk (my desk!) and elaborated on the terms of my employment: eight-thirty to six, Monday to Friday, evenings if there was something going on, and every second weekend to cover weekend events.

"Your over-time rate here is the standard time-and-a-half?" I asked, as blandly as possible.

He stared at me. "Yes. No. Sorry. Reporters are salaried employees, not waged workers. Didn't payroll tell you that?"

They did. I just hadn't appreciated the implication. I did the math. Every second week for sure, I'd be working for—geez—less than minimum wage!

"Why don't you start off here," he led me to the archives, "and get acquainted with our little paper?" He returned to his office. I pulled out yesterday's paper, sat down at the table, and turned to the jobs section.

Even though most jobs, apparently 80%, are not advertised. This, of course, forces the unemployed into what is, therefore, largely a wild goose chase: sending out resumes, making calls, making visits—to a long list of prospective employers shortlisted from the Yellow Pages. Said wild goose chase has the effect of further impoverishing said unemployed: resume plus cover letter plus manilla envelope plus postage equals about two dollars, times fifty and you're up to far more than I spend on food for a month. Said wild goose chase also has the effect of further demoralizing said unemployed: it's unlikely that even one resume in that fifty will be received by an employer who actually has an opening, for which one is actually qualified—constant rejection is, therefore, certain to occur. Which, in turn, has the effect of keeping said unemployed unemployed: the less optimistic—i.e., the more hopeless—one is at the interview, the more likely one is to *not* get the job, which makes one even more hopeless, which makes one even more unlikely to get the job, which makes one . . . With each rejection, it costs more to maintain hopefulness, until eventually the price of said hopefulness is sanity—only the deranged and deluded actually remain hopeful in these circumstances.

'Course it's possible that that's the point of such 'recruitment strategies': desperation (not to mention derangement and delusion) is a good indicator of workplace success. (Those who are not desperate tend to retain their dignity and, thus, their potential to be insubordinate.)

So, I thought to myself, let's see what job opportunities were advertised yesterday.

Lumber grader. I bet when you're evaluating a stack of two by fours, you take *off* marks for originality.

Food demonstrator. "Ladies and gentlemen, could I have your attention—*this* is *food*." Hm. Mark that one.

Bingo caller. Gee, *I* know the *whole* alphabet, not just those five letters. *And* I know my numbers. Telling six from nine can be tricky, but I think I'm up to it. Wait—"Experience required." Experience reading letters and numbers *out loud*? Experience reading *ping pong balls*? See what I mean by demoralizing? I haven't even got what it takes to be a bingo caller.

I went on to the next ad: "Energetic and dedicated person [slave] wanted to work in an open-skills, multi-project environment [expected to do everything, simultaneously] as part of a team [granted no autonomy whatsoever] with an open door attitude [we took away all the divider walls] in an innovative firm [we have no policies or procedures yet]." I moved along.

Avon Lady. Yeah right. Every time I pictured myself ringing a doorbell and singing out 'Avon calling', I burst into an idiotic grin. Especially since by the third door I was wearing that thick white face cream and lipstick the shade of scarlet worn only by retired ladies living in mobile homes and turquoise polyester pantsuits. Besides, I'd probably have to shave my legs. And they probably want a woman for the job. (And as several high school principals now know, I refuse to incorporate gender into my identity.)

Three female elves wanted to work in a mall during the Christmas season. Female elves? I don't think they're going to find *any* elves—male *or* female. They may, however, find three females to play the part. But really, aren't they exposing themselves to a discrimination suit with this one? I mean, what must a Santa's elf do that a man can't do?

Santa's elves are industrious; they're notorious for being hard workers. Well, men can be hard workers. Seriously. And elves are pretty handy in the workshop, making all those toys. Again, I think men can meet this requirement.

But in the mall, Santa's elves will probably have to stand on their feet all day. I must admit that I think women have an edge here. At least they do if I'm to judge by all the checkout cashiers and bank tellers I see, *all* of whom are women, all of whom are apparently subject to some ridiculous rule that prohibits them from sitting down on the job. (I've never understood that one: surely their work wouldn't worsen if they were able to sit down; in fact, it would probably improve—freedom from chronic back pain would have that effect, I should think.)

And, well, elving is a job that involves some heavy-duty multi-tasking. Ask any Santa who's had to work with an elf with an attitude. (I can give you the name of three.) A good elf intercepts the sucker that will get stuck in the beard; a good elf tells Santa the difficult names so the kid won't start bawling because Santa doesn't even know his name; a good elf has 'pee-my-pants radar' and uses it at all times. And a good elf does all that while *appearing* to be merely ornamental. I'm not sure men would be very good at that. Most men I've known who are important act like it. ('Course so do the ones who *aren't* important.)

Lastly, let's not forget that Santa's elves must be good with kids. And this one really makes me hesitate. Men can *make* kids, with hardly a second thought. But can they *interact* with them? *Can they pay attention to kids for eight hours at a time?*

Maybe the mall is safe after all—discrimination in this case may well be justified.

Then I saw the display ad. Not a twenty-five cents per word classified, but a two-by-three box with a thick black border. General Manager for an Arts Center. Well, I liked the Arts Center part. But what exactly does a General Manager do? I read on. "The successful applicant will balance the arts and business, be sensitive to multiple art forms, and be a host at ease with the community." Yeah. So what exactly does a General Manager *do*? The ad said the Center was "a $1 million venue". Scarey stuff, venues. I tried to picture myself as the General Manager. And realized I was a man. Hm. That's interesting. Then I realized I had an accountant to deal with that million. And a staff supervisor to take care of personnel. And a publicity officer to take care of, well, publicity. (Surely a man wouldn't be expected to draw all the little ballerinas for the Center's ads and brochures.) I even had a selection committee to attend arts showcases and decide which groups to book. So what exactly would I, as General Manager, be expected to do? Nada. Well, shit, I can do that. I tore the ad out of the paper and tucked it away.

Then another ad caught my eye. Poet for a greeting card company. Well, this is unusual, I thought to myself. A *job* for a *poet*! Who said a degree in English Lit would be useless! I started preparing my portfolio immediately.

"I'm sorry we fought last night. I'm much more vicious during the day."

"Heard you were ill, injured, whatever. Can I borrow your car this weekend?"

This was too easy. Keats and Byron, move over.

"You light up my life. Like an oncoming train."

"Sorry to hear about your loss. But hey, people die."

I was tapped on the shoulder. "Lunch time!," some woman cheerily announced, smiling at me. "Come on, I'll show you where we all go."

Right. Lunch already? Oh. Wait a minute. *Lunch.* "Um, I brought my own," I said quickly, glancing to where I thought I might have set a knapsack.

She looked put out, as well she should. I was snubbing her. But I wanted to keep this job. At least for a week. (I'd promised Kessie. She wanted one of those really big, and expensive, rawhide chewsticks.) (And she needed more bright green tennis balls.) ('Course she *always* needs more bright green tennis balls.)

Speaking of which (keeping the job, that is), I set aside the classifieds section as she left and took a look at the first section of "our little paper". I started to examine the stories. What got in? What didn't? And where did it get put? And how much space did it get? Surprise. This paper was pretty much the same as any other.

Which made me wonder once again, why oh why do people read the paper every day as if it were some civic duty? To keep informed? Bullshit. The paper doesn't inform. It excites. (Well, it does if you work in an office.) It presents conflict, conflict, and more conflict. (No resolution. Resolution is boring.) Every section is the sports section. And things that don't involve conflict are covered *as if they did*—as if there is some problem, some difficulty. And certainly any problem or difficulty that *is* there gets emphasized, even exaggerated. Covering 'both sides' is done not in the interests of fairness, but in the interests of presenting the story in adversarial terms. (Fairness demands presenting *all* sides, not just two.)

And even if the paper *did* inform, what's the point of 'being informed'? Does it make you feel *in control*? But you just *feel* in control. You're not really, as long as you do nothing with that information. (And anyone who cares feels *less*, not *more*, in control when presented with information about conflict they can't do anything about.) 'Course maybe that's the point—reading the paper reinforces powerlessness while seeming to engender feelings of control. A neat trick.

Next day, I was ready. I had my first story idea: Ontario Hydro was trucking tritium along Highway 11.

"It's not local," the editor said.

"What do you mean? Highway 11 goes right through here."

"Does anyone who owns Ontario Hydro live here?"

"Well yeah. *We* 'own' Ontario Hydro."

"But the executive officers, the ones in charge—they don't live here, do they?"

"Well, no."

"And the tritium. Is it something someone here produces?"

"No, it's—"

"How about the guys driving the trucks—are they local guys?"

"Well, no, probably not."

"This is a *local* paper. We cover *local* news."

"But that's crazy. People here, *local* people, may not be doing it, but they are *affected* by it!"

"How so?" he asked.

"Well if, when, there's an accident—"

"*Then*," he said, "then you can do a story on it."

I thought for a moment. "Okay," I said. "That can be arranged."

Over the course of the next couple weeks, I wrote up several stories. I covered the Chamber of Commerce awards dinner, a Board of Education meeting, various township meetings, several meetings of the Alzheimer's Society, the horticultural fair, the science fair, and the birth of a baby horse. (Now the birth of an *adult* horse—that would've been newsworthy.) And in every single case, the editor changed my carefully considered headline, my well-crafted crystal distillation. After the fifth time, I objected.

"You didn't even read the story!" I said.

"Most of the people who read the headline don't read the story either," he said back.

I had to admit there was a certain, peculiar, logic to that.

One tired Friday afternoon, suffering from a lack of Jean-Luc Picard and facing yet another Alzheimer meeting (they had them every Friday night), I decided to just use last week's report. It's not like anyone in attendance would know. When I presented it to the editor on Monday, he changed the headline (I'd titled it "The Three Stooges Meet Nietzsche's Eternal Recurrence") and sent it on to layout.

On Thursday, he called me into his office.

"I've been getting some letters about your stories."

"Oh."

"Here, read them." He handed me half a dozen sheets of paper.

"Oh that wouldn't be right, they're written to you." Okay, it was a pathetic stall.

"No, they're 'Letters to the Editor'."

I paused. "Aren't you the editor?"

"Well of course, but 'Letters to the Editor' aren't really letters to the editor."

"Then why don't you change *that* headline?"

He paused. Confused. I took advantage of that and left. And never did find out what the letters said.

The following week I got the break every journalist hopes for—a story fit for a Pulitzer. High levels of arsenic were found in the water of a certain lake. Yes, a *local* lake. I spent time on the phone with the

Township, I drove to the lake, I drove to the lumber mill, I spent time on the phone to the Ministry, and I interviewed residents. Then I wrote the story:

Traces of arsenic have been discovered in Lucky Lake, situated in Pickerel Township. Ministry of Environment officials attribute the presence of the toxic chemical to the local lumber mill, as arsenic is used in the process to pressure-treat lumber.

When asked for a comment about the situation, the owner of the mill said, "That's the price you pay. People want pressure-treated lumber, you gotta use arsenic."

When asked about improving the filtration component of the mill's byproduct disposal system, he screwed up his face in disgust and walked away, yelling over his shoulder at me, "Go back to your kitchen and find something else to worry about!"

The Township has decided not to file a complaint because they "don't have the money to win against the mill in court anyway, so there's no point in wasting taxpayers' money on a complaint."

When I called the MOE, a representative explained that their hands are tied as long as the Township refuses to file a complaint.

When asked whether the MOE's federal mandate of protecting the environment didn't override township governance, I was put on hold for three hours, essentially until the switchboard closed.

A citizens' group has been formed to protest and hopefully reverse the township's decision. To contact the group, call 421-6694.

Well. The editor skimmed it and said he couldn't print it as is.

"Well, you *can*," I said. "But you *won't*. Take some responsibility for your decisions."

"I *can't*," he glared, "print it as is because it's too one-sided. This is not a balanced, objective report at all. Your personal bias is all over the piece. You even use the word 'I'."

"Well, what am I supposed to use? *I* wrote the piece. You want me to pretend it wrote itself?"

"And if you're going to give out phone numbers for some artsy fartsy activism—which we don't do, by the way—at least don't just give out the one side's number!"

So much for my career as an investigative journalist. I was demoted to desk reporter. Which basically meant I was to write up the many press releases received by the paper. Mostly, these consisted of accident reports from the local police (10%) and announcements from various government bodies (90%).

I leafed through the releases received that day. He wants objective? He can't handle objective! To describe an incident with complete objectivity is to give a phenomenological account. And anyone who's taken Phenomenology 101—and yes, *I* have taken Phenomenology 101—knows how difficult that is. Even to say "There is a brown house" is to have made an assumption, is to have imposed your subjectivity. You can't see the house. From your perspective, standing in front of it, all you see is one wall, maybe two. You *assume* there's a third and a fourth. Your subjectivity fills in the gaps. *All the time.*

It gets worse. Is the glass half empty or half full? One description is positive, the other is negative. You've splashed your values all over your description.

And worse still. Consider something as simple as, well, an accident report. You begin with "A serious accident occurred—" Well, right away you're in trouble: Who says it's serious? How serious *is* serious? Serious to who? You've expressed your subjective opinion. Furthermore, you've assumed it was an *accident*. You didn't speak to the drivers. Maybe it was intentional.

So you try again. To say "Smith *ran into* Jones" is to describe the event in rather aggressive (i.e., emotional) (i.e., not objective) terms. "Smith *hit* Jones" is almost as bad. Besides it was not bodily assault. "A Honda Civic hit a Nissan Sentra" is a little better, though it suffers from anthropomorphism—cars don't exhibit such agency. And it probably exposes the paper to a lawsuit from Honda. "Car A *collided with* Car B" is better, but still you've suggested that A is to blame (because it did the doing—the colliding or whatever): maybe Car B *got in the way of* Car A. "Car A and Car B collided" is better still, but only "Car A and Car B occupied the same space at the same point in time" is *really* objective.

So I continued in this manner with the first of several accident reports, specifying the time as per Greenwich Standard, and specifying the space with longitude and latitude co-ordinates. I concluded with "Alterations"—'damage' implies a subjective value judgement—"resulted to both vehicles and two humans"—'people' confers personhood and that's another *huge* assumption. (Especially when we're talking about *local* residents.)

As for rewriting the press releases from the government, I browsed a few then wrote the following:

'Food Fight Breaks Out in the House of Commons'

Ricky and Peter started bickering again, and then Ricky called Peter a wuss, and then Peter stuck his tongue out at him. Then Johnny, who was on Ricky's side, started throwing clumps of something at Dougie, who was on Peter's side, and a bunch of other boys started yelling and hitting their desks to make lots of noise.

When the Speaker thumped his big stick and called for 'Order!', they all started accusing each other, pointing fingers.

"He started it!" Peter whined.

"No I didn't, he did!" Ricky whined back.

"Oh yeah?"

"Yeah!"

And then they started yelling and hitting their desks again.

I put the piece on the editor's desk, and called it a day. A week, actually. (As promised to the cute little dog now running around with a really big chewy in her mouth, knocking over everything at foot-high level.)

12

THE OFFICE

So now what? I was reluctant to venture into life as an office temp. After all, my first job had been in an office, and it had not been pretty. I liked the typing. It was like playing Mozart. And I liked the filing. A place for everything and everything in its place. (I have a very eighteenth century brain.) (Either that or I'm simply a compulsive.) (Or maybe the eighteenth century was simply full of compulsives.)

I especially liked Saturdays. (It was an after-school, Saturday, and summer job.) On Saturdays, there was just Joe the Janitor and me at the office. With the radio loud, piped through every intercom in the three-floor building, I remember dancing up and down the rows of filing cabinets, Jones over here JE-JY and Smith over here SA-SO—that's the way, uh-huh uh-huh, I liked it.

But Mondays, however, brought Muzak. And The Office Martyrs: the people living in fear and trembling lest a deadline not be met—*What if the policy renewal pre-reminders do not get in the mail 60 days before the grace period begins??*—the people whose days of their lives are measured out with coffee breaks (and for whom taking an extra three minutes is An Issue) and weekly indulgences of half a donut on TGIF. I could dance up and down the filing cabinet aisles and have a helluva time on Saturday, but come Monday, that kind of behaviour would be cause for Review. (And yet, some people actually *wanted* to work in an office. It's what they had actually *aspired* to.)

So besides learning that the MacPhersons and the McDunns of the world have no fixed place in the scheme of things, I learned that martyrs can't dance.

One day, after about a year and a half, the office manager (the Uber-Secretary) called me into her office and asked me to go through the 'Expired' files: the Winstone file was lost. No, sorry, I mean *The Winstone File Was Lost!* So I went down to the storage room and attempted to pull open the WA-WO drawer. I quickly surmised that the EXPIRED file cabinets had not been touched in quite some time. Rust was my first clue. I tried again, with both hands this time. The sound of metal scraping on metal indicated success. Well. 'Crammed' doesn't begin to do justice to their state of fullness. After several minutes of wrestling to part policies that would not be parted—some were actually stuck together with that red stencil-correcting fluid that used to come in little nail polish bottles—well, with what it turns into after twenty years—I managed to find and look between Winston and Winter. No Winstone. I spent an hour going through all the WIs for good measure. (Okay, and because I'm compulsive.) Unfortunately, I took out a six-inch chunk of Wes to do so. That chunk took five minutes to put back in. What can I say, I was only sixteen. I hadn't yet learned how to say 'Fuck it!'

I went back to the office manager and told her that the policy in question wasn't in the 'Expired' files. She looked serious. She looked perturbed. Yes, she looked seriously perturbed. The policy had to be found! The agent needed it!! Where else could it be??? Every secretary in the pool had already gone through everything on her desk. Everyone's 'In' box had been checked. Everyone's 'Out' box had been checked. Everyone's 'Pending' box had been checked. It wasn't in the 'Active' files. It wasn't in the 'To Be Renewed' files. It wasn't in the 'To Be Typed' files.

"Did you check through *all* the 'Expired' files?" she inquired.

"*All* of them?" I asked dumbly. "No," I said, "just the WIs."

"Well," she said, "look through all of them, it could've been misfiled." She smiled.

Well. My mother, a bookkeeper in the same building, found me three days later, on my knees in the dark and dusty storage room, trying to stuff a three-inch section of KOs into a half-inch space near the back of a bottom drawer. When I told her my task, she stormed to the office manager's office. (Uber-Secretary meets Uber-Mom.) The woman came down a minute later, smiling.

"The file's been found!" She showed it to me proudly.

"Where was it?" I asked quietly.

"On the agent's desk!" she laughed merrily. She laughed. Merrily.

And I quit. And I was devastated. It was the first time in my whole life that I had quit. (Remember? Compulsive?) It was the first job I had ever had, it was my initiation into the real world, into *real life*, and I had quit. Because I couldn't handle it. Of course I was devastated! I thought The Office was a microcosm of the world at large, I thought that everyone was like the people who work in offices, I thought that office workers were *ordinary* people, even *normal* people. (Fortunately, five years later, I realized that that wasn't true.) (Unfortunately, a few years after that, I realized that it *was* true.) And I had quit.

Little did I know it was to be the job I kept the longest.

But, alas, the Food Demonstrator position had been filled. (Too bad. I was hungry.) And I simply didn't have the experience required for the Bingo Caller position. So I made my way to the Office Temps office with a Monty Python gait of two steps forward and one step back. I aced the alphabet test, and my typing speed was still up there, so I was added to their registry.

Two days later, I was called. And in an unbalanced (and so perhaps fitting) sort of way, it turned out that the job I kept the shortest was also an office job. I was hired to address envelopes. In a small room, with a table and chair, and boxes. Lots of boxes. The supervisor's instructions were unnecessary. Really. I put a stack of preprinted address label sheets on my right and a box of envelopes in front of me, and right-to-left assembly line thing going: peel, pluck-press, pile, peel, pluck-press, pile. I thought I was handling the job rather competently. Apparently I was not. In fact, I was asked to leave. At lunch. I hadn't been doing the job fast enough. (What can I say, I had been pacing myself.)

After that brief employment opportunity (they don't call us temps for nothing), I decided that I may as well take advantage of my situation. I was a temp. By definition, I had no future. Ask anyone who's terminal: having no future does wonders for the present—the nothing to gain and nothing to lose elements combine in such a delightful way. Also as a temp, I was a non-entity—I was invisible and probably stupid as well. So, I figured, I was perfectly positioned for covert ops; I decided that I would Honour Truth and Inspire Outrage throughout the workplace. By doing silly shit. As often as possible.

So, while working in the mailroom of one company, I decided to re-route a few things. The custodians received the salary charts. The ride home on the subway was long enough for most to realize that since there were only 24 hours in a day, it was impossible for certain other people to work ten times as long as they themselves did. So they must work ten times as hard. But the walk home from the station, and up the too many flights of stairs, and especially the pause at the door hoping the kids were quietly watching tv or something, made them realize that that too was impossible.

The receptionists, who juggled three or four calls at a time for four hours straight with only a ten-minute break, and who had had their request for additional help denied, received the expense accounts of various sales representatives. They learned that lunch at a certain restaurant cost more than they spent on a week's worth of groceries. One caller, soon after, instead of hearing the even-after-a-hundred-times pleasant "Complete Clinique Computers, How can I help you?" was blasted with an irate "WHAT?!" However, the caller did not file a complaint with management because she was also a receptionist. At the She Sells Seashells Gift Shop. (And, instead, she burst out laughing in complete and unexpected identification.)

The President received a reprimand for taking too long in the washroom. Since the name of the intended recipient appeared only on the inter-office envelope which had undergone a dosey-do, he actually thought the reprimand was for him. (No comment.) So he stormed into the office of a certain supervisor who was soon to feel very much like Monty Python's ex-parrot.

And the golf invitations for Saturday went not to management trainees Robert, David, Michael, and Earl, but to trainees Meaghan and Jessica. Neither of them really played golf, but then nor did any of the others. (Except for Earl). Nevertheless, I heard they had a great time playing bumper cars with the golfcarts and yelling "FOUR!"—"FIVE!"—"SIX!" (They were, no doubt, great-grand-nieces of Edna, Alma, and Gladys.)

At another company, temping as a lobby receptionist, I replaced all the goldfish in the elegantly labelled 'Corporate Pond'. With piranha. (Though strictly speaking, I guess, 'replaced' isn't quite accurate.) I deliberated at length about whether or not to put up a sign identifying the new occupants. On the one hand, only upper management would actually reach into the pool to grab the shiny pennies tossed in by visitors. On the other hand, well, they wouldn't have an other hand—

Temping for inventory at a military base, I spent a day exploring their supplies of Adhesives, Binders, Corkboards, and Dividers, then wrote on the inventory sheets that they had "enough". I also told them they had enough AK-47s, B-52s, CS, and DU. I didn't get to Everything Else.

I spent a whole week on another placement listening carefully during conversations and staff meetings and keeping a record of how long people spoke and how often they interrupted each other. (To this day, I can't remember what I was actually supposed to be doing there.) On Friday, I posted the results of my research in the staff lunch room:

Men spoke on average for 78% of the total time.

Women spoke on average for 22% of the total time.

Men interrupted on average 6.7 times per minute.

Women interrupted on average 1.5 times per minute.

This was no surprise to the women, but the male employees were astounded. And indignantly so. One cornered me at the water cooler and spent 21.4 minutes telling me that I must be mistaken.

And whenever I temped during the holidays, I took along Chris Wind's *Christmas Album*. Slipped it into the cassette player right after Bing Crosby. And sang along.

Here comes an army tank
Here comes an army tank
Right through Tiananmen Square . . .

Then one of the temp jobs, something in HR to do with in-house training materials, morphed into a one-year contract position: they were delighted—okay, shocked—to discover that I had both a Literature degree and an Education degree. I was delighted—and, yes, shocked—to have a shot at a whole year's income.

Three months in, I was summoned yet again to my supervisor's office. And, unfortunately, to my supervisor. Who suffered from a management disorder. Characterized by a borderline personality, delusions of grandeur, passive-aggressive and histrionic tendencies, persisting traumatic stress, and the absence of a moral compass.

So. What is it this time? Last time, I wasn't being a 'team player'. (I had assured him I was. I just wasn't playing on *his* team.)

Time before that, he feared that my particular 'skill-set' was not 'appropriate' for this particular 'working environment'. (Gee. If *that* makes him afraid, I wonder what the threat of aggravated assault with a chainsaw would do.)

Life is so much easier, I've learned, when the word 'insubordination' is used. Actually, when I first heard the word, I laughed. To be subordinate is to be subservient. So to be *in*subordinate must be to *refuse* to be subservient. So what's the problem? Well, the problem is that at The Office, rank is everything. So, I thought, 'insubordination' must mean something like ignoring the chain of command or not following orders. And okay, yeah, I don't respond well to orders. Well, close, but not quite. "Insubordination" is, I was told, "*anything that questions your supervisor's authority or expertise.*" Yeah right. I laughed again. And that's 'just cause'? A valid reason for dismissal? You can't be serious! Oh yes, my union rep was serious indeed.

It was one of those eureka moments. Not the kind that sends you dancing naked into the street with delight, but the kind that stuns you so hard you just sit down. Understanding the transgression of insubordination made sense of so much that is wrong with the world. (I'd had only one such moment before—when I realized that our entire legal system, that system upon which we depend for justice, is based on *precedent*. 'Common law' is nothing but the collection of decisions previously made. And legal minds—*Mensa* minds—accept this house of cards! An appeal to precedent is nothing but an appeal to tradition, an appeal to 'Yeah—what he said'!)

And the time before the time before I was 'insubordinate', I had made the mistake of going to the New Year's office party. Now *there's* an oxymoron: office party. I had gone solo, of course. (Kessie wanted to go, but I refused to take her, reminding her of what had happened the last time she went with me to such a party, but she simply refused to remember her canine enthusiasm for the all-you-can-eat buffet.) When I arrived, I pulled up a chair to a table of six—three pairs. I made seven. Not an even number. Can't make pairs out of seven. Something's wrong. You wouldn't believe a table could become so silent so quickly. In the middle of a party. Later, I started dancing. On the dance floor. Almost immediately, some guy came onto the floor, faced me, and started doing what I can only assume he thought was dancing, smiling 'I'll be your partner' with *such* kindness. So just as the music stopped, I shouted loudly to him, "Are you having a seizure?" The following Monday I was spoken to about my 'people skills'. (Which is, of course a euphemism for 'suck-up skills' or 'screw 'em skills', depending on your rank.)

So what is it this time, I wondered, pausing at my supervisor's door. Oh. Wait a minute. What day is this? Friday? Casual Friday? I need two degrees to do my job, but apparently I just can't seem to dress myself. I need to be told what to wear. And I keep wearing casual dress on days *not* designated as Casual Dress Days. When I wear jeans—a most subversive fabric choice—does the quality of my work go all to hell? Gee, I don't think so. 'Course, how would they know? Ah. Perhaps jeans messes up their Total Quality Management program. I mean if good workers wear jeans, then, then, then maybe bad workers are wearing suits! Oh no! They couldn't judge by appearances any more! They'd have to look at—at what? Substance! Could they even do that? Hm. Better take off these Mickey Mouse ears. They're sure to be considered 'unprofessional attire' whatever day it is. I knock on my supervisor's 'always open' door and then enter.

Virtually indistinguishable from supervisors across the country, my supervisor was a middle-aged man in a middle-management position. He had a mid-sized car, a mid-sized house, a mid-sized family, and a teeny weeny dick.

"You weren't at the Seniority Luncheon," he said to me from behind his mid-sized desk in his mid-sized office.

"Very good, Sherlock," I replied, sitting down without waiting for his permission. I slouched and hooked my leg up across the arm of the chair. His face turned beet red, and I mentally reviewed the symptoms of cardiac arrest. I then wondered what it would take to kill him. My feet on his desk? A casual glance through his inbox? Wow. Who needs knives and shit.

"Why not?" He had recovered enough to frown thoughtfully and make a steeple of his fingers.

"Not that it's any business of yours, but I find this esteem for longevity rather misplaced." He didn't say anything. He probably didn't understand what I had just said. But he wouldn't ever, ever, admit that. "What's so impressive," I continued, "about working for the same company for a long time? Is it supposed indicate loyalty? Blind trust? And that's a good thing? More likely, it indicates complacency. Or cowardice. Or pure unadulterated self-interest, since pension increases with time served." Hm. "How fitting that they're given a watch," I added.

He'd had time by then to prepare a response that didn't require understanding what I'd just said. "But you're under my supervision, your absence reflects poorly on me."

"*You're* not my mom."

"I'm responsible for you," he explained, helpfully.

"You're *not* my *mom*."

"As your superior, I am responsible for what you do," he insisted, gently.

"As my *what*?" I stared at him.

"Your superior."

"Excuse me, but you are *not* my superior."

"I'm your *supervisor*," he corrected, smiling.

"Thatta boy." For people who are hard-wired for Hierarchy, it's a difficult distinction to make. I understood that.

He wasn't smiling anymore. "And *as* your supervisor, I'm responsible for what you do."

"No you're not!"

"Yes I am!"

"No you're not—how *can* you be? *I'm* the one who forms the intent to act, *I'm* the one who executes the act, so *I'm* the one responsible for the act. Basic theory of agency. Only the immature or incompetent are exempt." Hm. Must come back to that.

"Well, you can debate this all you like, but it's in my job description, that's how things are done: I am responsible for what you do here." Oh, three in a row! Dismiss the intellectual, appeal to the authority of document, *and* appeal to the norm!

"You may be responsible for *monitoring* what I do, but you are not, you can not be, responsible for *what* I do."

He was definitely not smiling anymore. "Look here, this is not open for discussion—" He pointed his finger at me. Wow, three more in a row! The retreat to commands, the Father-Knows-Best End-Of-Discussion thing, *and* the intimidation of the pointing finger! I hate the pointing finger. It's what *men* do, have you noticed? I *really* hate it—wow. He had quickly pulled his finger back. Uncanny. He must've heard about the time I grabbed such a finger and broke it.

"Look here," I said back, and stood, beating him to the Standing Over thing, "If I do not perform my job satisfactorily, who's accountable? Who gets fired, you or me?"

Shortly thereafter—*very* shortly thereafter, actually—standing on the other side of the plate glass doors, with my *Music for Inner Peace* tapes and my *Fuck It!* mug, I yelled up at his third-floor office, "I rest my case!"

This would definitely, absolutely, no question about it, be my last office job.

13

INCOME TAX FILLER-OUTER

Or not.

A week later, just in time for income tax season, I was qualified to do personal income tax returns. But despite passing the course with flying colours, I almost didn't get hired. I failed the application form.

Name. I like it that this question comes first. It's one I can answer.

Address. I also know where I live.

Phone Number. Three for three!

Sex. Other.

Marital Status. No. (Unmarried women have no status.)

Name Known to References if Different from Name Indicated Above. Hm. Bitch. (At this point, I began to feel my application form advantage slipping away.)

Education. Yes.

Scholastic Awards. Regional Math Quizmaster, Trout Township, 1972.

Employment History. Yes. Attach additional page if necessary. No.

(I'm not doing that anymore. I used to make out a complete list of all my previous jobs and attach it, as directed. I thought I was displaying versatility and a wealth of experience. A friend—okay, an acquaintance—pointed out that I was displaying stupidity. With a list like mine, she said, I'd be considered a flight risk, a bad investment. Employers wanted someone who could hold down a job for more than—she scanned my neatly typed list—a week.)

What aspect of your previous employment did you enjoy the most? Recess.

What aspect of your previous employment did you find the most challenging? Dealing with an asshole supervisor.

Describe any skills or experience relevant to to the position being applied for. Attention to to detail.

Hobbies. Snow shovelling, apparently. (It had been a very long winter.)

Have you ever lied? Yes. This answer is a lie.

Have you ever stolen anything from your previous employers? Yes. But only when my name was Heinz and my mother would've died otherwise.

Position Applied For. Income Tax Filler-Outer.

Other Kinds of Work You Might Be Interested In. Ship's Philosopher on the Enterprise.

And then I almost failed the arithmetic test because I felt like Q taking the Stanford-Binet, and I kept muttering insults to Riker.

When I went for my final interview, I had a sneaking suspicion that the Manager had read my application form, decided not to hire me, and then prepared the perfect list of interview questions to justify his decision. Not exactly standard procedure, but then he probably had the word 'discretion' in his job description. And he intended to use it, damn it. After all, he'd certainly been to enough management training seminars!

He couldn't wait to start the interview, and was practically grinning as he asked his first question.

"Well, yes," I answered, "actually I *do* have experience working with the criminally insane."

He sort of went blank for a moment, then stood up, shook my hand, welcomed me 'Aboard', and began what was no doubt a required orientation speech for new employees.

"Let me tell you a bit about our Total Quality Management Program." He was recovering admirably. "We pride ourselves on providing our employees with the opportunities to develop the skills required for success in the workplace: creativity, critical thinking, self-discipline, tolerance, and—"

"Well that's a bunch of crap," I said. He sort of went blank again. "The development of said skills is sure to lead not to success but to boredom or alienation or both—and a shooting rampage will seem the only response. Unless of course you're fired first for insubordination, due to a demonstration of said creativity and critical thinking."

Valiantly, he went on, exhibiting said self-discipline and tolerance, despite, no doubt, horrendous flashbacks to every management seminar he'd ever attended and the overpowering feeling that he was turning into a certain character from a Kafka play. "As part of our Total Quality Management Program, we value input"—at this point, he began, to his horror, to mumble—"regarding our enhanced support mechanisms and team implementation strategies." He paused and was obviously wrestling with the overwhelming desire to cease, desist, and scuttle across the floor.

"It's only for the month, you understand," he said then, though I'm not sure whether he was talking to himself or to me.

And so I went to my little faux-office with its faux-walls and its faux-files. Faux days went by, and like everyone else, my Inbox ranneth over. My Formbox too, with T1s, T4s, T4A(OAS)s, T4A(P)s, T4Es, T4RSPs, T222s, T778s, T1223s, T1229s, T5007s, and TWinkies. I added lines 101, 104 to 143, and 147. I subtracted lines 207 to 224 from 229 to 231. I ignored line 232. I entered line 150 minus line 233 (if negative, I entered "0"). I entered line 236 minus line 257 (if negative, I entered "mc^2"). I multiplied a few lines. Just for the hell of it. I entered the amount from line 7 or $250, whichever was less. I entered line 3 minus $4,000 times 2% (if negative, I entered "4,000"). I divided a few lines. Because I hadn't done that yet. Total payable minus total credits equals amount owing—TA DAH! $372,644.79 or the figure you came up with, whichever is greater. By Friday, my Outbox had an occupant ready for a signature.

"Hello, come in," I said to Mr. Whatever, who sat down on the other side of my faux-desk. "Now, before I get your signature here, would you rather buy a truckload of shrapnel or a truckload of nerve gas?"

"What?"

"The nine percent of your taxes that goes to the military—how would you like it used? Maybe more fuel for one of those low-flying planes still practising over the Innu? By the way, d'ya think they've got it right yet?"

"What?"

"'Course there's always the nuclear option. At the rate they lose the things, they could probably use the money." I start to sing. "'Oh where oh where has our missile gone, Oh where oh where could it be?' Don't know that one? Okay, how about 'Fly fly fly your cruise, gently through the sky, Merrily merrily merrily, we're all going to die.' Did you know that a while ago, the International Court of Justice considered whether or not the threat or use of nuclear weapons should be legal? Forty-five countries made submissions to the Court. Two-thirds argued for illegality; the U.S. and the U.K. were part of the other one-third. Canada didn't bother to take a stand one way or the other. Do you?"

"What?"

"That's probably our secret to being a peaceful people, don't you think?"

"What?"

"What."

"What?"

"Yeah." I pause and then go on, "According to Josef Rotblat—ever hear of him? He won the 1995 Nobel Peace Prize. According to Rotblat, the arguments presented by the U.S. and the U.K. assumed that nuclear weapons do not cause unnecessary suffering. I guess that means they just cause *necessary* suffering. Blowing your right leg off, that was necessary, but the left leg, gee, I'm sorry about that, that was unnecessary, wasn't it. Nor, apparently, are nuclear weapons indiscriminate—in the event of their use, civilians and territories of third-party states would not be affected. And pigs can fly. Backwards.

"The U.K. added that calling into question the policy of nuclear deterrence would be profoundly destabilizing. Hm. The 'Don't Rock the Boat' argument. It always seems to come from those already *in* the boat, doesn't it?"

"What?"

"Russia simply dismissed arguments against nuclear weapons as 'political and emotional.' This, from the country that had Chernobyl. Can you spell d-e-n-i-a-l?

"Germany and Italy presented an interesting opinion: a ruling from the World Court about the legality of nuclear weapons 'might jeopardize the complex and sensitive process of negotiating nuclear disarmament.' Well yeah. That's rather the point. If the stuff is deemed illegal, negotiations will indeed be jeopardized: they'll be over.

"France questioned whether the World Health Organization had exceeded its scope by requesting a ruling from the Court. Asking about weapons that could detrimentally affect the *health* of everyone in the *world* is exceeding the *World Health* Organization's scope? Could you run that one by me again? Granted, dead people have no health. But surely they could argue that nuclear weapons therefore decrease their client base. Oh, and they could also mention that nuclear weapons sometimes just injure people or make them very ill *before* they die.

"And the winner was? Well, we're not quite sure. The Court decided that the threat or use of nuclear weapons would be contrary to the rules of international law except 'in an extreme circumstance of self-defence, in which the very survival of a State would be at stake.' On that point, they tied seven to seven. Maybe. The way that part was actually worded—'The threat or use of nuclear weapons would generally be contrary to the rules of international law, however the Court cannot conclude definitively whether the threat or use of nuclear weapons would be lawful or unlawful in an extreme circumstance of self-defence'—was such that the yeas and the nays were a mess: yes, I agree that we cannot conclude, we can't make up our mind about the self-defence circumstance; yes, I agree that we cannot conclude, because to conclude about the illegality of nuclear weapons is not within our authority; no, I do not agree, we *can* conclude, and we can conclude that there is no 'generally' about it, nuclear weapons are illegal even in self-defence; no, I do not agree, we *can* conclude, and we can conclude that generally nuclear weapons are illegal but not in self-defence. Next to this, 'Have you stopped beating your wife?' is easy."

"What?"

"And of course the definition of 'self-defence' has me worried. Any law student can argue that one's self includes one's interests, and *voilà*! Iraq is a war of self-defence, bring out the nuclear arsenal, boys!

"So when the aliens see earth's tombstone floating through space, they'll read the epitaph 'We thought they were going to kill us.' Instead of *my* choice, 'I *told* you we were sick!'"

"What?"

"Now, why didn't we hear about any of this? Perhaps because at the opening press conference, there were no (no) media representatives from the English-speaking world. What, were they all still covering O.J. Simpson? (Ever hear of him?)

"Was it because they didn't care? Or was it because they know that any advisory opinion made by the International Court of Justice has about as much power as, well, a Canadian referendum.

"And it's not just nuclear bombs. They put radioactive waste from nuclear energy production into the bullets now. While this is marginally better than dumping the stuff into the ocean or launching it into outer space or using it to build schools—hm—so much for the portion of your taxes going to education, eh—there are, of course, ethical concerns."

"What?"

"I guess when you're hit, you glow in the dark. Which might be kind of cool. But there are drawbacks. I mean, when the war is over and all the bullets have been fired, the area will still be radioactive. We'll have to wait 4.5 billion years just for the uranium's *half*-life to expire.

"Oh, you're leaving? But you haven't signed—yes, right here. Thanks. Now, this copy is yours, and this one I'll put in the mail for you." I paused. Wait for it . . .

"What?"

With the next person, I decided to change focus.

"Now, as for the portion of your taxes that goes to healthcare, would you like to buy one whole Kleenex or half a teaspoon of O Neg?

"And would you like to append a letter of protest against the pathetic amount of your taxes that *is* directed to healthcare?"

"Yes!" she replied vehemently, "I would! I had to drive my neighbour to the hospital for surgery last week. But then we had to turn around and drive right back home. It's an hour each way. Turned out they didn't have a bed available. So unless my neighbour wanted to just walk out of the OR after having his gall bladder removed . . . "

"You'd think the person who scheduled the surgery would've thought to check that."

"You'd think," she agreed.

"Do you have a regular doctor, by the way?"

"Yes—"

"Do you know if he or she is taking new patients?

"Why do you ask?"

"Well," I said, "the doctor I had for fifteen years recently moved—to the States, of course—and I automatically became a patient of his replacement, Dr. Whosis. Talk about a No Quality Management Program. I had some abdominal pain one night, bad enough to not lay on the one side, and I couldn't remember which side my appendix was on—or my gallbladder—so I called for an appointment first thing in the morning. He saw me four days later."

She nodded.

"We talked about the pain. He scheduled a separate appointment for an examination. For a month later."

She nodded again.

"Why can't you just do an examination now, I asked. Well, he had another patient in five minutes, he'd just squeezed me in because I'd reported pain, and besides he didn't like doing physicals until he knew his patients a bit more. Excuse me? We're talking about a medical examination, what's to know, it's a body.

"I was able to come back a mere two days later for a blood test. But then I had to make yet another appointment for his assistant to take my blood pressure. Which of course by this time was higher than normal."

Another nod.

"So six months after the pain had occurred—one month after the physical examination which resulted in a referral for an ultrasound examination, which took another three months to schedule because they were so busy, guess there's only one machine in the whole district, and then it took a month for my doctor to get the results of the ultrasound, guess they don't have a fax machine, and then another month before he could see me to discuss the results—so six months after the pain had occurred, I found out what it was. Sort of.

"'According to the ultrasound report,' he said, 'there are a few masses but they're small and likely to be normal. No pathology is suspected. Since the pain hasn't recurred—'

"'Wait a minute,' I said—I was reading the report upside down—'that says one of the masses is 8.2 cm. That's rather large, isn't it?'

"'Oh. Yeah. That must be a typo. I'll call about that.'

"Well, either this guy hadn't read the report before my appointment, or he had but didn't notice the 8.2 cm measurement, or he did notice it but didn't bother to call the clinic to confirm. Either way—"

She nodded yet again.

"It was then that I found out how lucky I was to even *have* a doctor. Four of the 'family physicians' I called were not accepting new patients. Two were, but only if you lived in their township. A third also was, but only if you didn't already have a doctor because they weren't accepting transfers. That left Dr. Whatsis.

"Now at my first appointment with Dr. Whatsis, he asked a lot of questions. A *lot* of questions. I couldn't answer the ones concerning my birth, for obvious reasons. As for the rest, I wouldn't've had to answer them if Dr. Whosis had just given my file to Dr. Whatsis—they were in adjoining offices—but it would've cost me fifty bucks to have my file 'transferred'. Five bucks a step, I guess.

"Anyway, again, I had to make another appointment for a blood test. And another for a physical. It finally dawned on me that these guys get paid per appointment. No wonder there's no money left over for hospital beds."

"Exactly," she said.

"So I said, 'Look, I'm not sick, I don't need a blood test, I don't need a physical, I just wanted to officially change doctors, I'll see you in the Fall for my annual check-up.'

"'You'll find it easier to remember if we schedule your annual check-up in the month you were born, so that's what we'll do,' he said.

"'For the past fifteen years, I've had my annual check-up in the Fall. So I'll find it easier to remember if we keep it that way.'

"'We'll schedule an appointment for April.'

"So in April, when I showed up for my physical, the first thing he did was ask me to take off my boots and stand up tall against the wall. 'As tall as you can!' he urged cheerfully. 'You're 5'4",' he told me. Oh what a clever doctor you are! Then after he listened to my breathing for a bit, he asked me to lie down and said he was just going to feel around on my tummy. My tummy? At that point, I couldn't decide which was worse, not being listened to or being treated like a child. Then it occurred to me they were the same.

"Hence," I sighed, "my question: is your doctor taking new patients?"

"Well, she is, and she's great—she actually assumes you know more about how you're feeling than she does—but—"

"I'd consider moving," I said, as she nodded, sadly.

We finished the income tax stuff then. She signed her return and decided to enclose three letters of protest (I'd had several prepared by then, on a variety of issues). I countersigned it and put it in my outbox.

"Nice meeting you," I said, shaking her hand.

"Likewise," she said, as I then walked her to the faux-doorway of my faux-office.

My next client wanted to claim her dog as a dependent. Since she (the dog) was under eighteen years of age, living with the claimant, and had a net income of $653 or less, I saw no problem. And suggested deducting vet expenses (line 330) and obedience school tuition (line 324). While I made up some figures, she made a passing comment about how her dog is absolutely obsessed with tennis balls, with new, bright, fluorescent green tennis—hey! We decided to consider the purchase of tennis balls tax-deductible—and entered $3,000 on a line we hadn't yet used. (Note to self.)

Unfortunately, I'd forgotten how faux my faux walls were, and the income tax filler-outer in the next cubicle (I didn't know his name—I never actually saw him—well, except for his feet, always visible through the foot-and-a-half gap where the faux walls don't actually reach the floor—he wore hushpuppies) apparently wasn't overly fond of dogs: he'd been bitten by a huge dog named Pacman when he was a child—the income tax filler-outer, not the dog—though I suppose the dog could've been a child at the time too, perhaps even a puppy hushed once too often, I'll bet no one thought to take that into consideration.

Anyway, he—the income tax filler-outer, not Pacman—overheard my conversation with that last client and went to the Manager, and well, yes, I suppose I should be grateful they didn't press charges—we *do* certify that the information given on our returns is correct and complete (line 487), and tax fraud *is*, well, a bit of a faux-pas.

14

WAITRESS!

Of course no resume would be complete without, in addition to the office temp entry, a waitress entry. I worked in a restaurant with pretensions to artsiness. Outside, two tables pretended to be a European sidewalk cafe. Inside, dim lighting revealed a decor in turquoise and teal, with rusted wrought iron accents. Across from the large tv screen showing a never-ending football game, there was an equally large all-grey just-grey painting. It even had a little spotlight and a title card. The title card was empty. So on my very first shift, I remedied that by neatly printing, on said card, "Flock of Pigeons in the Fog". Then I added, "Discussing Existentialism".

Speaking of which, inspired by the muse of servitude (daughter of the muses of dance and comedy), I often wondered who came up with the notion that one person should serve another person their food? Why don't people, why can't people, just get it themselves? It's not like it requires any special skill. In fact, anyone out of toddlerhood can put food on a plate and take it from a kitchen to a dining table. Serving food (or anything, for that matter) is an ego thing, pure and simple. But how? What logic turns the apparent helplessness of infancy into a status symbol? The answer came out of my own mouth: "May I take your *order*?"

So when the next person sat at one of my tables, in a three-piece suit no less, I went over with my pad and pen and said, "So what do you need Mommy to bring you today?" It changed everything. He actually stammered, just like the little kid he was.

And who came up with the idea of a tip, I wondered, as I pocketed the change left on one of my tables. Either it's a compensation for poor wages and you feel like a charity case, or it's a bonus for a good performance and you feel like a trained seal.

Some people entered the restaurant then, and in defiance of my telepathic persuasion, sat down at one of my tables. I finished clearing the table I was at, put a few glasses of ice water from the bar onto a tray, and went over to them.

"Aarf, aarf! Aarf!" I barked at them. They looked at me for a moment, then got up and left. Wow. That was easy. Gotta remember that one.

I turned around, carefully, with my tray of ice water still held in one hand at shoulder height, and headed back toward the bar. As I passed one of the restaurant's dim lights, I stopped and removed its teal and turquoise tissue paper globe, tilted my head back, and ever so carefully balanced it on my nose. I then proceeded toward the bar, doing rather well, I thought, as I really hadn't mastered the tray thing yet. I thought maybe I should carry my tray two-handed in front of me as I usually do (my hands don't bend over backwards like, apparently, they're supposed to), but then I thought, Hell no! I hadn't dropped it yet and my ball was still balanced on my nose! Bring on the roller skates! Then I walked into the manager.

"What the—?!" he said. Yes, ice water is cold. Sort of by definition.

"Aarf, aarf!" I replied. He didn't leave. It wasn't working. "Aarf!" I insisted, then looked sadly at my teal and turquoise ball as it rolled under a table.

"What the—?!" he repeated.

I pondered his limited vocabulary and regretfully admitted that in any cross-species interaction, it is incumbent upon the more intelligent one to speak in the other's language. "What the *fuck*?!" I said, helpfully.

"Yes! No! What, may I ask, did you think you were doing?"

"Practicing?" He didn't get it. So I said, "Why don't you raise all the prices by ten percent, inform the customers they aren't obligated to tip, and then simply pay us a decent wage for a job well done—for pleasant and efficient service?" He thought I was joking. I thought he was an asshole.

And pleasant and efficient service *is* what I provided to my customers. A middle-aged couple sat at one of my tables one evening. I took over two glasses of ice water and two menus.

"Good evening, how are you tonight?" Besides overfed. People in this country eat *way* too much. The 'Food Guide' is really just an advertising campaign, sponsored by a consortium of food-producing companies who would love it if we all pigged out three times a day. Seven servings from five food groups? What bullshit! We can live healthily on a daily diet of 1,000 well-chosen calories.

"Fine, thank you," the woman smiled. The man didn't acknowledge my presence. Guess I'm not important enough. Well fuck you.

"Tonight's specials are the Pasta Primavera, with fresh spring vegetables," fresh from a bag of frozen No-Name Mixed Carrots and Peas, "and the Fish Platter," note that we don't actually identify what kind of fish is on the platter, the cod's all gone, so is the haddock, the tuna's down to twenty percent, "the entrées come with soup or a salad, and you have your choice of baked potato or french fries."

"I'd like to order an appetizer," the man said, turning to the front page of the menu. But of course—since you're obviously eating for two. And if her dress didn't have that little red belt, those two medium-sized rolls would be one large-sized roll. I dropped my pen, just to see one of them try to bend over and pick it up. Instead, they both looked down at it, then up at me—as if faced with a problem of etiquette, not a problem of fat. I left it there just to bug them.

"So are you ready to order now," I asked, smoothly taking a spare pen out of my pocket, "or would you like a few moments?" They looked at my spare pen, then down at their menus.

I could tell before he picked up his fork that he'd bend close to his plate and half-throw the food into his mouth. He'd toss and chew, toss and chew, quickly, without interruption, until he was done. Then he'd push the plate away and make a noise equivalent to 'Finished!' as if the meal was a race. Then let out a belch, the checkered flag. So I was ready with a stopwatch as I stood near the bar, watching him watching me.

And she'd cut her food into tiny pieces and seem to pick at it, delicately, but her plate would be empty when I came to clear.

"Would you like coffee or tea? Dessert?" They ordered coffee and dessert. Under the counter strewn with pretzels, chips, and beernuts, there was a display case filled with deliciously decadent desserts: Chocolate Volcano, and, um, Chocolate Volcano, and—well, there were about half a dozen different kinds, but hey, that's the only one that mattered. (Okay, that one and the butter tart pie. Kessie's favourite.) Such desserts are wasted on people like this. Food, especially dessert, should be savoured. But thanks to fast food, epicureanism is dead. But so too will be these two. I give them ten years tops.

Alas, culinary innovation is also dead. I regularly made suggestions to the kitchen staff: tossed salad with chocolate syrup, sauerkraut and ice cream, rice with barbecue sauce, peanut butter and jam milkshakes, deep fried tomatoes. They ignored me. Especially after the deep fried tomatoes.

Once a week I gave out my Most Idiotic Customer of the Week Award. A free dessert. The manager didn't know, of course. I preferred to keep my good deeds unnoticed. And I must say the winners almost always lived up to their award by being idiotically delighted to have won.

One of the winners had asked, "What's in the turkey sandwich?"

"Beef," I replied. He didn't bat an eye. I kid you not.

Another one had scanned the menu and said, "Gee, it all looks so good." What? Either his standards were pathetic or he was trying to impress me with his lively personality. Either way, he won that week's award. (Though he almost lost to a guy who kept telling me his sales figures—units sold, commissions earned, bonuses received, and on and on. "My what big numbers," I had said adoringly. That was a mistake.)

"Want some help?" I had asked of my gee-whiz customer, bored out of my mind.

"Sure!" he replied, eagerly waiting for inside advice on the day's specials, I suppose.

"Okay, how do you turn a rainforest into a desert?"

He looked at me. In utter incomprehension.

"Eat a hamburger."

Speaking of hamburgers, once I had this family of four in my section, the kids were getting impatient, and the mother stopped me to ask if I could bring the kids' dinners now.

"They're not ready yet."

"You mean you actually have to cook the hamburger?"

"Ma'am, we actually have to kill the cow, drain its blood, scrape out its guts, and chop up what's left. Did you want fries with that?"

Which reminds me, I read that people are protesting elk farms as unethical. Hello—what about cow farms? Aren't they just as unethical? I mean, what, are cows the niggers of the ungulates? Hath not a cow four legs? If you drive past them, do they not dumbly stare?

And speaking of turkeys, once a customer asked, "What's a chicken delight?"

"It's a rice salad made with boneless chicken." Pause. "Yes, that does make life in the barnyard a little difficult."

One of the things that made life as a waitress so difficult was being constantly told to smile. Told, not asked. And only by the male customers. Who never told the waiters to smile. What the fuck is going on with that?

Do men need to feel attracted to every woman in the world—in order to feel assured of their maleness—and it helps if we're smiling?

Do they think they're responsible for us, for our happiness, and so an unsmiling woman is a reproach?

Do they insist on reserving seriousness (i.e. non-smilingness), and by erroneous extension, importance, for themselves?

Or do they think we should simply be delighted to see them?

Yeah right. One customer—an overweight and out of shape guy, the kind you usually see in manual labour positions—who was a regular, unfortunately—always horked up a gob of something before he came in and spat it into the bushes beside the entrance. Delighted indeed.

Why is it, by the way, that only *men* spit? (Hey, a new set of stupid names for sex-separate washrooms: "Smile!" and "Spit.")

I mean, is it physiological? Do males produce a larger amount of saliva? Even so, why the need to spit it out? Why not just swallow it? Would that remind them of swallowing semen? Which is female, effeminate, gay? (I'll ignore for the moment the assumption that all, or even most, women swallow semen.)

But no, that can't be right; it seems too—too reasoned. Spitting seems to be more of a reflex, a habit, a that's-the-way-I-was-raised sort of thing, a cultural thing, a *sub*cultural thing: to spit is to be manly. Little boys spit to appear grown up. Grown up *men*. So what's the connection between spitting and masculinity?

Well. Let's consider the way men spit. It's not a chin-dribbling drooling kind of getting rid of saliva. Instead, it's a somewhat forceful ejac—ah—is that it? Is spitting a little pseudo sex act? Every time a man spits, does he experience a sort of orgasmic release? Both do involve an expulsion of bodily fluids.

Hm, the pissing contest now comes to mind. So what is it about expelling one's bodily fluids with some degree of force that proves one's manhood?

Is it just the forcefulness? Whether it's throwing a ball or—hm—this may also explain the unnecessarily loud, Kleenex-devastating way men blow their noses. Bodily fluids there too. But then why don't men wail when they cry? There must be something more to spitting.

Maybe it's—there seems to be a certain contempt in the gesture. Certainly to spit *on someone*, like pissing on them, (and ejaculating on them?), is to defile, is to degrade them.

But what about the man just walking down the street who hacks up a gob and spits every few seconds? Is that then just a *continuous* display of contempt—for everything? *I am male: I am better than everything.* That rings true. (As does the corollary: *I am so insecure I have to display my superiority every few seconds.*)

Perhaps men see saliva, like mucous, as germ-filled and rightly expelled from the body. Spitting on the street, then, is doubly contemptuous, showing, additionally, an utter disregard for the other, the one who shares the sidewalk he has so inconsiderately contaminated. (For they could, of course, spit instead into a handkerchief or a Kleenex.)

'Course it could just be that men are slobs. But, again, what's the connection? Why do men associate lack of hygiene with masculinity? I recall a female car mechanic explaining that the perpetually greasy hands thing was totally unnecessary, just a macho thing. Why are clean hands unmanly? Surely few women want to be touched, inside or out, by greasy black fingers. (And isn't touching women proof of one's manhood?) (No. *Entering* them, *invading* them, *occupying* them is.) Maybe it's just that it's so opposite to women: *women are clean, so if I am a man, I am dirty.*

And maybe there's something about the liquidity of saliva. Liquid is soft; soft is feminine. (Real men don't eat yogurt.) So men must dissociate themselves from it, get rid of it. After all, you don't see men hacking off their tough, hard, fingernails and hurling them away so contemptuously. Actually, maybe you do—long fingernails are a female thing.

So—do men think hard stools are more masculine than soft stools, do real men brag about hard it is to shit? (Is that what that pile of magazines in their washrooms is all about?) Do they feel better when they've had a hard shit?

Speaking of which, the gobber came in one Thursday, as he always did, and sat at one of my tables, as he always did.

When I took him his steak and potatoes plate, which he always ordered, he looked up at me and said, as he always did, "Smile, why dontcha!" I ignored him. As I always did.

And he acted, as he always did, as if I had personally insulted him. "Hey all I asked for was a smile!"

So I spat onto his plate of steak and potatoes. It had a paralyzing effect. He didn't move. He didn't say a word. He just sat there completely unmoving. Wow. Gotta remember that one too.

Unfortunately, the little whiner went to the manager, eventually, and complained. And, well, who'd've thought you'd get fired for spitting on someone's food?

15

SALES

So the next day, I applied for a position in sales. Major Appliances. A week later, I showed up for the interview I'd been granted.

"Hello, uh, Ms.—" said the manager, who looked at me oddly as I entered his office. He then looked at my application form, a bit confused. But not on account of my last name.

"You were expecting a man," I said, closing the door behind me to muffle the Shoppers' Muzak that had assaulted me like a wad of cotton candy the minute I'd entered the store. It wasn't my last name I'd omitted on the application form, but my first.

"Well, yes," he smiled, apologetically, no doubt eager to avoid a discrimination complaint from someone who wasn't even an employee yet.

"Hm." I sat down as he gestured to the chair across from his desk. "Why?"

"Excuse me?" He smiled again.

"Why were you expecting a man?"

"Well, it's just that . . . " he trailed off. He had no idea.

"It's usually men who apply for jobs in Major Appliances," I said.

"Well, yes," he smiled yet again. Gee. He should apply for a job as a waitress.

"And why do you think that is?"

"I'm sorry?"

"Why do you think it's usually men who apply for jobs in Major Appliances?"

"Oh," he shrugged as if it weren't that important really, "I suppose it's because major appliances are, well, refrigerators, ovens, washers, dryers—they're fairly big items, aren't they?"

"So?"

"I beg your pardon?" Was this guy slow or just unaccustomed to having a real conversation?

"Well," I said, "we just have to sell them, don't we? We don't have to *move* them."

"Oh, no," he chucked, "no, of course not—"

"So I don't have to be a Schwarzenegger," I said. I got up then and went to the window overlooking the Major Appliances area of the floor. "*He's* certainly not," I said, pointing to one of his salespeople, the one waddling down the aisle. "And *he's* not," I pointed to another, rather lanky-looking, fellow. "And that one couldn't even move a bar fridge," I pointed to a third. "*I* could though," I said, sitting down again.

It took him a moment. "You could move a bar fridge?" he asked, doubtfully.

"Yeah. Ever hear of a forklift?"

"Yes, yes, of course," he chuckled. Then didn't know what else to say.

"Why are you chuckling?"

"Excuse me?"

"Is there something funny about forklifts?" 'Cuz if there was, I wanted to know!

"No, no . . . " he trailed off. Hm. And this guy is actually considered competent to interview someone?

"I suppose next you're going to tell me that appliances are, after all, machines of a sort—they plug in, at any rate—and since I probably didn't take shop in school, I don't know how they work."

"But *you did* take shop, didn't you," he said, a little pleased with himself. And justifiably so, given his responses so far.

"No, I didn't. Wasn't allowed to."

"Oh. I see."

"But shop or no shop, it seems to me it's *men* who don't know how a dishwasher works. Or an oven. Or a washer and dryer. I, however, have been using major appliances of various makes and models since I was twelve. Was that true of the last guy you hired?"

"Well, no, but . . . "

"But?"

"Well, no."

"And frankly, if I were to come shopping for, say, a vacuum cleaner, well, I'd want to speak with someone who's actually *used* one. Because I'd want to know whether the damn cord is going to get sucked in when I run over it, whether the thing'll stay on the stairs when I put it there, and whether I have to vacuum all over again after I change the stupid bag. *And* whether it's cat-friendly," I added.

Took him a moment, but then he looked up in alarm. I simply raised my eyebrows.

"Who sells the sewing machines here?"

"Ah—um, I'm not sure," he said. "I'm not sure we carry sewing machines."

"'Course, sewing machines aren't *big*, are they," I muttered to myself, abandoning that line of thought.

"Have you ever worked on commission before?" He seemed to suddenly remember that *he* was the one who was supposed to be asking the questions.

"Aarf, aarf," I replied. He was, understandably, puzzled. "Straight commission?"

"No, we pay a minimum wage, with increments based on length of service. Our commission program is complementary to that, based on merit."

"Merit?"

"On number of units sold."

Ah yes, 'merit'. "And *price* of units sold."

"Well, yes, of course."

"Maybe *that's* why men get the jobs selling major appliances."

"Excuse me?"

"Well, they need the big bucks, don't they?"

"Ah, yes, I see. Yes, I suppose that explains it."

"I mean, *I* don't have mortgage payments to make. Someone *gave* me my house. For free! And I don't have to pay property taxes—female property owners are exempt, right? Car payments? Not me! If you're a woman, Honda will just *give* you a car! And they'll pay for repairs for as long as I own it! Insurance? The insurance companies don't charge you if you're a woman, isn't that the case? And food? It just falls from the sky, right onto my plate."

"Yes, I see," he said, smiling. Nervously. "When can you start?"

On my very first day, my very first customer told me all about the development of refrigeration technology. He went on and on, from ice boxes all the way to state-of-the-art CFC-free stuff. Apparently, I needed to know. And he was just the man to fill me in. At great length. In easy-to-understand but thorough detail. Eventually he somehow moved from that to the evolution of the human species. "It's amazing that we developed as we did," he finished, at last, proudly.

I looked at him. "Yeah well, shit happens."

And I decided to avoid customers from then on.

Turns out the lanky-looking fellow was an actor. Which, when you think about it, makes a lot of sense for a position in sales. Actually, when you think about it some more, being an actor would enhance one's job performance—ah! *performance*!—in a lot of positions. At the very least, I thought, it would reduce the likelihood of being fired for insubordination. Though playing an idiot would surely get tiresome after a while.

It was a joy to watch Lance work. One day, this newlywed and six months pregnant couple came in to buy a fridge. So Lance walked them around to three or four different models, talking about freezer capacity, and produce drawers, and moveable shelves, and ice-makers, and then he opened the door of the largest one. The woman screamed. There was a rather blue infant lying inside. He'd brought in a prop from the theatre.

"And that's why," he dead-panned, "you should always remove the door from a refrigerator that's not in use."

I could learn from this guy!

Shortly after, on a slow day, I found him in the back room, looking rather gothic in a vampirish kind of way I couldn't quite place, tinkering with one of the vacuum cleaners.

"Modifications," he explained. I had no idea what he was doing, but he was certainly more interesting to watch than Bert. Bert was the fat slob I'd seen waddling down the aisle during my interview. He'd lie through his teeth to make a sale. And did so, every day. Last year, he'd bought a swimming pool with his commissions. Too bad he never used it.

Lance put the vacuum cleaner back together, took it out to the floor, and set it beside the demo box. The demo box was sort of like a sandbox, half tiled, half carpeted, filled with assorted debris—sand, yes, but also lint, pieces of thread, paper clips, a few pennies, a marble, and some unidentifiable bits I probably didn't want to recognize. We used it to demonstrate the power of our vacuum cleaners.

Bert was with a customer, well on his way, apparently, to a vacuum cleaner sale. As he led the customer to the demo box, Lance started humming the old Munsters theme. Of course! *That's* what—I quickly moved out of the anticipated line of—what's the reverse of 'vacuum'? But there was no need. Just before turning to the sandbox, Bert always, Lance knew, held the nozzle toward the customer, while delivering some cock-and-bull pseudo-science about diameter and suction. What can I say. It was a Kodak moment.

"You are such a shit disturber," I said admiringly.

"So you agree that what we have here is shit," he grinned at me.

And then there was *WKRP* week. What a week! Monday, Lance was Les Nessman. He had the geek glasses and the squeak walk. Didn't sell a thing. Though he tried. Earnestly. He was as proper and polite as his bowtie, but utterly lacking in confidence.

Tuesday, he was Herb. Brash in his checkered suitcoat, full of confidence that was utterly baseless, he was at once both the perfect salesman and the perfect American tourist. Interesting. Gave Bert a run for his money.

Wednesday, he was Jennifer. Blond bombshell wig. And all. And that was an amazing day. Some guy entered Major Appliances, saw Jennifer, walked straight to her, and said, "I'll buy this"—then thought to point to whatever she was standing beside.

"Bert?" she said, in that sweet, seductive, beguiling voice, sort of raising her hand, but certainly not looking at him. Bert rushed to do the paperwork that completed the sale.

Then it happened again. A guy walked in, headed straight for her, and bought something. Anything. And again. And again. Some guys looked like a deer caught in headlights (a pair of headlights, of course) and some looked like Walter Mitty transforming into James Bond (but never quite making it). And they bought it all. Washers, dryers, refrigerators, vacuum cleaners, humidifiers, dehumidifiers, air conditioners. One guy practically *ran* to her, arriving before she was in position. He insisted on buying the customer service counter. All Lance had to do at the end of the day was stroke out 'Jennifer' on the receipts and write 'Lance'. Sold enough that one day to get to a dozen very out-of-town auditions.

So Thursday, he was Jennifer again. Good thing too. I swear all the guys from Wednesday sent their friends on Thursday.

Near the end of the day, like Odo having trouble maintaining his form, Lance started flipping from Jennifer into Les and Herb. That was amazing too.

"What can you tell me about this water heater?" a customer asked.

"Well," Les said hesitantly, quickly thumbing through the technical specs. "It has a temperature/pressure relief valve for safety and includes an energy-saving pilot" he read, then beamed proudly at the customer.

"*Everything* you need to know," Herb said, swaggering as if he was approaching a dame in a bar.

"Oh you really don't need to know anything about it, do you?" Jennifer asked in that honeyed voice. He shook his head, like a spaniel, then bought it.

Friday, Lance was Johnny. Complete with shades and bell-bottoms. Johnny took one look at the first customer then headed to the back room, in his purposeful slouchy kind of way, where he put his cup of coffee down long enough to put on some headphones and crank up some rockin' blues.

The next customer caught him before he could make his escape.

"Could you tell me how much energy this model uses?" he said, pointing to a fridge.

Johnny looked at the fridge. "No." He looked at the guy. "It keeps stuff cold though," he said, as he opened it and took out a can of beer. Then headed to the back room, leaving the customer standing there.

Anticipating Johnny, I had gone to Food Stuffs and bought a brownie mix, and at lunch we baked some really good brownies in one of the ovens. The manager found us at closing time sitting in front of a washer, staring at it with fixed eyes, completely captivated by the wonder of waterfall, the eternal cascade, the rise and fall, and rise and fall. The XL Front-Loader had become a Perpetual Motion Tsunami Machine. We smiled up at him, blissfully, and offered him some Doritos.

So Monday found Lance transferred to Sports ("Oh yeah," I'd heard him say, "the *guy* always knows about sports"), and I was on my own. In Cosmetics.

"Does this *really* make me look young?" some woman asked about a face cream.

"No," I said, "but smearing chocolate pudding all over your mouth will do the trick. At a much cheaper price," I added helpfully.

Another woman was trying on different shades of red lipstick. "What do you think?" she asked, puckering her Scarletta No.7 lips.

"Great advertisement for fellatio," I replied. She gasped and stomped away. "Wasn't that what you wanted?" I called after her.

For a while, there were no customers. So I thought I'd go over and visit Lance, perhaps bring back some fishing lures with colourful feathers and big sharp hooks to accessorize the cosmetics display.

But then I noticed the still unpacked box of Basic Cover-Up. In Skin Tone. Twenty-four medium-sized bottles of gunk. In beige. Well, that's not right, I thought. So I went over to Food Stuffs and discovered that licorice flavouring is clear. I went to Paints and Paper and discovered that no one but me painted their rooms black. Office Supplies! I came back to Cosmetics with a huge bottle of printer ink and proceeded to tint all twenty-four bottles of Basic Cover-Up. In Skin Tone.

Then I got hit with a basketball. And Lance ran up to the Cosmetics counter and asked in his best just-this-side-of-losing-it Goldthwait-from-*Saturday-Night-Live* voice, "Can you come out to play?!?!"

Well, yeah.

Within five minutes, we had a full-out game going, seven on seven, with three refs—or at least, three people from Discount who had a ready supply of polka-dotted whistles. Pass 'n' go! Pass 'n' go! Someone dribbled the ball down the aisle to Men's Wear, but we hadn't found a basket yet, so he threw the ball to someone else, who feinted left and right, and left and—Catch! I got hit with another ball!

We were up to nine on eight, no, ten on nine, with two balls. Make that three balls, one of which was a brand new fluorescent green tennis ball in the mouth of a little brown dog. Who was clearly *very* happy to be playing with us. (And not tucked under the counter. Where she'd been told to stay.) Then suddenly we had three and a half teams, and the entire Discount Department was reffing with impressive enthusiasm. Pass 'n' go! Pick! Switch! A bounce pass was intercepted! Here! There! Customers abandoned their purchases. Some of them joined in. I'm open! Here!

Then someone from Home Entertainment found "Sweet Georgia Brown"—and access to the store's speaker system. We had located several baskets in Kitchen Wares, conveniently placed at less than regulation height. Three more balls—basketballs—got tossed into the game, and Globetrotter dreams came true. We were dribbling fools. We were ball-handling magicians. Lay-ups, jump shots, slam dunks, and a five-pointer lobbed from halfway to Automotive!

Who knew Crystal Wares was right behind Kitchen.

16

FIREFIGHTER

Then someone suggested I apply for a job as a firefighter. Apparently, they were in desperate need of women (women firefighters, I assumed he meant), and I was certainly physically fit, what with all the record ten-miles I'd been running lately. Plus, since even with degrees in both English and Education, and several years' experience teaching high school English, I didn't even get an *interview* for a job as literacy *assistant*, way up in *Moosonee*, I figured I was so underqualified—okay, *un*qualified—to be a firefighter, it might just work out.

I walked into the recruiting office and spoke to the woman sitting at the desk behind the counter.

"Hello, I'd like to become a firefighter!"

She looked at me. Like I was nuts. Then she opened one of her desk drawers, pulled out an application form, and handed it to me. I filled it out. Aced it, in fact. So far, so good.

She took the application form, then said "You'll also have to take a written examination and a physical test."

"Okay!"

"When would you like to schedule them?"

"Right now!"

She looked at me. Like I was nuts. Then she got up, pulled open a drawer in the filing cabinet, pulled out what was presumably a copy of the written examination, handed it to me, then pointed to a small room off to the side.

I went in and got to work. I'm good at writing. Therefore, I'm good at having written. Therefore, I should do well on a written exam. Too bad it wasn't a logic exam.

Question 1: When water flowing through a pump is suddenly stopped, what is the sudden surge of pressure called? Hm.

Question 2: If an explosion in a small warehouse results in the ceiling's collapsing, but no crater is observed, what is most probably cause of the explosion? Hm.

Question 3: What color code is used for water reactive flammable solids? Hm.

Oh well, not to worry. It was multiple choice. I used the scrabble method. You know, ADD, CAB, BEAD . . . You just keep choosing letters that make words. Worked wonders on my third year Psych final when I didn't know a thing. I got a C. I wondered if a C was good enough to become firefighter. Probably. It's not like any of my A or B students ever wanted to become a firefighter. (And yet here *I* was . . .)

After a quick stop at home to change, I went to the physical test center, located at Station #5. The physical test included so many instances of sex discrimination, I don't know where to begin. Okay, the push-ups. Push-ups favor bodies with a high center of gravity. For the most part, male bodies rather than female bodies. So, struggling, severely, once I hit thirty, I gasped, "I bet I can do fifty *sit-ups* with no trouble, though!" Sit-ups favor bodies with a lower center of gravity.

"Okay," said the male who was taking me through the test. "Let's see you."

Well not *now*, I wanted to say. Now, I thought I'd just lay there for a bit. Tomorrow, maybe. Or the next day. But I rolled over, hooked my feet under the table, and did fifty sit-ups. Nah, nah, I looked at him. He just nodded.

"Aren't you going to mark *that* on your clipboard?"

"Sit-ups aren't part of the test," he said.

Great. So now I've wasted all that energy—energy I would sorely need for what came next. Which was more sex discriminating—okay, the rest of the tests weren't *sex* discriminating, so much as *size* discriminating. They were clearly designed for over six-foot-tall bodies that weigh closer to 200 pounds than 100 pounds. Several of which had mysteriously appeared in the test center to watch.

For example: the timed test for getting a folded hose off the racks and carrying it twenty feet. The racks were about five and a half feet off the ground. Shoulder height if you were six feet tall. If you were five-four, it was over your head. And shoulder height was nice if that's kind of where your center of gravity was. Hip height would be nice for me. Around three feet off the ground.

It quickly became obvious that this test was like the Chinese paper tube finger thing. Impossible. No matter how hard I tried. For me to lift the hose off the rack *and keep my balance*, I had to stand with my feet apart and my knees bent. But then I wouldn't be able to reach it. To *reach* the hose, I had to stand on my tippy-toes, feet together. Which meant I'd topple backwards as soon as I got it off the rack. Which is exactly what I did. Five times in a row. Cameras flashed.

Speaking of Chinese, that's why I call it size discrimination rather than sex discrimination. If I were taking the test in China, I'd be doing okay. *There* I'm the size of most men. *There* they'd store the hoses at a height I could reach without falling over.

The next test required me to perform eight revolutions of a fire hydrant valve stem using a wrench. I huffed and I puffed, and huffed and puffed, and puffed, and then huffed, "If this is so damn important, why don't I see you guys out there WD40-ing these things from time to time?"

I finally got the job done, well after the entire neighbourhood had burned to the ground.

My tester announced the next test. "Run an eight-minute mile." Sure. Piece of cake. I can do that. "Fully equipped."

I paused. "Is that for when the guy forgets to return the truck to the station with a full tank of gas?"

Okay. So I put on the heavy coat. It was way too big and flapped down around my ankles. I hoisted on the oxygen tank and whatever, then put on the gloves. Also too big. They kept coming off. Unless I held my hands together in front of me. Not the easiest way to run. Then the boots. Also too big. I kept tripping. Cameras flashed. Took me an hour to cover a mile.

Then, climb ten flights of stairs. So equipped.

I just glared at them. "Ever hear of an elevator?"

Next test: take a sledge hammer to a beam and knock it over. With pleasure. I was *so* pissed off. Unfortunately my hands were so slick with sweat, I set an indoor record for the hammer throw.

Lastly, the ladder test. Climb a seventy-five degree ladder to an elevation of fifty feet, and then descend to ground level. Well, the good news was he didn't say *how* I had to descend. The bad news was the task had to be done—of course—fully equipped. What with the flapping coat, the fumbling gloves, and the flipper boots, it'd be suicide for me. Actually, even under normal circumstances, it'd be, well, scary. For some reason, I had completely failed to anticipate this. I don't do ladders.

He saw my hesitation. "You're afraid of heights, aren't you?"

"No. Not exactly. I just get severely disoriented when my feet leave the ground." 'Course half the time—all of the time if I'm in Europe, apparently—I get severely disoriented when my feet are *on* the ground . . .

I considered retracting my application. Because the bottom line is these guys saved lives. And I couldn't think of anyone I'd run into a burning building to save. Except Kessie, of course. But, apparently, like doctors, firefighters can't pick and choose who they save. (Pity.)

Turned out I was hired. Because of their affirmative action policy, the Fire Department *had* to hire a woman. Which was so wrong. Not only would I not save anyone, I'd probably get my own crew-mates killed. Not because I was a woman, but because I didn't know what I was doing.

So I wrote a letter to the Chief, explaining what a stupid policy it was. If anything, the policy should state that *all things equal,* a woman should be hired over a man. And then all things should be made equal. I'll bet there are lots of women out there who, with properly fitting equipment, and a firehouse built as much for their average size as for men's average size, would perform as well as men.

But, too, it should be noted that a good firefighting crew should include all sorts. Yes, we need the brute force bodies. They can hold up the roof when it's collapsing. But we also need the small and limber bodies to crawl through the air vent to rescue the kid who's hiding there. And we need the kind of body that can perform well on infrequent breaths of oxygen—the kind of body a synchronized swimmer or tuba player has, for example. And so on.

I'd sent a copy of my letter to the local newspaper as well (the *other* local newspaper), so the day after I was hired, I was relieved—so very relieved—of duty.

17

JELOOFAH'S ATHEISTS

So I created my own job.

Knock, knock.

"Hello, and how are you this fine morning? I'm out and about today to spread the good news about Jeloofah!"

"Who's Jeloofah?" he asked.

"Good question! Jeloofah is a god-like entity that doesn't exist."

He stared at me.

"Yeah, yeah," I conceded, "and the King of France is bald, but since there is no King of France, the statement 'The King of France is bald' is neither true nor false, so if 'Jeloofah doesn't exist' is true, then there is no Jeloofah, so it can't be true, it has to be neither true nor false, which sort of puts Jeloofah in some Ever-Ever land along with Schrödinger's cat. I'm aware of all that."

"Who's the King of France?" he asked.

Knock, knock.

"Hello, and how are you this fine morning? I'm out and about today to spread the good news: God is a big fat liar!"

His eyebrows raised.

"I'm sure you know your *Bible*—recall Genesis 17:3,8. 'Abram fell on his face and God talked to him, saying "I will give unto thee, and to thy seed after thee, the land wherein thou art a stranger, all the land of Canaan, for an everlasting possession."' Genesis 13:15 and Exodus 32:13 say pretty much the same thing. But check out Acts 7:5, which says 'He gave him no inheritance even though he promised that he would give the land to him and to his seed after him for a possession.' Promises, promises, eh?"

"That retraction is in the New Testament, which isn't recognized by those of the Jewish faith," the man at the door said smoothly.

"Not to worry," I replied without missing a beat. "There are lots of lies in the Old Testament too. God said that Adam would die on the day he ate the apple, but he didn't. Jehoiakim was told that he wouldn't have a son, but he did. God promised Jacob that he would return from Egypt, but he didn't. And Nebuchadnezzar was to have captured and destroyed Tyre, but, surprise, he didn't."

"Those are just historical errors."

"I see. One might expect God to know his history, but that's okay, what about the blatant contradictions? 'For by grace are ye saved through faith, not by works'; 'By works a man is justified, and not by faith.' Well, which is it? 'Peace I leave with you, my peace I give unto you'; 'Think not that I am come to send peace on earth'—"

"Again, those from the New Testament."

"Okay, 'Israel shall rise again'; 'Israel shall not rise again'. She loves me, she loves me not."

He started to close the door.

"'Every living thing shall be meat for you'; wait, changed my mind—'These shall ye not eat of them that chew the cud or of them that divide the cloven hoof'. 'Thou shalt not kill'," I shouted through the closed door, "'Put every man his sword by his side and slay his brother, companion, and neighbour'." I stared at the closed door. "You're *okay* with all this?"

The next guy started lecturing me on Pascal's wager. "If *I'm* wrong, and there *isn't* a god or a heaven, when *I* die, it won't matter, because I'll just be dead. But if *you're* wrong, and there *is* a god and a heaven, when *you* die, *you* won't be allowed in." He was so *very* pleased with himself.

"Yeah, okay," I said, "but what if there *is* a god, and heaven is only for those bright enough to recognize there's no *proof* that he exists?" That shut him up.

Eventually, I realized that if this was supposed to be a *job*, there had to be some income. (Unless, of course, it was a volunteer job.) (Though one might well ask at this point, when does a volunteer job become a hobby?) (Or a public mischief?)

So I created a pamphlet to sell on my door-to-door tours of duty. I called it *The Wholly Libel*. Issue #1 hit the streets the next day.

Krishna, an ancient god, was born of a virgin twelve hundred years before Jesus. He was visited by wise men at his birth, performed miracles, and was crucified.

Indra, another god, was born of a virgin seven hundred and twenty-five years before Jesus. He led a life of celibacy, walked on water, was crucified, then ascended to heaven.

Mithra, yet another ancient god, was also born of a virgin, on December 25, six hundred years before Jesus. Some Magi brought gifts, his first followers were shepherds, there were twelve of them, he was slain on a cross to atone for humankind, and his ascension to heaven is celebrated in Spring.

Buddha was—wait for it—born of a virgin, named Maya, six hundred years before Jesus. He performed miracles, was crucified, descended into Hades for three days, then ascended into heaven.

Quexalcote, yet another god, was born of a virgin five hundred and eighty seven years before Jesus. He spent forty days fasting and resisting temptation, and was eventually crucified along with two thieves, but was resurrected on the third day after his death.

Now is all this just coincidence or what?

Knock, knock.

"Hello, and—"

"I've heard about you, young lady—"

Young lady. I should've aborted the mission right then and there. No doubt I was also Eve incarnate. Scheming temptress, responsible for the downfall of man. Never mind that she couldn't possibly have known it was wrong to eat the apple—until she ate it. It was *from* the tree of the *knowledge* of good and evil, remember? And anyway, why did God forbid it? Why did he forbid knowledge of good and evil? Could it be he didn't want us to know what a messed up sonuvabitch he was? Given that he ordered mass murders left, right, and center, and we *still* think he's overflowing with love and kindness, well, he obviously didn't have anything to worry about. And because of Eve, because of this knowledge of good and evil, we're all born sinners. So, what, blessed are the psychopaths?

He was still talking. "—and I am a *believer*, yes I am , and I will *not* have you—"

"You believe in God?"

"I surely do, yes."

"And why is that?"

"Well *The Bible* says so!" He was incredulous. I didn't know?

"And *The Bible* is the word of God, right?"

"Yes, it surely is."

"And that's why you believe what it says."

"Yes, I do."

"Isn't that just a little like saying you know that Santa Claus exists because he said he did in a letter he wrote? Even a ten year old can see through that one."

"Now look here—"

"It says a lot of other stuff in *The Bible*," I continued. "For example, in Matthew, it says that if you do something wrong with your hand, you should cut it off. Do you believe that too? Matthew also says you shouldn't plan for the future."

"The Lord is a wise and righteous—"

"I mean, if you're going to pick and choose, and believe only what you want to believe, why involve *The Bible* at all—why not just start from scratch on your own?"

"*The Bible* is the greatest book ever written! Don't you forget that!" He was jabbing his finger at me. Not to be distracted, I continued.

"*The Bible* is a piece of shit. The plot's confusing, the thematic development's superficial, the characters are unlikeable, the dialogue, unrealistic, and the tone, puerile. And much of it is just fucking incoherent."

"Look here, young lady!"

"No you look here, old man!"

"God created us in his image!"

"Which one of us exactly?"

"The good Lord works in mysterious ways!"

"And why is that again?"

"I will not entertain godless heathens at my door! You will surely burn in hell!" He turned away.

"Yeah, yeah, we're the spawn of Satan. But hey, it wasn't godless heathens who submitted a good number of people to assorted tortures during the Inquisition! It wasn't godless heathens who burned at the stake women suspected of flying through the air and having sex with Satan!" Not necessarily in that order, I suspect. "It wasn't godless heathens who herded Jews and Gypsies into boxcars! It wasn't godless heathens who led the lynch mobs! And it's not godless heathens bombing nightclubs, blessing landmines, and hijacking planes!" He'd closed the door long ago.

"The raspberry farts during the Lord's Prayer at City Council? Okay, yeah, that's us."

I took the next day off—you can do that when you're self-employed—and prepared Issue #2.

"Now kill every male among the little ones" (Numbers 31:17).

"They shall have no pity on the fruit of the womb" (Isaiah 13:18).

"Thou shalt eat the fruit of thine own body" (Deuteronomy 28:53).

"Their infants shall be dashed to pieces, and their women with child shall be ripped up" (Hosea 13:16).

"Dash their children, and rip up their women with child" (2 Kings 8:12).

"Happy shall he be, that taketh and dasheth thy little ones against the stones (Psalms 137:9).

So I guess you're not really Pro-Life then.

Knock, knock. No one home. I moved on. It's interesting, I thought, given that everyone says they're Christian—

Oh but, they hasten to add, they're not necessarily *practising* Christians. Which is a really interesting notion. I'm a non-practising saint.

Knock, knock. No one home here either. It's almost as interesting as the notion of being *born* a Christian, something else I'd heard said a lot. Almost as an apology, as if they had no choice, they can't really be held responsible, they were just born that way. HELLO. We're talking about *beliefs*. You can't help what you believe? (Quite apart from the fact that when you're born you don't have the cognitive capacity to *believe anything*, let alone that there's some all-knowing, all-powerful, all-good supernatural entity that created a world full of all-stupid, all-feeble, and all-bad people . . .)

Knock, knock. Where *is* everyone today? And then you've got the ones who say they're Christian, but not necessarily *good* Christians. What kind of ass-covering move is that?

Anyway, oddly enough, given that everyone says they're Christian, I'd noticed that people who noticed I was holding a copy of *The Bible* were not as welcoming as I would have thought, let alone as welcoming as I would have liked. So I'd started carrying instead Darwin's *Origin of the Species*.

Knock, knock. The door opened. "Hello," I said. "Do you consider yourself a Christian?"

"What?"

"Are you a Christian?"

"What?"

"Did I do your income tax a while back?"

"What?"

"Is your name Willy by any chance?"

"What?"

"Do you believe in God?"

"Yeah, I guess so."

Yeah, I guess so. Wars have been fought, people have been killed, for 'Yeah, I guess so.' "Well, do you or don't you?"

"I don't know."

"You don't know?"

"Yeah. I mean no."

"What?"

"Okay, yes."

"You *do* believe in God. Okay." Now we're cooking. "Why?"

"What?" With fire from two sticks rubbed together. Though I'll bet *this* guy descended from the guy who kept letting the firestick go out. 'Course, *that* guy would've been killed and barbecued. (Not necessarily in that order, I suspect.) (And not, apparently, soon enough.) "Do you have any kids yet?"

It was time for another day off. And Issue #3.

According to The Bible, Adino killed 800 men in a single battle, Abishai killed 300, and Jashobeam killed 300. Even if the battles in question lasted 24 hours, that's at least 12 people per hour, which is one guy every five minutes—for 24 hours straight. Now I've never killed a person, with just knives and swords and shit, but it can't be that easy. One guy every five minutes for 24 hours straight?

In another battle, the Israelites killed 120,000 people in one day. During World War II, the German and allied forces together, using heavy tanks, artillery, mortars, machine guns, hand grenades, landmines, fighter planes, and bombs, managed to kill only 176,000 people over a period of six weeks.

So. Inquiring minds have to ask: did any of these guys ever catch any fish? Yeah? How big?

The Bible also records that God masterminded the deaths of 10,000 Moabites, 10,000 Perizzites and Canaanites, 24,000 Israelites, 100,000 Syrians, 120,000 Midianites, 120,000 Judeans, and 185,000 Assyrians.

This rounding off to the nearest thousand—is that a lack of attention to detail or are individual human lives just so, um, unimportant?

After one particularly unrewarding day, I decided I needed a teaching aid. So I enlisted the services of a chimp named Washoe V. Yes, descendent of the late and great. Funding for the language lab at which he had been employed had been discontinued and he found himself suddenly out of a job. (I sympathized.) For a while he despaired of finding any employment commensurate to his aptitudes and abilities. (I sympathized.) But when he saw my ad, he swung at the chance. So here I was with my copy of Darwin and a chimp with a vocabulary of I don't know how many words. And really, I was *not* going to dress him up. No streetcorner Bojangles thing, no King Kong costume. But he insisted on wearing a hat he'd found somewhere. It was a Shriners' Great Poobah hat, no less (which made me wonder if he was also related to Sultan). So what the hell, I bought him a pair of bright Bermuda shorts to go with it.

Knock, knock.

"Oh, my, what have we here?" the lady was delighted to see us. Our appearance was probably the highlight of her day. As well it should be. How often does someone come knocking at *your* door with a copy of Darwin's *Origin of the Species* and a chimp in a Shriners' hat and bright Bermuda shorts?

"Yes—oh, come on out here, dear," she called to her husband, presumably, who was in the other room watching television, "You've got to see this!"

"Game's on," I heard him grunt, and I could see the edge of a six-pack beside a lazy-boy chair. Ever notice that *which* game is never specified? Just like *which* god. An assumption that there's only one? Or is it that it doesn't matter—one game, one god, is just like any other. I heard a can of beer pop open.

She sat me down, offered me a cup of tea, gave Washoe V a banana (which was not what he'd asked for), and waited for me to speak. I delivered my *Coles' Notes* version of evolution, and showed that it was a far better explanation of how we came to be than the Adam and Eve theory.

"Oh, no," she said when I'd finished, "we did *not* come from apes." She looked at Washoe V with something like a 'He's adorable but—' expression on her face. He burped then, but politely covered his mouth with his hand. (Or not. I realized his third finger was somewhat extended.)

"I will not agree with you on that, I'm sorry. We are not at all the same." At that, a much louder belch erupted from the living room. Recognizing a Q.E.D. when we heard one, we left.

Then one day I saw in the distance a conservatively well-dressed young couple—Barbie and Ken meet the boy and girl next-door—going door to, well, to the next door. They too had a bag full of pamphlets. And a very nice leather bag. (They didn't have a chimp though. Had them on that.) I decided to follow in their footsteps.

Knock, knock.

"Did that young couple just snow you with the argument from design?" I asked the woman who'd answered the door.

"They did point out that it's unlikely the world just happened by accident, yes," she replied. "Because everything fits so nicely together, you see."

"Well *yeah*," I said, waving my copy of Darwin. "The stuff that *didn't* fit together with everything else *died*!"

The nice young couple moved on a few houses. I, spawn of Satan, moved on a few houses.

Knock, knock.

"That nice young couple just convinced you God exists, didn't they?"

"Well, I—"

"And I'll bet they gave you that old 'first cause' song and dance, right?"

"Oh I don't—"

"Well if God made everything, who made God? And if he 'made himself', then why couldn't everything else just have made itself? And if he just 'always was', then couldn't everything else just have always been? You can't have your cake and eat it too: you can't say everything needs a cause, therefore God, and then suddenly change your mind and say no, not everything needs a cause, God doesn't!"

"I can't?"

Shortly after they got the restraining order, I thought 'Wait a minute, I can do better than this!' I mean there I was, trailing a carefully measured hundred metres behind them, never close enough to hear what they said, having to guess at which refutation to follow with—I can do *much* better than this!

The first church I went to was Roman Catholic. I walked up the broad stone stairs, through the heavy doors, up more stairs, past the marble holy water font, through more heavy doors, and into the church proper. Wow. Rows and rows of polished wooden pews, tall stained glass windows, an altar way in the distance. I walked half way up the center aisle and took a seat. The priest was in vestments of ivory and gold, he had half a dozen altar boys assisting, and there was a choir in the balcony.

I stood, sat, knelt, stood, sat, and stood—then said fuck it and just sat. Several ushers started circulating through the church, and I realized I was in time for the Collection.

"Don't you think there's something a little incongruous about begging with a gold-plated plate?" I said loudly as the usher put said gold-plated plate in front of me.

"Shhh," said the person beside me.

"This isn't begging, m'am. We're merely asking for a donation." He was soft-spoken and oh-so-polite.

"Yeah, I guess it takes a hell of a lot to heat this place, what with the ceiling wa-a-a-y up there." I craned my neck to look up, past the statues, past the stained glass windows, past the arched architecture. I started to take out my wallet. "And you're probably still paying off the furnishings. What did all this cost?" I ran my fingers along the polished wood. "Bet you didn't get this at that don't-pay-a-cent-till-May place. Still," I made a show of putting my wallet back in my pocket, "if you can afford this stuff, you don't need *my* money. And if you overspent, well, why should *I* bail you out? I mean *I* don't have marble accents at *my* place. And I *live* there." He moved on to the next person, and I saw the priest staring at me.

I stared back. "Hey," I called out. (Wow. Cool acoustics.) "People give $80 million a day to God. $80 million a day! Just what the fuck has he been doing with all that money? And," I glared at him then, "when do you think he'll be able to start paying taxes—for roads, schools, hospitals, and stuff?"

Again I stood, sat, stood, knelt—then said fuck it again and just sat. And then everyone started lining up for Communion. They were going to *eat* the Body of Christ! Eew. Everyone in my row got up, then stared at me expectantly.

"You're gonna eat bits of some guy's body and drink his blood?" I asked the people who had realized I wasn't getting up and were bumping my knees to get out of the pew. "That is so sick!!" I looked around in disbelief. Everyone was getting in line, with an almost vapid slowness, like they were—like they were zombies! The choir was singing—"Humbly We Eat Thee" or something—as they knelt at the altar, one by one. The priest moved along the line saying to each one, in a disturbing monotone, "The Body of Christ," "The Body of Christ," and they replied, in an equally disturbing monotone, "Amen," "Amen"—and then opened their mouths to receive said body of Christ. Well, a piece of said body. Then they all shuffled back to their pews, faces expressionless. Scary stuff. I figured the Kool-Aid might be next so I got the hell out of there. Picked up a veggie pizza on my way home to get the taste out of my mind.

I think the next Sunday was Presbyterian.

"Let us pray," the minister began, opening his arms in invitation.

"Why?" I called out. He scanned the congregation, looking for me. I helpfully raised my hand. "If God knows everything," I continued, "he surely knows what I'm going to ask for, so why do I have to say it out loud? Besides, it's not like I'm going to change his mind: 'Hey, Supreme Being and Ruler of the Universe—this is what *I* think should happen here, okay?'" People fidgeted.

"We need not limit ourselves to prayers of beseechment," the minister said gently. "We can also offer prayers of gratitude—"

"Well, doesn't he *know* that I'm thankful? And if I'm not," I thought to add, "I sure as hell can't put one over on *him* now, can I?"

"Let us pray," he repeated, reminding me very much of an ostrich.

So I crossed myself and chanted along with the others, "Hocus pocus, abracadabra, doobee doobee do!" I added some fun arm movements, but alas, no one joined me. Not for the first prayer. Nor for the second. I gave up when he started on the third.

"God the Father—"

"God the *Father*?" That caught my attention. "Talk about a deadbeat dad!" People turned to look at me. So I elaborated. "He left almost 2,000 years ago. Said he'd be back real soon. Right. 'Wait 'till your father gets home.' That got tired real quick.

"He never writes. He never calls.

"And child support? It's not just that so many of us don't have enough to eat. A lot of us are starving to death! We have no roof over our heads. And we could use new clothes. 'Cheque's in the mail.' Right.

"Role model? 'Like father, like son' is an understatement. Lots of us have a temper, and we're a vengeful lot. We kill, we torture, we loot, we lie. We're racist. And women, well, they're just not very important.

"They say the typical dad interacts with his kids for just two minutes each day. Half of you would weep with gratitude just to hear his voice for two seconds, wouldn't you?" I look at them. "Yah bunch of snot-nosed pathetic losers!"

The following Sunday—Methodist? Lutheran?—I engaged the minister in meaningful dialogue during his sermon.

"Amidst our trials and tribulations, it is comforting to know—"

"Did you hear about that cute little toddler who got run over by the driver of a Mack truck three times the other day?" I called out to him. "And is still sort of alive?"

He looked rather blankly in my direction, then smiled graciously at me. "Yes, I did, thank you. Let us offer our prayers for—"

"Oh I wasn't suggesting we pray for her. I was wondering what God was doing at the time."

He looked confused.

"Well, shouldn't he have stopped it? I mean, isn't he all-loving and all-good?"

"Well, yes, it is unfortunate, but remember we are all of us capable of doing good as well as bad. Our Father in his wisdom created us with the capacity to *choose*. Let us pray that we choose—"

"You're saying that's the price we pay for free will?"

"Yes," he nodded sagely.

"Hm."

"The child will surely be rewarded in Heaven."

"Well I think 'rewarded' is hardly the word, since the child wasn't old enough to have *done* anything to be rewarded for. 'Compensated' is more like it."

"Amidst our trials and tribulations—"

"Did you hear about that little baby deer that was discovered burned to death in that fire?"

His smile wasn't quite as gracious this time. "Well, there again—"

"*Forest* fire."

"Yes, and—"

"Started by *lightning*."

He glared at me.

"Not matches."

"And it is comforting to know—"

"If God knew it was going to happen, why did he even let it be born?"

The minister took off his glasses with—could that be exasperation? "We can't presume to know the ways of our Almighty Father, but perhaps it was an example—"

"*Geez.* Can't we do without those kinds of examples? I don't know about the rest of you," I looked around, "but *I* can learn right from wrong without little kids being run over by Mack trucks and baby deer being burned to death. What does he think we are, idiots?" A few people nodded.

"But if God were to suspend the laws of nature whenever you thought it appropriate that he do so . . . ," he tried to smile benevolently. "Trust that this is surely the best possible world."

"You're saying this is the best he could do. Little kids getting run over by Mack trucks and baby deer being burned to death."

"I'd like to remind the parishioner this is the *sermon*. I'd be happy to discuss these matters—"

"No you wouldn't. I've tried for two weeks to get an appointment, but it seems you're always 'out'. No doubt visiting the sick. Pediatrics, perhaps? The burn ward?"

He very suddenly and totally lost it then. "Look here! *I* do the talking!" He jabbed his finger at me. "You do the listening! This is my fucking sermon!"

A collective gasp rose from the congregation and a little old lady in the front row fainted. The little old lady beside her was heard to say in the ensuing silence, "Oh get a fucking grip, Agnes!"

At the next church, as soon as the minister started his sermon—on miracles—I wasted no time and went straight to the pulpit myself.

"He can walk on water?" I grabbed the mic. "We can race across it at a hundred miles an hour.

"He can rise up to the clouds? Hell, we've been to the moon and back."

I turned to those on the left. "He can heal the sick? We can make them sick in the first place and *then* heal them."

I turned to those on the right. "He fed 5,000 people with loaves of bread? What, no fries with that?

"He transformed water into wine? Check out what we've done with the Great Lakes.

"The virgin birth? Duh. We *invented* the turkey baster.

"He can resurrect the dead?" I put the mic back into its holder. "Well that's just gross."

"May I ask why you're here?" A gentleman touched my shoulder as I headed toward the following Sunday's church. "I'm an elder here at the God Save You Chapel." Clearly he'd been forewarned.

"Certainly," I said, as officially as possible. "I'm apprenticing to be Ship's Philosopher. On the *Enterprise*," I added.

I was escorted back to the sidewalk.

"But my presence here is a program requirement. Ask Jean-Luc!"

I didn't make the mistake of actually entering the chosen premises the following Sunday. Instead, I got there early and set up a booth out on the sidewalk. The sidewalk on public property. I had a power supply, some electrodes, and an article written by Dr. Michael Persinger. He's the guy who's discovered the part of the brain which, when stimulated, elicits 'a god experience'. Rather like the patients of the famous neurosurgeon who discovered the part which, when stimulated, elicits a seizure ("I can smell burnt toast!"), Persinger's subjects, when that part of their brain was given a little jolt, would say things like "I feel a divine presence!" or "I feel such peace and serenity!" (Though a few said "Oh wow!" and "Cool, dude!") (And, yes, one said "Burnt toast!")

I put up my signs and opened for business. "A Religious Experience! Five cents!" "Feel God's Presence! Ten cents!" And, since it *was* breakfast time, "Toast! Fifteen cents!"

Turns out my last offering was especially fitting since shortly thereafter, thanks to 911 (or the Crisis Hotline) and the appearance of the local fire department (yup, that one), as well as a reporter from the local newspaper (yes), that's pretty much what I became.

18

WALKING (WITH) THE DOGS

Since that went so well, I thought I'd create my own job again. I decided I'd become a dog walker. Well, I was already a dog walker. I took Kessie for a walk several times a day. As she, to all appearances, took her bright green tennis ball for a walk. Don't leave home without it.

And now we had Snookums too. Snookums was just a little baby. A sweet little bundle of licks and kisses. About twelve weeks. And six pounds. She (too) had me wrapped around her little paw. Her teeny little paw with the still baby pink pad. The one she lifted when she wanted me to carry her. In the snuggly sling thing I wore for just that purpose.

So, since I was already going for walks with Kessie and Snookums, what I meant was that I'd decided to become a *professional* dog walker. I'd *get money* to do it. I wouldn't do it any better, mind you. I'd just get paid for it.

I put up signs in the neighborhood, and within a week I'd received three responses. Not from the dogs, of course. As far as they were concerned, they could walk on their own. Most had been doing so pretty much since birth. Which is more than I can say for members of my own species.

So a week later, Kessie, Snookums, and I were on our way to pick up Hunk. A male Doberman who was aptly named, but not quite as big as his owner wanted him to be. Nor, he indicated, as smart. After a few days with Hunk, however, I decided the guy was wrong—and realized it's true: it takes one to know one.

While we stopped to get Hunk, Kessie was patient, but indifferent. After all, she had a bright green tennis ball in her mouth. As for Snookums, she peeked with curiosity from the safety of her snuggly thing. At the dog! The BIG DOG!! She squiggled in excitement. She likes nothing better than being part of a pack. Even if it is from the safety of her snuggly thing.

Our next stop was to pick up Little Miss Bo Peep. Little Miss was a female Standard Poodle. So she had outgrown the 'Little' but not the 'Miss'. Where the 'Bo Peep' came from, I have no idea.

Kessie was again patient, Snookums was again excited, and Hunk was—interested.

Next stop was for Spunky Doo. Half mutt, half clown. Unlike Hunk's architect and Little Miss Bo Peep's lawyer, both of whom didn't have time to walk their dogs, Spunky Doo's owners *did* walk him. In the morning before they went to work, in the afternoon as soon as they got home, and again at night. And still Spunky Doo was a one-dog demolition crew. So the idea was that if I walked him during the day, he'd work off the excess energy he'd been channeling into deconstructing the living room furniture. Or maybe the walk would alleviate the boredom that led to his daytime amusements. In any case, if Spunky Doo wasn't *in* the house, he couldn't wreck the house. No argument there.

So things were going rather nicely. We even had the multiple leash thing worked out. After experimenting with several arrangements, we discovered we did best with Hunk and Little Miss Bo Peep together in my left hand, Kessie and Spunky Doo in my right, and Snookums mostly in her snuggly thing. I set her down occasionally, but there was a real concern that she'd get landed on, by Spunky Doo, by mistake. Also, of all the paws she saw from her vantage point at ground level, she wasn't quite sure yet which ones were hers.

Spunky Doo was clear on that point, but it didn't seem to help. I must have put his harness on a dozen times. But still he didn't seem to get it. *This* paw goes in *this* hole? Or *this* one? And my head goes *here*? No, here. No, wait, I remember. My head goes here. I was paying only half attention once, got him all harnessed up, clipped the leash on, and we were all set to go, Hunk and Miss Bo Peep in my left, Snookums in her snuggly, and Kessie and Spunky Doo in my—wait a minute—Spunky Doo was grinning at me from ear to ear as he was—facing me. That's not right. (He probably would've walked backwards too.)

One day, although I'd noted quite clearly on my signs that I was offering to walk *dogs*—'course it could have been *because* I'd noted that quite clearly—a cat decided to join us. It sauntered over to us, took the lead, and, well, led. Hunk, big male dog as he was, felt *compelled* to compete with it. I had no idea what the object of the competition was. Let alone the standards of judgment. I suspect Hunk was clueless on this matter as well, because he kept losing. I thought it likely the standards kept changing. The cat would strut, Hunk would strut, then the cat would give him a scathing look, and he'd know he'd lost. He'd hang his head and put his tail between his legs. Then the cat would resume strutting, and so would Hunk. And he'd lose again. Each time, Hunk would stick his chest out even further, lift his head even higher—and lose even more dismally. Little Miss was not impressed.

We eventually got to the dog park. "Well, here we are at the *dog* park," I said pointedly to the cat. It gave me a scathing look. I gave it the finger and took a moment to decide which way we wanted to go. Some guy walking three dogs approached me, as I stood there with my five, and, after a moment, said "You've got me beat!" Took me a minute, 'cuz he didn't have a flashlight, but then I understood—and introduced him to the cat.

After a few weeks, we all got tired of the dog park. And frustrated with the whole leash thing. There was really no need to keep anyone leashed except Hunk, and that was only because people freaked out when they saw an unleashed male Doberman. And Spunky Doo, because he'd take off. In a heartbeat. Not because he didn't like being with us. But just because he had to be everywhere at once. People kept giving me dirty looks when they realized Little Miss and Kessie weren't leashed. Even an unleashed Snookums was cause for serious moral disapprobation. So I decided it was time for a field trip.

To a field. There was one near my place—it was relatively large and surrounded by quiet streets. The dogs could get some real running time and still be safe. I hadn't used my car for a bit, so I went out and opened all the doors to get rid of the stuffy smell. Shook out the dog blanket in the back seat and moved out a few things to make room for Hunk, Little Miss, and Spunky Doo. Then I went back in the house to get Kessie, who was all set with her tennis ball in her mouth, and Snookums, who was now seven pounds.

When we got back out to the car, there was a large dog sitting in the passenger seat, nice as you please, all ready to go. Looked like a lab cross. Kessie took one look and bounded into the car all happy to meet him. That doesn't usually happen. Snookums is the social butterfly. Kessie isn't interested in other dogs. She's got her tennis ball. I followed her into the car and checked his tag. Chum. Phone number, no address. I pulled out my cell phone and called his people, but there was no answer. Well, okay, sure you can come. He thumped his tail.

We picked up Hunk, then Little Miss, then Spunky Doo. All three got into the back seat, Hunk claiming the open window on the driver's side, Spunky Doo, the one on the passenger side. Little Miss sat primly between them. Kessie had claimed the prime spot—my lap, with her nose to the air vent—and Chum was in the seat beside us. Snookums was—car sick. All over Miss Bo Peep. She was not impressed. Hunk licked it off her. Eew. *That* impressed her.

Ten minutes later, we pulled into the field. Yippee!! Free!! We're free at last!! Thank God Almighty, we're— yeah, yeah. Kessie knew the score because we'd been coming here for years. She carefully put her tennis ball into my hand, then assumed her ready position—sprinter's crouch in the starting blocks. I threw the ball and she raced after it, leaving Asafa Powell or whoever currently held the 100M record in the dust. (And she's not even black.) She trotted back with it, put it snugly into my hand, and got ready again. I threw it again. She raced after it, trotted back with it, put it into my hand again. We could do this for hours. Had done so, on many occasions.

Snookums, on the other hand, wasn't much of a ball chaser. She'd run after it, but when it stopped, she stopped. She wasn't much of a tug of war player either. Actually I hadn't yet figured out how to play with her. Didn't know what her natural desires were. But today, she trotted off without hesitation, and did whatever it is that puppies do in fields—chase butterflies and birds or something.

Chum, in the meantime, had found one of the million tennis balls Kessie had lost there. Turns out he was a ball dog too. No wonder it was love at first sight. Especially since he understood he was *not*, *ever*, under *any* condition, to go after Kessie's ball.

Hunk and Little Miss were pretty much sidewalk and dog park dogs, so we were a bit uncertain at first about what to expect. They ventured a short distance away, then returned to me when I called; I told them what good dogs they were. They ventured out again on their own, returned when I called, and were again told that they were very good dogs. Thus assured, they were soon running full out to the end and back with relative abandon.

Spunky Doo needed no such assurance. He was beside himself with joy. (And was already convinced he was a good dog.) He didn't know where to go first. So he tore off to the right, then tore off to the left, then ran straight ahead, then turned, kicking up dust, and ran straight back. Straight—into me. Knocked me flat on my ass. Kessie carefully put her tennis ball into my hand.

Then I saw my sweet little Snookums in the distance playing with something. Tossing it in the air, again and again, so—gleefully. It was bigger than a butterfly. It was bigger than a bird. It was—a rabbit. An ex-rabbit. (I hoped.) She trotted over to me, carrying it, more or less, in her mouth, tripping over whatever was trailing—eew. She had blood, and whatever, all over her muzzle. But she was oh so very proud. Baby's first kill. She was not, no way, giving it to me, mind you—she was just showing me. She wasn't done playing with it yet. My gruesome little Snookums.

Meanwhile, Spunky Doo was still tearing around in all directions, right, left, forward, backward, up—what? Did he just—? Yes, he did. He just chased a squirrel up a tree. Scrambled right up the trunk to the first branch, and then lunged up—made it!—to the second branch. Oh. He looked down. That's a bit of a jump. Now what, he looked at me. Yeah. Duh. Now what. For a second it looked like he thought about jumping down. NO! Damn it, what was the word for "Stay!" his owners had taught him? It was something I knew I'd never remember in an emergency. "Stay, Stay Put, Freeze, Don't Move, Wait, Be Still"—ah—"Remain Immobile!" He looked at me, and then, somewhat impossibly, lay down on the branch, legs dangling on either side.

I looked around. And saw no ladders nearby. Not that Spunky Doo would know how to use one. I sighed, then pulled out my cell phone and started dialing the Crisis Hotline. Then thought the better of it and called 911 instead.

"What is the nature of your emergency?"

"I have a dog stuck in a tree."

"I'm sorry. You have a *dog* stuck in a tree?"

"Yes."

"Name, please."

"Spunky Doo."

The operator paused.

"I meant *your* name."

"Oh, sorry." I gave my name, phone number, and location. By now, the other dogs had gathered around. This was too good to miss. An opinion validated when they heard the firetruck siren. And saw people streaming out of their houses to come see.

The truck pulled into the field near the tree. A Station #5 truck. Of course. An extra-full crew of firefighters disembarked, took in the situation, then tried hard not to laugh. They held a brief consultation. And took some photographs. Then they decided that getting Spunky Doo into the basket on the end of the crane might be tricky. So the plan was, instead, to ease him over the branch into a net which they would then lower with the crane.

They positioned their truck.

"Remain immobile!" I shouted up at Spunky Doo. They all looked at me. I shrugged.

Once up there, they realized that one guy in the basket would not be able to get Spunky Doo safely into the net. But, they also confirmed, there was no room for Spunky Doo in the basket. Down came the crane with basket. Out came the guy. Back up went the empty basket.

They all looked at me. What? Oh.

"Jump!" I shouted up at Spunky Doo. "Hop! Leap!" No response. "Eject!"

Spunky Doo looked at me. What? Oh.

He looked down into the basket now positioned right under him. He looked at me. He looked at the firefighters. Who had their cameras ready. Then he lunged into the basket, face first. A cheer went up from the crowd. Unfortunately his hindquarters kind of got stuck and he didn't have any wiggle room. The crane started lowering the basket, Spunky Doo's ass end in the breeze. Cameras flashed.

As soon as the basket hit the ground, one of the guys opened the door, and Spunky Doo flopped out—but then couldn't decide whether to prance around or put his tail between his legs. So he pranced around with his tail between his legs. I thanked the firetruck crew, and they left. After a few more photographs, posed shots with Spunky Doo. The neighbors trailed away as well.

Okay! Field trip's over! Kessie trotted to the car, ball in mouth, Chum behind her, ditto. Hunk and Little Miss, and Spunky Doo, of course, and—wait a minute, where was Snookums?

"Snookums!" I called out. No Snookums. I called again, "Snookums!" Then just before panic took over, I saw the tall grass move in the distance. Had to be her. "Snookums!" The grass moved again. Not much further than the first place. Was she hurt? "Snookums" I started running toward the moving grass. Suddenly it dawned on me. She was trying to bring the rabbit with her. Eew. "Leave it!" The grass continued to move. "Drop it!" Still moved. "Let go!" By now, I had reached her. She was insistent. She would not leave the rabbit. I was insistent. I would not touch it.

The others came to see what the problem was. Hunk was the first to understand. He walked over to Snookums and before I knew it, took a bite. I heard the soft crunch of cartilage. He gave the rabbit's ear to Snookums. Little Miss was impressed. Snookums was delighted, and ready to come home.

Or not. Not in the car. No way. I have to admit, I empathized with her: motion sickness is not pleasant. This time, Chum resolved the situation. He gently picked up Snookums, rabbit ear flopping—okay, and a little bit dripping—from her mouth. He set her gently into the front passenger seat and climbed in after her.

We dropped off Hunk and Spunky Doo with no problem, but Little Miss' person was home. She peered in at the passenger side then drew back quickly as Snookums put her little front paws on the window, barely reaching, to proudly show the somewhat unidentifiable object in her mouth, blood and whatever smeared on her—well, smeared on her.

"She got into some strawberry syrup and—"

Big Miss waited.

"Some beige pudding," I finished lamely.

Our next trip was to the beach. Fewer trees. No rabbits. It was a longer drive, though, so it was a whole day thing. No problem, said Hunk's guy. Okay, said Big Miss, a little cautiously. Sure, said Spunky Doo's people—please. And Chum? He had gone home on his own after the field trip, but I'd remembered his number.

"Oh, he'd *love* to go to the beach with you! I'll get his beach ball out." His beach ball? Turns out it was a severely waterlogged rubber ball. Essentially a sponge ball. Chum was waiting at the door, his beach ball in his mouth, clearly understanding he was GOING TO THE WATER!! Of course. He was part lab.

Little Miss Bo Peep was also waiting at the door. In a bikini. Oh my god. It was an itsy bitsy, teeny weeny bikini. A yellow, polka dot bikini.

Hunk pretended not to notice. As did Chum. Spunky Doo wouldn't have noticed in any case. And Kessie didn't really care what other people wore. She had a bright green tennis ball in her mouth. And Snookums—Snookums threw up. I pulled over and with Bo Peep's permission, and I suspect, her approval, took off her bikini and used it to clean up Snookum's throw-up.

Half an hour later, we arrived. I parked the car and let the dogs out. Yippee!! That was me, this time. I love sun, sand, and sea. Again, Kessie knew what she wanted. She'd been here before. She put her ball in my hand, got ready, then tore off down the runway of hard packed sand by the water's edge, racing after her ball. Sheer bliss.

Chum put his beach ball down at my feet, then looked expectantly out to the water. Of course! I threw it out as far as I could. He heard the plop, noted its position, then threw himself into the waves after it.

This was Snookums' first time at the beach. What would she do? Turned out she was fascinated by the water's edge. She toddled along the edge, beside me, as I walked along on the firm part. Splish, splash, plunk, plunk. She was very focused. On what, exactly, I wondered. Shiny grains of sand, perhaps? Rotten bits of fish flesh?

Spunky Doo was running ahead and back, barking at the waves. Little Miss was walking on the other side of me, careful not to get her tootsies wet, lifting them higher than was really necessary. And Hunk. Hunk was a surprise. I don't think Dobermans are known for their swimming ability. And suddenly he was out there, howling, and yipping, and squealing, and splashing at the surface with his huge paws, having the time of his life, and gulping water—oh my god, was he drowning? I looked at Chum, who, as part lab, was our designated Lifeguard. Until this moment, he had been repeatedly plowing through the waves with masterful and determined strokes after his soggy and increasingly forlorn beach ball. But upon hearing Hunk, he stopped, looked, and listened. And then resumed plowing through the waves with masterful and determined strokes. After his soggy and increasingly forlorn beach ball. Okay then. Little Miss had also looked to Chum. She understood he was not concerned, but she wasn't entirely convinced. She kept her eye on Hunk as she walked beside me.

Apparently Spunky Doo didn't get the memo. He dove into the water after Hunk. Whether he intended to rescue him or whether he just thought he'd join in the goofiness, we'll never know. We do know that once Spunky Doo reached Hunk, the rescue situation had to be reassessed. Again Chum stopped, looked, and listened. I looked at Chum. As did Little Miss. Even Snookums paused. (Kessie used the moment to put her ball securely into my hand.) But by then Hunk had extricated himself from Spunky Doo and had struggled ashore, muttering. ("Dumb ass dog," no doubt.)

Okay, it was definitely time for ice cream. We headed to the ice cream place down the beach a bit. I loved it, because they gave tasters—little plastic spoons with a dollop of whatever flavor you wanted to try before deciding which one you really wanted.

Okay, one mint ice cream cone for Kessie. And Snookums liked butter pecan. Though she leaves all the pecan bits. First time that happened, I thought she'd lost all of her puppy teeth at once.

Chum, what would you like? I asked for a taster of Very Cherry. No. Of course not, what was I thinking. Not Hawaiian Pineapple or Tangerine Orange either. Ah. I asked for a taster of Peanut Butter Swirl. Bingo. One Peanut Butter Swirl, please.

Little Miss Bo Peep, let me see . . . French Vanilla? Yes, got it in one! She delicately licked the spoon clean then waited politely for her cone.

Hunk . . . Tiger Tail Licorice? Oddly enough, yes, he liked it. 'Course, he also liked the little plastic spoon. Double scoop of that one, please. Better have lots of coating for that spoon.

Spunky Doo, what do you want? Amaretto, Praline Delight, Peachy Keen, Triple Chocolate Brownie Fudge—woof. No, sorry, you can't have that one—dogs can't have chocolate. Terrific Toffee,

Candy Floss, Espresso Express—woof. I looked at him. I looked at the mile long beach. What the hell, if not now, when? Okay, one small cone of Espresso Express for Spunky Doo.

I ordered the Triple Chocolate Brownie Fudge for myself. Spunky Doo stared at me. Because I can, I told him.

The neat thing about having ice cream cones at the beach, if you're a dog, is that they can be stuck into the sand for easy consumption. And the water nearby makes for easy clean up. Unnecessary this time, however, as Snookums went around and took care of everyone's ice cream face.

We started to head back. Actually, Spunky Doo had already headed back, returned, headed back again, and returned again. When he started out a third time, Hunk accidentally stretched out his foreleg and Spunky Doo went flying. I saw him grin. Hunk, I mean. Though, Spunky Doo was probably also grinning.

After a little bit, Snookums got in front of me and lifted her cute little pink paw. Carry me, I'm tired, I'm just a little baby. I picked her up, eight pounds now, and put her in her snuggly thing, where, much as she tried, she couldn't keep her eyes open.

Good idea, I thought. I headed to a shaded spot, and sat down. Almost immediately Hunk, Little Miss, and Chum dug holes to get to the cool sand, then curled up in them. Spunky Doo also dug a hole—and curled up beside it. I got comfy too. Kessie was curled up on my left, with her ball—*and* Chum's beach ball—how did that happen? And Snookums was still nestled in her snuggly thing on my right, fast asleep, wagging her tail as she dreamt. How sweet is that?

After a while, I woke up. What? I hadn't intended to fall asleep! I quickly counted the dogs—one, two, three, four, five, six, whew! Wait a minute—seven, eight, nine—what the—*fourteen* dogs were curled up and mostly asleep all around me. Snookums was awake and giggling at me from ear to ear. Aha! *She's* the one responsible for this! Probably invited every passing dog to "Come join us!"

As she then demonstrated. The largest German Shepherd I'd ever seen came our way. I snuck a look at Hunk. He was still asleep. Good. Snookums toddled over to the Shepherd, all happy, and did her thing: she squiggled into a sort of log roll, ending up belly up under the dog's jaws. At first I was dismayed when I saw that this so-called submission behavior was her norm. But then I realized it was just her way of getting all the competitive stuff out of the way as quickly as possible—yes, yes, you can be the alpha dog, I'm a happy little beta, now LET'S PLAY!!

The Shepherd didn't play. It opened its mouth. My, what big teeth you have. Hunk was still asleep. *Not* good. Then the Shepherd, unbelievably, put his jaws around Snookums' whole head. Snookums' whole head was in his mouth. What to do?

I took my cue from her. She didn't seem to mind. Maybe it was a sign of affection. After all, he wasn't biting down. And if she was really afraid, she'd have run to me and flown into my open arms. Literally. Once I wasn't expecting it—she had been afraid of a garbage can—and I wasn't ready. She thumped into my chest and I had to scramble to catch her as she tumbled down. But she wasn't running. She squiggled a bit more, then reached out a paw, a cute little baby paw, to touch the Shepherd's mouth. He licked her. My, what a big tongue you have. She giggled. Then he decided to lay down beside her. Okay then. But he wasn't going to fit into the car, I told her.

Our next outing was to the toy store. The one that lets you bring your dogs inside. With the understanding that you'll keep your dog leashed, I know, but trust me—keeping all six leashed would have been—worse.

So we went in after I made sure they understood they could each buy one thing. *One* thing, got it? Okay.

This was Snookums' first time, and she was a little afraid, so I had to go with her to pick out her toy. I set her down, and she toddled up and down the aisles, looking back to make sure I was still with her, to make sure she was still with me. We went right through the stuffed toys aisle, and through the treats aisle, past the grooming aids, and the fashion accessories to—the cat section? There she discovered a bin full of squeaky mouse toys. She didn't just stick her head in and get one. Of course not. She jumped right into the bin. All nine pounds of her. Once in, she pounced—*squeak!*—and pounced again—*squeak!* She giggled at me. And pounced again—*squeak!* I reached down and picked her up, one moist squeaky mouse in her mouth. She burrowed into her snuggly thing, completely disappearing. *Squeak!* Okay, one down, five to go.

We found Hunk and Little Miss Bo Peep at the collar and leash display, sitting politely, though with controlled interest, waiting for me to get what they had their eyes on. They couldn't reach—well, they could, but they weren't going to. Good dogs. I moved my hand—*squeak!*—from one item to the next until I got a bark. From Little Miss BoPeep. At the thick black leather studded collar. Okaaay. A few seconds later, Hunk barked. I had my hand on the pink rhinestone encrusted collar. Hm. Either they're engaged or they're experimenting with cross-dressing.

Chum came trotting around the corner, a smallish basketball in his mouth. Of course. He's a ball dog. Or maybe he'd just watched Air Bud way too often.

Kessie found us next, dragging something, with great effort, ass end in the air. I couldn't see what—ah—a 100-pack of bright fluorescent green tennis balls.

Okay, off to the checkout. We stood in line. *Squeak!* The cashier smiled, as she dealt with the customer ahead of us. *Squeak!* She smiled again and snuck a glance at the lump in the snuggly thing that was Snookums. Then it was our turn.

"Hi, how are—" *Squeak!* "What have you got in there?" She baby-talked to Snookums. "Let me see," she coaxed, "what have you got?" *Squeak!* She gently pulled back a corner of the snuggly. A teeny little nose appeared. Then a teeny little muzzle appeared, jaws clamped tight. "Have you got a mouse?" Snookums shook her head back and forth, a tail hanging out of her mouth.

"Do you need me to get the tag for you?" I asked.

She looked at our line-up. "It's only a buck. Don't worry about it."

"Okay, thanks." I reached down then to get Kessie's bag of tennis balls. She wouldn't let go. Silly me. What was I thinking? I picked her up then, still holding on to her bag of tennis balls, and set her on the conveyor belt. She stood there, the bag as big as her. The cashier activated the belt. Surf city, here we come! She scanned the tag as Kess went by.

Chum was next in line. He put his paws up, set his basketball carefully onto the belt, and gently rolled it toward the cashier with his nose. Okay, he *had* watched Air Bud too often.

Hunk and Bo Peep walked past next, each with the other's collar—or not. They graciously allowed me to take the collars, get them scanned, then give them back.

Then we heard a crash over in the stuffed toy section. Spunky Doo—where was Spunky Doo? Dare I call him? And hear half a dozen more crashes to the ground as he came racing to answer my call? No, give him another couple seconds. We heard another crash, a little closer. That made just two, please note. Then we saw him bounding around the corner and—what the—? He was wearing his toy. A giant purple furry octopus was somehow wrapped around his neck, its garish head appearing to rise out of his own, making him look like some ridiculous two-headed cartoon alien. *And* he had a huge caveman rawhide bone in his mouth. Must've been three feet across. That was two things. But okay. The mammoth bone was probably going to save a dining room set. He got in line with us at the checkout, relieved to have made it in time. With no idea how ridiculous he looked. Then again, given the grin on his face, he was probably perfectly aware of how ridiculous he looked.

Seeing that it was his turn, he eagerly stepped forward. Whack! The mammoth bone wouldn't fit. Spunky Doo backed up and stepped forward again. Whack! Oddly enough, it still wouldn't fit. He backed up and stepped forward a third time. Whack! (Then again, about that dining room set . . .) Hunk, until now sitting patiently beside Little Miss on the other side of the checkout, lay down. This was going to take some time.

"If we don't help him, how many more times do you think he'll do that?" The cashier asked, barely concealing her laughter. Good question.

Spunky Doo backed up again. "No, wait!" I reached out my hand. He looked at it curiously, then he looked up at me, then back down at my hand, the octopus head bobbing up and down as he did so. What? Hunk groaned.

"Give. Let Go. Release." No response. "Look, it won't fit sideways, give it to me and I'll carry it through for you, the other way." Oh. Why didn't you say that?

So we got Spunky Doo through the checkout and then headed out to my car. Once there, everyone looked pointedly at Spunky Doo's mammoth bone, then at the car, then at the bone, then at me. Right. Someone's liable to get knocked out. Probably me. I opened the trunk and put the mammoth bone inside. Spunky Doo jumped in after it, his purple octopus head bobbing up and down. No—okay, yeah—no, get in the back seat, you.

Our last outing was to the dog show. 'Course, I didn't know it was our last outing. Then again, I didn't know dogs shouldn't be taken to dog shows. Go figure.

The show was held at the city's huge arena. Inside, different areas of the arena were marked off for different shows or competitions or whatever. The first one we came to was the puppy agility course. You know the course I'm talking about: it has various obstacles the dogs have to jump over, climb through, walk across, run around, and so on. We all settled into the bleachers to watch the first group of puppies. Five of them were let loose at the starting line and given various encouragements to more or less head off in the right direction.

One simply had no idea. It sat down. Two scampered off together toward the first obstacle, but then got tangled up before they got there. They snarled and snapped at each other—they couldn't wait to be big dogs. Which would probably happen next week. The fourth puppy stopped to piddle. Then forgot what it was supposed to be doing. The fifth one ran *into* the obstacle. Fell down, laughed. The sixth little one made it to the obstacle, and even made it over, but was then so delighted with itself it had to run over to—us. "See what

I did? Did you see? I climbed over it! I did!" Unfortunately, leaving the course gets you disqualified. However, if you're not formally entered in the first place . . . We all congratulated Snookums. Yes, we did see! We know! And not only did you climb over the obstacle, you did it with a mouse in your mouth! What a clever little girl! Then we stuffed her into her snuggly thing and moved on to the next area.

Which was the tennis ball relay race. Two dogs race to jump on a springboard, which releases a tennis ball, which they catch, then race back with, so the next dog on their team can race down the stretch to the springboard, and so on, four dogs to a team. We settled into the bleachers to watch. Kessie leaned forward, her interest rather—intense. Suddenly I felt her gently put her ball into my hand, but before I could tell her this was not the time nor place, she shot off the bleachers, and in an amazing feat of speed, timing, and coordination, intercepted the tennis ball in mid-fire and flew back to her spot in the bleachers. Leaving the Border Collie—the breed reputed to be the genius of the species, I might point out—staring dumbly at the hole, waiting for the ball to pop out. Kessie put her newly acquired ball into my hand. I looked around innocently as I slipped it into Snookums' snuggly—*squeak!* Then Kess shot off the bleachers again. I put the second ball into the snuggly—*squeak!*—then grabbed her just as she crouched for her third launch, and moved us all quickly to the next area.

It was the show portion of the show. We were in time for the poodle class. First one poodle, then another, strutted down the runway, all fluffed and shaved and manicured and be-ribboned. Cameras flashed. Hunk started howling. His equivalent to a wolf whistle, I guess. 'Cuz it distracted Contestant #3. Contestant #4 actually 'lost her carriage'—or whatever the correct dog show phrase is for 'tripped'. Then Contestant #5 howled—at Little Miss Bo Peep. Well. Hunk was confused. He didn't know poodles came in male. Or that male dogs did the show thing. (Though, of course, if any male dog did, it would be a male poodle.) So he didn't know whether he wanted to howl at the next contestant or attack the previous one. His next howl had a growl at the end. Well, that got Contestant #6 all excited. She hit the floor, paws down, rump up, in the classic invitation-to-play posture. Well, okay, the classic invitation to—her rump was *facing* Hunk.

Then Contestant #7 was announced.

"No, sorry," the announcer stumbled to correct himself, "there doesn't seem to be—"

I don't know where she got the bonnet from, let alone who helped her put it on. No, wait. Yes I do. It was on backwards. But there she was—too sexy for Milan, too sexy for Milan, and as she did her little turn on the catwalk, Hunk lost it. He let out a howl as he flew off the bleachers straight to Little Miss Bo Peep, and they did the deed right there on the runway. Doggy style, of course. Cameras flashed. They made the third page, local news. Same day as Spunky Doo.

Maybe it won't matter. Maybe I can put up signs again. And become a cat walker. That'll work. Maybe—Snookums! My little social butterfly! I'll make up some clip-on business cards, the three of us'll go back to the beach, have a nap, and when I wake up, I'll have a job again!

www.ingramcontent.com/pod-product-compliance
Lightning Source LLC
Chambersburg PA
CBHW031229210726
48287CB00003B/719

* 9 7 8 1 9 2 6 8 9 1 4 8 4 *